The Pulos Family and Their Peculiar Kin

HARRIET PULOS
She is young for a matriarch, but being rich helps.

DMITRI PULOS
Harriet's gorgeous, young, second husband. He married his favorite teacher.

ALEXIS PULOS
Dmitri's brother, who lives off Harriet's money.

MARIANA PULOS
Dmitri's sister, ditto.

THALIA HOLLY
The beautiful but orphaned ballerina is the odd girl out in the family.

REBECCA HOLLY
Harriet's ailing former mother-in-law might be slightly unbalanced.

MILLIE EARL
Harriet's cousin. She, her husband, and the kiddies are all reluctant to leave the well-fleeced nest Harriet has provided for them.

A DEATH FOR A DANCING DOLL

E. X. Giroux

BALLANTINE BOOKS • NEW YORK

Library of Congress Catalog Card Number: 90-29899

ISBN 0-345-37609-9

This edition published by arrangement with St. Martin's Press, Inc.

Manufactured in the United States of America

First Ballantine Books Edition: July 1992

This book is for Marjorie
and for my brother,
Gordon Limbert Giroux

CHAPTER ONE

UNDER NORMAL CIRCUMSTANCES, ROBERT FORSYTHE possessed an even temperament and exercised courtesy and patience, but the present circumstances were hardly normal. He was suffering from a combination of jet lag, indigestion, and pain. The flight from Heathrow in London to the Vancouver International Airport had been unpleasant. He had dozed fitfully, had eaten little, and his bad knee, injured years ago in prep school, had stiffened up so badly that he needed the support of the cane on which he was leaning. His secretary, Abigail Sanderson, although many years his senior, was in better shape and was managing to be polite to the manager of the Vancouver Harmony Hotel. The manager's name was Malone, but he had a Gallic nature and couldn't appear to speak without arm and hand motions. If Miss Sanderson had been free to keep her distance from him, it might have been tolerable, but in an elevator crowded with her employer, two bellhops, and a mound of luggage, she was shoved against Malone's sizable paunch. She noticed enviously that Forsythe had managed to work loose of the pack and was standing in front of her, silently and morosely glaring at the elevator door.

To her relief, the elevator drew to a smooth stop, the doors slid back, and she stepped into a spacious foyer. Forsythe, without glancing around, limped toward rather impressive double doors, waited for a bellhop to unlock them, and disappeared into the suite. Malone flung out a hand, hit her handbag with it, and said anxiously, "Mr. Forsythe seems in a bad mood. Have I done anything to offend him? Mr. Harmon's orders were to extend all courtesies to Mr. Forsythe and, of course, to you."

Bad mood is an understatement, Miss Sanderson thought. Robby has been acting like a bear with a sore paw and Mr. Malone, if anything, had been too fulsome with his courtesies. Of course, it was to the manager's professional advantage to make them happy. Robby not only was Mark Harmon's friend but was also a guest in the penthouse suite of the owner of the Harmony Hotel chain. She managed a reassuring smile. "Robby's simply exhausted, Mr. Malone. It was a long flight and his bad leg stiffened up. About ten hours sleep and he'll be in fine fettle again."

"I could send the hotel doctor up to—"

"No. Not necessary." She held out a dismissive hand. "Thank you."

His large hand engulfed her slender one and he retreated to the elevator while she moved into the hall of the suite. Directly in front of her was an archway, and long halls led both to the right and left. The bellhops were patiently waiting near the wheeled racks of luggage. The shorter one flashed a smile and asked, "Would you like to select your bedrooms, ma'am?"

"How many are there?"

"Four bedrooms." He jerked his head. "And four baths."

Ye gods, she thought. She fished in her handbag, extracted her wallet, and handed him a bill. "Stick the cases in any two of them and leave the keys on that table."

The archway led into an enormous living room with the rear wall entirely of glass. A door had been slid open and she spotted Forsythe on the patio, leaning against the parapet, sunlight glistening on his smooth hair. She joined him and gazed down at the city and then lifted her eyes to the rugged crests of mountains silhouetted against the northern sky. "Marvelous setting this city has, Robby. Looks like a precious gem."

He grunted. "May look like a gem, but Vancouver is merely another city suffering from crime and drugs and general mayhem."

"Blimey, but you're a little ray of sunshine and good humor today! Keep on like this and you're in a fair way of ruining the beginning of a much anticipated and much needed vacation."

"Sorry, Sandy." He turned to face her. "Put it down to jet lag. Physically, I feel like midnight and it's barely afternoon. A drink may be in order. Located Mark's bar yet?"

"Haven't even located a bathroom yet, but that should pose no problem. The bellhop tells me there're *four*."

He grinned. "Wouldn't have done any good if you had looked. Mark keeps his liquor supply well hidden. Before we left London, he rang me up and told me the important things. The bar's location and where the keys for the cars would be."

"Cars? Meaning more than one?"

"One for each of us. A Mercedes and a BMW for our use while we're in residence in this palatial penthouse."

"I'm impressed. Tell me, just how long have you and Mark Harmon been buddies?"

"We're only acquaintances. Mark is a friend of Jennifer's and we met when I was visiting her in Los Angeles last spring."

"He must have taken a fancy to you. Offering the use of this place and his cars anytime you wish and for as long as you want to stay."

Forsythe's face sobered. "More like gratitude. I did Mark a service, Sandy. His young sister had got into a mess and I managed to extricate her."

Miss Sanderson stared at him. "You never mentioned it."

"Doesn't bear talking about. Sordid business and the girl was barely sixteen."

"Apparently what they say about casting bread upon water does come true occasionally. Lead on to the booze, Robby."

He stepped back into the living room. "What's your opinion of the decor?"

She cast a critical look around. "Shows the skilled hand of an interior decorator, expensive and with about as much personality as those room groupings they used to put in department-store windows."

"The type of room where one is nervous of spilling ash or disturbing a cushion. Let's hope Mark's library is cozier. Wonder where it is? Let's try that door near the fireplace. Ah, now that's more like it."

"Looks like our host might have taken a hand in this himself." Miss Sanderson gazed around. The library wasn't much smaller than the living room, but it had a feeling of warmth and comfort and ease. Walnut paneling covered the walls, handsome carpets glowed against oak floors, the bookshelves had glass fronts, and leather and brass predominated. She frowned. "No sign of a bar, Robby."

He laughed and limped around behind the desk. "Mark said there's a brass button here and all you do is press and . . . voilà!"

A walnut panel slid silently back and disclosed a lighted recess complete with a short marble counter and rows of bottles, decanters, and a multitude of various-sized glasses faithfully duplicated on mirrored shelves.

"Blimey! An alcoholic's paradise." She slid behind the counter. "What's your pleasure?"

"Laphroaig, and make it a double."

Miss Sanderson splashed whiskey into glasses and handed one to Forsythe. He sank into the custom-made chair behind the desk and his secretary wandered across the room to the fireplace. She inspected her image in the oval mirror over the mantel and smoothed gray waves back from her brow. Her hair looked fine but her long, austere face was as drawn and weary as her employer's. The room was warm and she slid off her green linen jacket. No doubt there was air conditioning, but she didn't suggest using it. Forsythe loathed artificially cooled air. She turned to look at him. Mark's chair could have been designed with Robby's long, slender, ele-

4

gant frame in mind. "Tweed seems a bit warm for mid-July in this area, Robby."

He rubbed a tweed-clad knee. "Heat doesn't bother me, Sandy; it's the cold that raises hob with this ruddy knee."

Her mouth snapped open to mention she had been urging he have that knee operated on for years, but she reconsidered—hardly the time or place. Instead, she said, "Nice of Gene Emory to urge we take three whole months for our vacation. I could hardly believe our luck."

"We both needed it, Sandy." He took a sip of his drink. "But when I told you that Gene and his partner and I were considering combining our two practices, you didn't appear overjoyed. I thought you'd be jumping with joy. Not only a chance for more time off from the grind but also an opportunity to get out of those cramped old chambers you've been complaining about for years."

Sinking into a leather chair opposite him, she stretched long, shapely legs. "Getting rather set in my ways, I suppose. After all the years with your father, then with you, I was used to the firm of Forsythe, Forsythe, and Forsythe. It will take time to accept Forsythe, Emory, and Mertz. But I must admit having a real office instead of a cubbyhole sweetens the deal. When we go home, I'm going to get those furnishings out of storage that Aunt Rose gave me when she took off for Corfu. I've been longing to use that desk, those chairs, and that wonderful old Bokhara but couldn't squeeze them into my flat."

The barrister regarded his secretary with affection. Miss Sanderson had been much more than a good right hand to both his father and to himself. His mother had died when Forsythe was a toddler and his father had never remarried. His father and his secretary had raised the young Robert and she was the only mother he could remember. He finished his drink, debated whether to have a second, and decided against it. He contented himself with lighting his pipe. "Have you made plans for your vacation?"

She stretched luxuriously. "The first month and the last one are mine alone and I'm staying loose on them. But from the middle of August to middle September, I have a number of duty calls to make: a brother in Idaho, an aged cousin in Seattle, a childhood friend in the Yukon. I'm looking forward to the Yukon. Shades of Robert Service and *The Face on the Barroom Floor*.''

He grinned and puffed out a cloud of aromatic smoke. ''Just make sure your face isn't one of them. Aren't you going to ask me about my plans?''

''No need to. The middle month you're spending with Jennifer Dorland in California, and I know you have a number of jade auctions—''

''Nothing so crass as auctions, Sandy. Collections where one wanders around staring covetously and writes amounts on discreet little cards and tucks them into—''

''The highest bid takes the coveted jade object, doesn't it?''

''Certainly.''

''Then it's an auction.''

''It is *not* like the usual auction.'' He glanced at the desk calendar. ''The day after tomorrow, there's an estate showing I simply must attend. The star of the collection is Han dynasty.'' He stared raptly off into space. ''Lady with Heavenly Peaches.''

His secretary's mind was on another lady. ''Jennifer's certain she will have that month free, Robby?''

''Positive. It wasn't easy, either. She's not only writing the script for the documentary but she's been asked to direct it, too.''

Miss Sanderson's cool blue eyes glinted with pleasure. Next to Robert Forsythe, Jennifer was her favorite person. ''You really should snap her up. Not only is she pretty but—''

''Jennifer is *not* pretty.''

''Well, she is attractive and intelligent and witty.''

He hammered the pipe bowl into an ashtray. ''Might better leave the marriage counseling until this jet lag wears off. Right now, I might take a large bite out of your ankle.''

She decided not to pursue the subject. Robby and Jennifer were in love and it was only their careers keeping them apart.

Best to change the subject. "What shall we do for the rest of the day?"

"I'm going to have a meal, soak in a hot tub, and fall into bed."

"And I shall emulate you. I'd better order up a meal from that gourmet kitchen Mr. Malone was babbling about."

He shook his head. "Didn't he mention our larder had been stocked?"

"Repeatedly. But—"

"Soup and sandwiches. I'll be cook, Sandy. If we order from room service, the manager may trot the meal up himself and do some more hand licking. Trying to gain more brownie points with Mark Harmon."

"You were frightfully rude to the poor chap. And I have a hunch Mark Harmon was only part of the manager's reason for being in awe of you. Mr. Malone might have read that article published in the American magazine a couple of months ago. Remember?"

"How could I forget?" He pushed his fingers through light brown hair. " 'England's Contemporary Sherlock Holmes'! A mishmash of errors, exaggeration, and downright sensationalism." His lips relaxed into a faint smile. "You received honorable mention, too."

Miss Sanderson demonstrated her amazing memory. " 'This modern Holmes,' " she quoted, " 'has his Doctor Watson. Abigail Sanderson, the barrister's secretary, plays this role to the hilt. Miss Sanderson, a maiden lady in her mid-sixties—' " Breaking off, she snarled, "Mid-sixties, indeed! Off by ten years!"

"Which way, Sandy?" He dodged the cushion she tossed, and laughed. "Enough violence. I'll dig out the car keys, and to make amends, you may have your choice. Which will it be—Mercedes or BMW?"

"Mercedes," she said with no hesitation. "What's in the envelope?"

He tore open the envelope. "Communiqué from Mark Harmon."

"Oh, oh! Now we get the price tag for all these goodies."

7

"You have a suspicious mind." He scanned the letter. "Mark's simply extending a welcome. Refers us, quite unnecessarily, to Malone should we require anything and . . ."

"And what? Does he have another sister to rescue?"

"No. But there is an elderly woman—a friend of his mother's—he'd like us to speak with. Appears she's having a spot of trouble." He looked up. "Mark doesn't sound as though he's taking it seriously. Says he thinks it's all in her mind. If we need more information on Mrs. Rebecca Holly, he says to ring up George Barton."

"And just who is George Barton?" Miss Sanderson asked frigidly.

"The attorney for both Mark and Mrs. Holly."

"How cozy."

"Now who's being a ray of sunshine? Don't look so glum, Sandy. Might as well ring up the lady and get it over with. Probably I can solve her little problem with a call."

"Get your hand off that phone and stop being an optimist. Mrs. Holly will hustle right over here to tell all and we're not up to it. You can make that call tomorrow."

He snapped a salute. "Aye, aye, sir!" He reached for his cane and pulled himself up. "Now I'll keep my promise and heat up soup and cut some sandwiches."

"In a pig's eye you will! You'll have a hot tub and crawl into bed. I'll locate the kitchen and get the food."

"But—"

"No buts. When you're steadier on that leg, you can take over kitchen duties. I'll bring you a tray. Scoot!"

"Why do I sometimes feel as though I'm back in the nursery?"

"Because sometimes you should be."

He limped through the living room and paused in the hall. "Where is my bedroom, Nanny?"

"The bellhops carried the luggage that way. Don't bother unpacking. We'll get settled in the morning."

Forsythe turned down the left-hand hall and Miss Sanderson opened the doors lining the right-hand one. In quick succession, she discovered a broom closet, a storage room, a utility room, a formal dining room, and, finally, a kitchen. She gazed around covetously: the kitchen of her dreams, including a breakfast nook, glass doors leading to a patio featuring a glassed-topped table and four rattan chairs ringed by a small garden of potted shrubs and flowering plants.

She cut sandwiches, and while the soup heated she stepped out on the patio and gazed down at the streets far below. As she looked, she thought of Robby's words about cities and knew he was right. Every city, no matter how lovely, had a Janus-like nature. Like the god of the portals, this wonderful place wore two faces, one all beauty and sunlight and charm, the other a horror of crime and violence. She devoutedly hoped that Vancouver would not display its dark face to Robby or her.

CHAPTER TWO

FORSYTHE MADE THE CALL TO REBECCA HOLLY SHORTLY after breakfast, and before eleven the woman was seated in one of the leather chairs in front of Mark Harmon's desk. Forsythe was obviously feeling much better, his color was normal and the cane was not in evidence. Miss Sanderson, holding a notebook and pen, sat at the far end of the desk. She found she was intrigued with their visitor. Mrs. Holly had explained that she was in her seventies and was a semi-invalid, having suffered for years from a heart condition. She didn't look her age and she didn't look ill. She was tiny and her hair, piled high on a finely shaped head, was silver-white. Her skin was fine and smooth and her eyes were that shade described by novelists as gentian, a bright and unfaded blue. She was modishly dressed and on the lapel of her jacket a corsage of violets nestled. At first sight of the woman, Miss Sanderson had thought of lavender and old lace. She soon found her assessment was totally wrong. Rebecca Holly was not a sweet old lady. She had an acrid turn of speech and was able to discuss her problem with no signs of emotion.

Mrs. Holly was talking rapidly and Forsythe held up a hand. "You say your granddaughter died in a town called Hollystone. Was this place named after your family?"

"Partially. A Holly and a Stone founded the town. My family—I was a Holly by birth as well as marriage; my husband was a second cousin—were merchants and business-men. The Stones were teachers and artists and writers. Oddly enough, through the years the two families didn't intermarry. They dwindled in numbers until there were only a few Hollys left—my two sons, my granddaughter, myself. There is only one Stone—Harriet. She was a teacher and when she was nearly thirty, she married my older son, Kenneth, finally uniting the families.''

Miss Sanderson consulted her notes. ''And Thalia Holly, your granddaughter, was the daughter of Kenneth and Harriet?''

''No. Kenneth and Harriet had no children. Thalia was the daughter of my younger son, Reggie.'' Rebecca's lips relaxed in a tiny smile. ''Reggie was the direct opposite of his older brother. I was fond of Reggie but I never could stand Kenneth. Reggie had no knack for making money but a wonderful ability for spending it.''

Forsythe raised his brows. ''You speak of both your sons in the past tense. Are they dead?'' She nodded, and he asked, ''Why did you dislike your older son?''

''Because Kenneth had only one good point. He could make money. Even as a boy, he was in the image of my father-in-law. He was a drinker, a womanizer, and, when he was drinking, Kenneth enjoyed giving abuse—''

''Physical abuse?'' Forsythe asked.

''He only beat Harriet once and that was shortly before he died, but there are many types of abuse. When he was drink-ing, Kenneth taunted his wife—sometimes before guests—about his other women, about Harriet's lack of physical attraction. I've no idea why Harriet married him. I won't pretend I like Harriet but I do respect her. During her mar-riage to my son, she put up with humiliation and abuse that no woman should endure. Many times I urged her to divorce him, but she kept saying, 'He's only a child, Mother Holly, a little boy who has never grown up. When Kenneth sobers up, he's always so remorseful.' ''

''How did your son die?'' Forsythe asked.

''His own wicked excesses finally killed him. He was

dreadfully drunk and that time he didn't only abuse Harriet verbally but gave her a terrible beating. He also threatened Thalia—''

"Your granddaughter was living with her aunt and uncle?''

"Thalia had been with them for two years. Her parents were drowned in a boating mishap off the Italian Riviera. Reggie and Ann were not model parents, Mr. Forsythe. Until Thalia was old enough to send to boarding school, she was left in the care of servants. Reggie and Ann didn't even have the child with them for vacation breaks. Occasionally, I'd take her for a week or so, but, as I mentioned, I've never been well. Perhaps when my son and daughter-in-law died, I should have raised Thalia myself but . . .'' Unfaded eyes looked into a past only Rebecca Holly could see.

Guilt, Miss Sanderson thought, the sin of omission. Aloud, she said, "Sometimes it's most difficult to raise children. Even if one is young and well.''

"That's what I told myself at the time, Miss Sanderson. Now . . . I'm not so sure. Perhaps I really didn't want Thalia. Kenneth was brutally honest, as he always was. He flatly refused to take his niece, wasn't going to be bothered with an eleven-year-old brat, as he told Harriet and me. Finally, Harriet talked him around and they did take the child, but Kenneth never became reconciled to her.''

Shifting in the leather chair, Forsythe asked, "Was Thalia fond of her Aunt Harriet?''

"Fond? She doted on the woman! Considered Harriet the mother she'd never known. Called her Mommy. Thalia had two passions—Harriet and ballet.''

"Did Harriet return this devotion?''

"Thalia was convinced Harriet loved her but . . .'' Rebecca Holly twisted a sapphire ring on one thin finger. "You'd have to know Harriet to understand, Mr. Forsythe. She inspires a devotion that I find mystifying—''

"Is she beautiful?'' Miss Sanderson asked.

"Far from it.'' Mrs. Holly smiled faintly. "Harriet has a type of magnetism that I simply can't explain. Of course, I'm one of the few people who appear to be immune to Harriet's appeal. I suspect even that group of leeches living on the estate have fallen under her spell. Granted, they want all the financial help she gives them, but they seem to adore her, too. But I see my daughter-in-law clearly, and Harriet has an obsession. Overdeveloped maternal instincts. She was kind to Thalia but she didn't love her. She desperately wanted children of her own. Kenneth wouldn't give her a child, but as soon as she married the Greek—''

''Whoa,'' Forsythe broke in. ''You're getting ahead of the story. *How* did Kenneth die?''

''Sorry. I do get a bit carried away. But to think of a woman who was born a Stone and married a Holly being the wife of the son of a fruit peddler . . . No, I'm being unfair. Dmitri's father ran a fruit and vegetable store in Hollystone. Kenneth's death? As I said, he'd been on one of his periodic binges and that time had beaten Harriet. I live in Vancouver and Harriet came to me, bringing Thalia with her. I was shocked. No matter how Kenneth behaved, Harriet always stayed with him. He was a diabetic, you see, and alcohol was dangerous for him. But even Harriet has her limits, and she wouldn't stand for being a battered wife. Also, she thought the servants would be in the house with him. But Kenneth was very violent and he frightened the servants so badly that they left the estate. Three days later when Harriet returned, she found Kenneth dead. Either he'd forgotten to take his insulin shots or had misjudged the proper amount. He'd gone into a coma and died alone. Harriet was shattered and she had a nervous collapse.'' Mrs. Holly shook her silvery head. ''Best thing that could have happened to her. Four years of hell!''

''She did remarry,'' Miss Sanderson pointed out.

Gentian eyes turned on her. A fascinating woman, Miss Sanderson thought. Completely cold. Rebecca Holly might feel a measure of grief and perhaps guilt, but the secretary had a hunch the grief was stirred by the death of the last Holly, not for Thalia personally.

''Harriet remarried in less than a year after my son's death, Miss Sanderson. An unsuitable union. Not only was Dmitri

13

Pulos her social inferior but he's years younger than she. In fact, she was his teacher in high school. According to all reports, Dmitri loved Harriet passionately from the time she was his teacher, and after Kenneth's death he lost no time in pressing his suit.'' The smooth brow furrowed. ''I fail to understand him, either. He's not only too young for Harriet but he's extremely handsome.''

''A love match?'' Forsythe asked.

''The love is one-sided. All Harriet wanted from him was children. At thirty-four, she must have felt time was precious— and they wasted no time, either. Her daughter, Iona, was born less than a year after their wedding. Then Harriet had a series of miscarriages. Dr. Brent begged her not to try for more children, but she persisted and three years ago she gave birth to a son. Leander's birth nearly ended her life.''

Forsythe templed his fingers and regarded them. ''Would you give us the names and relationships of the people at Holly House at the time of your granddaughter's death?''

Mrs. Holly's mouth twisted. ''Harriet bought suitable relatives for her precious children—to, as she said, give them a well-rounded childhood. Thalia and I were the only holdouts. I flatly refused to live at Holly House and Thalia felt she must be in Vancouver to further her dancing career. Thalia and I were close to paupers, but I must admit Harriet is generous and she gave us allowances—''

''Didn't you inherit from your husband's estate?'' Miss Sanderson asked.

''We most certainly did. The furniture factory, lumber mill, and other property were left to Kenneth, but Reggie and I received the equivalent in cash. Reggie and Ann managed to fritter away their portion and I . . . well, I made bad investments and went to Reggie's financial assistance too often. But''—she straightened frail shoulders—''Hollys are proud and Harriet couldn't buy us. Which is more than I can say about that ragtag bunch living on her now.''

''Their names?'' Forsythe prodded.

''There are Mariana and Alexis Pulos, younger brother and sister of Dmitri. Then there is the Earl clan. Supposed

14

to be distant cousins of Harriet. Where she found them, I neither know nor care, but they're a trashy bunch. Four children, one less attractive than the next. And, of course, there's Brice Stevens-Parkes. Local solicitor, hopelessly smitten with Harriet. Brice doesn't live on the estate but he's always hanging around there. I mustn't forget Fabian Harcourt. Harriet doesn't want *him* around and I don't blame her, but he's Mariana Pulos's boyfriend and tags around after her.''

''A ready-made family,'' Forsythe mused.

''All with their roles for Harriet's children: an aunt, an uncle, cousins, an old family retainer. Thalia was supposed to be the brilliant artistic older sister and my role was live-in granny. Leander and Iona are *not* my grandchildren.''

''Is it a happy household?''

''It was. I suppose some would call it a type of paradise. All living on Harriet's bounty, pretending to be working at one of her concerns to save their self-respect. Until Iona was killed.''

''The little girl was killed?''

''A tragic accident on the first day of May. Iona fell into a falls at the estate and was swept to her death. Thalia was looking after the child at the time and she was blamed for Iona's death. Most unfairly.'' Rebecca Holly finally showed a touch of emotion. Her mouth quivered and she bent her head. ''Two months later, Thalia died.''

Forsythe regarded the bowed head. ''Do you have doubts about the little girl's death?''

''If you're asking if I think it was foul play, the answer is no.''

''But you don't feel your granddaughter's death was suicide?''

''Absolutely not!'' Mrs. Holly extracted a glossy photograph from her purse and handed it to him. ''Does she look like a potential suicide?''

Miss Sanderson rose and looked over her employer's shoulder. The background was dark but the figure in the foreground was clear: grace and beauty, timeless and alive, frozen forever in a classic ballet position. Balanced on her toes, her arms were raised gracefully above her dark head. She was a girl who looked much like Rebecca Holly must once have looked—fragile, tiny, an oval face, dark hair drawn back into a huge chignon.

"I was the one who found her," Rebecca said brokenly.

She described how she had found Thalia: hanging from a slashed drape cord knotted to a hook in the ceiling, long hair mercifully loose and almost hiding the mottled features, misty green chiffon not hiding the curves of the young body, strong dancer's legs no longer graceful but dangling aimlessly. The slender feet that had effortlessly danced the pas de deux now pointed at each other in an awkward, infinitely poignant, and childish position.

Rebecca Holly was speaking again, rage muffling her voice. "Mr. Forsythe, Thalia was murdered."

Pain tugged at the corners of the barrister's mouth as he stared down at the photo. "If she was, Mrs. Holly, her murderer must be found and punished."

The lines of tension in the woman's body relaxed and she asked, "Then you will look into this?" He nodded and she continued: "When Mark Harmon and my attorney, George Barton, suggested I consult with you, I sensed they were only trying to placate me. I know both of them consider me a silly, deluded old woman. But I was glad to meet you. I've read so much about your work in criminology. When I first saw you, I must admit I was a bit dismayed."

"Why was that, Mrs. Holly?"

"You look so young." She gave him a charming smile. "I'll phone Harriet and tell her you will be at Holly House and to have everyone gathered to speak with you. Shall I say tomorrow?"

Forsythe looked dismayed and Miss Sanderson said quickly, "Robby has an appointment tomorrow but I'm free. I'll drive to Hollystone and handle the interviews." The older woman gave her a dubious look, and it was Miss Sanderson's turn to give a charming smile. "Do you consider *me* too young, Mrs. Holly? I assure you I'm quite competent."

"To be associated with Mr. Forsythe, you would have to

be. Very well, Miss Sanderson, I'll tell Harriet to expect you.'' She turned to the barrister. "Have you further questions?"

"A number."

Forsythe asked questions, Mrs. Holly gave crisp concise answers, and Miss Sanderson applied herself to her notebook. After a time, the questions were exhausted, the barrister shook Mrs. Holly's tiny hand, and Miss Sanderson escorted their visitor to the foyer and the elevator.

When she returned to the library, she found the bar recess had been opened and Forsythe was making a drink. "Make that two," she told him, and sank into the chair recently vacated by Mrs. Holly.

He handed her a glass and started pacing up and down. She was relieved to note he had only a slight limp. "Sandy," he asked, "what did you think of Rebecca Holly?"

"Not exactly an emotional type and certainly neither silly nor deluded."

"You believe her granddaughter was murdered?"

She shrugged. "I believe she *believes* it. But best to keep in mind the police call it a suicide. Still, it sounds as though it's worth checking into."

He paused by her chair and patted her shoulder. "Which you gallantly offered to do. Thanks, Sandy."

"Couldn't have you missing that jade nonauction and the Lady with Heavenly Peaches."

He stared down at her. "Sandy, I'm feeling pangs of conscience. We're on vacation and I should have told Mark Harmon I wouldn't get mixed up with Rebecca Holly's problem and—"

"Relax." She touched the hand resting on her shoulder. "After all the lavishness laid on by your friend, it would have been in the worst possible taste. Besides . . ." She hesitated and then said slowly, "Do you remember when you were laid up with that broken ankle and were bored silly? You told me you thought you'd become addicted to criminology and I—"

17

"And you said *you* certainly hadn't, that after that messy business in Maddersley-on-Mead—"

"Robby, I know what I said. But I think I might have caught your bug. Vacation or not, I'm quite looking forward to going to Hollystone and delving into the death of Thalia Holly. Besides, it will give me a chance to try out Mark Harmon's Mercedes."

"Better keep in mind you're not used to right-hand drive and you'll be going through mountainous terrain."

"Do I have to assure *you* that I'm competent, too? Not to worry, Robby. I'm certain our Mr. Malone will be delighted to provide me with a road map and perhaps half an hour in directions."

"I still want you to be careful."

"Blimey!" She flashed her gamine grin. "Who's acting like a nanny now?"

CHAPTER THREE

Abigail Sanderson was an excellent driver and right-hand drive gave her no problems. She checked the road map provided by Mr. Malone, followed his instructions, and had no difficulty turning onto the road that led through the mountains in a northeasterly direction. The road was narrow and winding and the scenery was spectacular. To her right, rocky cliffs soared up and to her left, only a low guardrail protected from steep plunges into valleys below. She found the drive exhilarating and as the big car glided smoothly down toward Hollystone, she took her eyes off the road to scan the sprawling town below.

The hotel Rebecca Holly had mentioned was located on Main Street. It was large, obviously old, and the facade had been tarted up with neon and chrome and false brick. Before that had been done, it probably had had a pleasant appearance. Well, at least the place was supposed to be comfortable and the food palatable.

After pulling Mark Harmon's car into the parking area at one side of the hotel, Miss Sanderson clicked off the motor, reached for her overnight bag, and walked around to the front entrance. The lobby had been renovated to match the ghastly exterior and sported chrome and spindly furniture and a great deal of imitation wood. Glaring neon over archways spelled out Holly Room and the Stone Lounge. Looking much out of place were two elderly men playing checkers at one of the plastic-topped tables. As she crossed orange carpeting to the desk, they lifted wrinkled faces and watched her. The man behind the desk, who instantly reminded her of a weasel in a three-piece suit, raised indifferent eyes, swung around the registration book, and muttered, "One night? More?"

"One. And I'd like a bath."

"All our rooms have baths. Dining room's over there." He pointed at the Holly Room. "Coffee shop's down that hall. If you want a drink, try the Stone Lounge."

Hardly cordial, she thought, but then the Hollystone Hotel was the only hotel in town. He was looking not at her, but over her shoulder. She glanced around. A waitress was putting a coffee tray on the checker players' table. As the girl leaned over, her dress pulled tightly over shapely hips and an intriguing behind. Miss Sanderson glanced from the weasel's avid eyes to the nameplate at his elbow. BOB WESTON, MANAGER. She decided she didn't care for him. "When I drove into town," she said to Weston, "I noticed the library is called Mary Anne Stone and there's an Ernest Stone Secondary School."

He was still ogling the waitress but he volunteered, "Named after Mrs. Pulos's parents. There's also an office block called Holly Building and a medical clinic named Kenneth Holly." Weston smiled and managed to look even more like a weasel. "This is a company town and the Puloses own everything in it, including me. Mrs. Harriet Stone Pulos comes in here and I jump to attention, say yes, ma'am, no ma'am, three bags full, ma'am. They own this hotel, too." Suddenly, he seemed to realize he was talking too freely and broke off.

Miss Sanderson took pleasure in her next question. "Could you give me directions to Holly House?"

For the first time, he looked directly at her. She gave him an icy smile and he wilted. "Hey, don't take what I say seriously. I'm always kidding around." He called to the checker players. "Boys, I'm a great little kidder, aren't I?"

One of them lifted his head and gave Weston a nasty grin. "Never heared you kid in your life, Bob."

The manager was definitely deflated. He babbled directions to Holly House, scurried around the counter, scooped up her bag, and said in a hoarse whisper, "You won't say anything to Mrs. Pulos about me kidding around about her, will you?"

Miss Sanderson didn't bother answering. She glanced at the neon signs and then walked down a short hall to the coffee shop. The only patrons were a couple of women sipping coffee at one table. Miss Sanderson perched on a counter stool and the waitress with the good figure moved toward her, a smile on her wide face. "Afternoon. Want the lunch menu?"

"Coffee and soup will be fine." The secretary glanced at the sign on the wall. "What's the soup du jour?"

"Tomato and rice." Judy—the name was embroidered on the pocket over one swelling breast—lowered her voice. "Not so great. The clam chowder's good."

She opted for the chowder and it was good. So was the coffee. She drained her cup and Judy picked up a glass coffeepot. "Like a refill? No extra charge."

"No, thank you." Miss Sanderson handed the waitress a bill and waved away the change. "Your manager doesn't seem too happy about the Stones and Hollys."

"Old Weston? He's not happy about anything. 'Course a lot of people in town don't care much for that bunch out at Holly House. Haven't anything against Mrs. Pulos but figure those Earls and Puloses are a bunch of upstarts."

Another ready talker, Miss Sanderson decided. "Why is that?"

"Beats me. The Puloses are nice enough. Alexis took me out a couple of times and first off I didn't want to go. He's got quite a reputation. Figured he'd spend all evening groping me, you know, but he was a real gentleman and treated me like a lady." Judy smiled widely. "More'n I can say about others in this town, including old Weston. Now, there's a real tomcat!"

21

The secretary steered her back to the Puloses. "I understand the Pulos family once ran a shop here."

"Fruit and veggies. That's probably why folks don't like them. They ran the store and lived in a dinky little house on Oak Street, but after Dmitri Pulos married Mrs. Harriet Holly they all moved onto the Holly estate. Now they drive around in swell cars and have everything."

"Many people can't stand success."

"That's the truth. And the Puloses really have gone up in the world. Mrs. Pulos—she was Miss Stone then—used to teach at the high school. My older brother Mac had her for English Lit. Mac chummed around with Dmitri Pulos, too. All the fellows used to kid Dmitri because he had one awful crush on Miss Stone. Mooned all over the place about her. Even after she married Kenneth Holly, Dmitri hung around her. Now, there's a good-looking guy! Much better looking than his brother Alexis is."

Judy gave a heavy sigh and Miss Sanderson decided the waitress was mooning over the handsome Dmitri Pulos. She climbed down from the stool and Judy asked, "You staying in the hotel?"

"For tonight."

"Passing through?"

That's what your manager thought, Miss Sanderson told the girl silently. Aloud, she said, "Business trip. I'm going out to Holly House now."

The girl's face brightened. "Say hi to Alexis for me. Sure wish he'd ask me out again. We double-dated with his friend Billy and Billy's girlfriend. Went to Salmondale to a disco. Perfect gentleman, Alexis was. Didn't even try to hold my hand."

When Miss Sanderson retraced her steps, she found Weston was no longer behind the desk. A youth with an undershot chin was holding the fort. As she passed the checker players, one of them looked up and winked at her. She smiled back.

CHAPTER FOUR

THE MAN WHO SWUNG OPEN THE HEAVY GATES OF HOLLY House cut quite a figure. Cowboy boots, skintight jeans, and a garish shirt clothed his wiry frame. Under the brim of a Stetson, his face was old and wrinkled. His jaws chomped steadily as he marched up to the Mercedes and peered down at Miss Sanderson.

"You that Miss Sanderson I was told to look out for?"

"Yes."

"Don't hardly seem right. Deaths in the family, you know, and everybody still pretty broke up."

"I know, but I'm only doing my job."

"Guess we all has to do that. Take me, I open and shut these gates. Used to handle all the gardening but told I was too old for it. My boy, he comes in from town to do it now but I'll tell you straight, Eddie ain't as good as his daddy was. See you looking close at my duds. Always had a hankering to be a cowpoke. Too old for that, too, but I can sure dress like one. Folks poke fun at me but I don't pay 'em no mind."

She smiled up at him. "I think you look great."

Shifting his cud, he beamed tobacco-stained teeth at her. "Shows you got taste, lady. You can drive up to the house. They're expecting you."

She looked down the road. In the distance, she could make out a cluster of buildings. "Which house is it?"

"Ain't none of them. That's where the staff and the Earls live. Wife and me—she's the cook—got a nice place there. Mrs. Pulos sure looks after her people. Drive right by them places. Main house is beyond them a piece." He stuck out a hand. "Name's Granger. Bert Granger. Rather be called Tex."

She clasped the hand. "Pleased to meet you, Tex."

As she drove up the road, she glanced in the rearview mirror. The old chap was standing in a crouch, his arms dangling by his sides, looking for all the world like Wyatt Earp at the showdown at the O.K. corral. Shifting her attention from Tex, the overaged gunfighter, she concentrated on the estate. It looked like a sizable one, stretching out on both sides of the road. To her right were trim cottages, one painted blue, the other white. On the other side was a larger house, half-timbered, with leaded panes. All it lacked to look like a replica of an English inn was a sign. Beside it stood a powder blue Cadillac. The last house was the prettiest of the lot. Charmed, Miss Sanderson stared at it. Gingerbread house, she thought, small and cozy and built of weathered cedar with ornamentation along the roofline, across the tiny veranda.

The Mercedes rounded another curve and directly ahead was the main house. The road circled in front of it and then straggled off into a cul-de-sac. Holly House probably looked much the same as the hotel must have before it had been given the face-lifting. It was old, rambling off at odd angles, built of the same silver-gray cedar as the gingerbread house was and with a deep, shaded veranda.

She drew the Mercedes into the cul-de-sac and parked it beside a Lincoln Continental. Mark Harmon's car was keeping suitable company. Besides the Lincoln, there was a Morgan, a Jaguar, a Bentley, and a dashing red Alfa-Romeo. She could see what the waitress in the coffee shop had meant about the Puloses driving in style. There was also a motorcycle—a vintage Harley-Davidson—that looked out of place among the expensive vehicles. Getting out of the car, she strolled toward the house.

She had half-expected to find the entire family waiting for her, but there was no one in sight. She mounted three shallow steps and gazed at comfortable wicker furniture cushioned in faded chintz. The front door was ajar and near it was a portable bar, lined with bottles, a canister of ice, and glasses of assorted sizes and shapes. As she lifted a hand to knock, the door was pulled wide and the man facing her asked, "Miss Sanderson?"

"Yes."

He stepped out on the veranda, lifted a hand as though to shake hers, considered, and dropped it. "I'm your welcoming committee," he told her with no trace of welcome in his voice. "Alexis Pulos."

The brother, she decided, the one with the reputation who had dated Judy. "Judy asked me to say hi," she told him.

He smiled, showing an appalling line of great white teeth. "Ah, little Judy. A real sexual acrobat." One eye closed in a wink. "Quite a girl. But, I'm forgetting my manners. I was about to stir up a pitcher of martinis. Care to join me? Or, if you'd prefer, I can mix you something else."

Sinking into one of the chairs, she told him, "A martini would be fine."

"The others will be here shortly. Harriet's tied up with her lawyer but she ordered a full-scale turnout. She said to tell you she'll be as fast as she can."

She murmured there was no hurry and watched the young man as he deftly mixed ingredients at the bar. At first sight, she'd thought him handsome. He wasn't. The dark tightly coiled curls left only a narrow strip of brow and the crown of his head was balding. An effort had been made to comb hair over the bald spot. His lips were fleshy, parting automatically when he spoke in a wide, insincere smile that displayed the huge teeth. He had a smooth olive complexion and eyes like brown pansies, however.

He handed her a frosty glass and she took a sip. Alexis could make a first-rate martini. He opened his mouth but the

25

voice she heard came from behind her. "I'll have one of those, too, Alex."

A slender girl in tight jeans and a loose sweatshirt bounded up the steps and pulled to a halt in front of Miss Sanderson. "You must be Robert Forsythe's secretary," she said. Miss Sanderson nodded and the girl beamed down at her. "I'm so pleased to see you. I've read so much about you and Mr. Forsythe. I admire his work in criminology. Tell me, did he really—"

"You have rotten manners, Mar," Alexis said. The teeth flashed at Miss Sanderson. "Doesn't even bother introducing herself. This is my sister, Mariana, baby of our family and spoiled rotten."

"I am not!" Accepting the glass her brother was extending, she sat down beside the secretary. "This is thrilling! Tell me all about your cases."

"I'm afraid that would take more time than we have."

The girl pouted and Alexis came to the rescue. "Where's the faithful swain, Mar?"

"Back at the swimming pool." She touched damp hair clinging to her head and neck. "We were having a dip. No reason for Fabe to be here, anyway. He wasn't even on the estate the night when Thalia—"

"Harriet said everyone. That means Fabe. Better get him."

"You want him, you get him."

Muttering, Alexis slammed down his glass and ran down the steps. Eagerly, his sister turned to Miss Sanderson. Rather a pretty girl, the secretary thought, with her brother's eyes but without his thick lips and unfortunate teeth. Mariana had a better brow, too, high and rounded under the wet hair. "Now," Mariana said, "about—" She broke off and said, "Damn!"

Miss Sanderson swung around and followed the girl's eyes. A powder blue Cadillac was slowly making the turn into the cul-de-sac. It came to a halt beside the Alfa-Romeo, dwarfing the small car. Doors flew open and children tumbled out. More sedately, a large woman and a small man followed.

Remembering Rebecca Holly's description of the family members, Miss Sanderson asked, "The Earls?"

"The damn bloody Earls," the girl said gratingly. "And their damn bloody brats."

"Better introduce me."

"I won't have a chance. With Millie Earl around, few people can get a word in."

She proved to be correct. The woman panted up the steps, dropped a baby carelessly on a chair, and stuck a fat hand at Miss Sanderson. "Millie Earl. This is my husband, Randolph, and our kiddies." She pulled a gangling girl forward. "Our daughter, Edith. Eleven. Say hello to the nice lady, Edith."

The child looked Miss Sanderson insolently up and down and closed her lips firmly. "Shy," her mother said, brushing limp hair back from the child's narrow face. She turned to her husband. "Randolph, say hello."

As Randolph obeyed, Miss Sanderson glanced from Millie's perspiring face to her husband. He had a thin face topped by crisp russet hair. A hairline mustache, a darker red in color, perched on his upper lip. Millie looked slovenly but her Randolph was turned out with a degree of sartorial excellence. *Natty* was the word for the little man. Miss Sanderson could visualize him as he would have looked in an earlier decade, dressed in a straw boater, white pants, spats. They'd have suited him perfectly. She glanced past him at the two young people waiting their turns. Swinging around, Millie hauled the girl forward. "This is our big girl, Suzy. People claim she's the spit of her mama."

Suzy was indeed a younger edition of her mama—tall and even at her age going to fat. The boy looked like his father. "Floyd, our oldest. Nineteen." Millie sighed. "Soon to fly the nest, I'm afraid."

Mariana hissed in Miss Sanderson's ear. "As long as Harriet keeps feathering that nest, little birdie Floyd will be right in it."

"What's that you say?" Millie glared down at the girl.

27

"Always bad-mouthing my kids. Mariana, you don't like children."

"Most children I don't mind. But you missed one of your kiddies."

"So I did." Millie lumbered over and snatched up the chubby baby.

"His name is Dmitri," Mariana told the secretary with a grin. "They call him Demmy for short."

"That's right." Millie shoved the baby at Miss Sanderson. "Like to hold him?"

"Better not," Mariana cautioned. "Little Demmy is probably sopping as usual."

"Will you stop that! Randolph, speak to this girl. I won't have her talking about my children that way. I keep telling Harriet, 'Harriet,' I tell her, 'that Mariana is a smart mouth.' "

Mariana paid no attention to her. She spoke again to Miss Sanderson. "Little Demmy was named after my brother. If he'd been a girl, Millie would have called her Harriet. Millie sure knows how to lick ass."

This time, Randolph had to physically restrain his wife. Hanging onto her meaty arm, he implored, "Calm down, love. Mariana's only teasing." He glanced around at the other members of his family. "All of you sit down and behave. You, too, Millie. You know Harriet hates bickering and she could come out here at any moment."

His words had an immediate effect. The Earls scurried for chairs. Thumping down on a divan, Millie felt the baby's bottom. "You are a little damp, hon. Suzy, run out and get baby's bag."

Randolph took a chair, hiked up his sharply creased trousers, and regarded Miss Sanderson sternly. "It may not be my place to say this, but I do feel your being here at this sad time is an intrusion on this family's grief."

"I'm only following orders, Mr. Earl."

"I still think—"

"Amazing, Randolph, I had no idea you could." Alexis strode up the steps, passing Suzy on her way for baby's bag, and showed his teeth at Miss Sanderson. "I see you've met the Earls. Now you have another treat." He gestured at the man behind him. "My sister's faithful suitor. He rejoices in the name of Fabian Harcourt but prefers to be called Fabe."

The secretary had only a fleeting impression of Fabe, an impression of enormous size and an incredible amount of hair. He wore a pair of low-slung denims and had not only shoulder-length hair and a beard but his shoulders, wide chest, and arms were covered with a luxuriant growth. He was also soaking wet, evidently having come directly from the pool. Fabe ignored her. Heading directly to Randolph Earl, he seized the man and wrenched him out of the chair. Fabe held him effortlessly up to his own eye level. Randolph's gleaming shoes dangled a foot off the floor.

The latest arrival had a voice to match his size. "You little worm!" he bellowed. "Been waiting to get my hands on you. Sneaking around behind my back, turning everybody against me. I've a notion to twist that scrawny neck of yours!"

Millie nearly dropped the baby and gave a shrill scream. It was Mariana who moved. She put a hand on her boyfriend's bulging biceps. "Turn him loose this instant! You're only making it tougher on both of us."

Muttering, Fabe dumped Randolph back on his feet. The smaller man straightened his jacket and whined, "I only did what I was told, Fabe. No hard feelings, huh?"

Alexis drawled, "Must admit you have me interested. What's Father Earl been up to now?"

Mariana snarled, "Ruining every chance Fabe has to get some place to set up his business. He had that garage behind Mercer's hardware lined up and all of a sudden Sid Mercer changed his mind. Same deal with the shed behind the drugstore."

"Even my landlady's gone sour," Fabe growled. "I've been there for over a year and Libby's never minded me tinkering with bikes in her backyard. Then she tells me this morning, 'No more fooling around with those dirty machines on my property.' Admitted who'd gotten to her." He glowered at Randolph. "You, you little cockroach!"

Randolph retreated a few feet and then he drew himself up to his full height. "It was nothing personal. I was told to and I had no choice."

"Harriet," Mariana moaned. "She's trying to run Fabe out of town."

Alexis patted her shoulder. "Correct, little sister, and if Harriet has decided to, I guarantee she will."

Mariana's pointed chin lifted. "If Fabe goes, I go."

"Good riddance," Millie told her. She'd finished diapering baby and now took a plastic bottle of an orange-colored fluid out of the bag. She smiled at Mariana and it was a smile of malice.

Blimey! Miss Sanderson thought. One happy family. No wonder Thalia and Rebecca Holly had stayed clear of the Holly estate. She had the feeling that Mariana and Alexis were fond of each other, Fabe and his Mariana were obviously much in love, but the three of them just as obviously loathed the Earls and the emotion seemed to be returned. She tried to make conversation. "You're interested in motorcycles, Mr. Harcourt?"

Alexis laughed. "He should be. See the tattoo on his brawny arm? Hard to tell with all that fur but it's a skull and crossbones with a double *L* above it. Stands for a tough bike gang called the Lucky Lucifers. Fabe wasn't lucky. Spent a little time behind bars, didn't you chum?"

"You can be so cruel, Alex!" Mariana whimpered. She looked as though she was about to burst into tears.

Fabe put an arm around her shoulders. "Never mind, baby, I'm used to it. I'm not ashamed, either. Hell, I was only a kid." For the first time, he looked directly at Miss Sanderson. He has nice eyes, she thought, clear and honest. "Yes, I'm interested in bikes. Can dismantle them and repair them blindfolded. I've been trying to get a business going, but every time I figure I've nailed down a place, along comes that lousy Earl and kills the deal."

"Why don't you try the coast?" she asked.

"I'd like to set up in Vancouver, but that takes more money than I can lay my hands on. Anyway—" his arm tightened around Mariana's shoulders—"I've been hanging around here because of this girl. We're going to be married."

"Not if Cousin Harriet can prevent it," Millie said.

Fabe's wet beard jutted. "Mrs. Pulos isn't God. Mariana's of age. We can get married anytime we want to."

Alexis bared his teeth. "Granted we can't stop my sister from marrying you, but Harriet will cut off the purse strings fast and I can't picture Mariana giving up her Jaguar and other perks to live in poverty with *you*."

Neither Fabe nor Mariana rebutted that. Sinking into a chair, Fabe pulled the girl onto his lap. Millie raised disapproving eyes and stared at them. She'd been aiming the nipple of the plastic bottle at baby's mouth and Demmy lifted a chubby fist and sent it flying. The bottle bounced across the boards and down the steps. Millie gave the child a shake and said, "Naughty Demmy! Randolph, dear, get baby's bottle for Mama."

Her husband trotted down the steps and bent to retrieve the bottle. As he stooped, a large dalmatian, a piece of rope dangling from its collar, galloped around the side of the house. With no hesitation, it leaped high in the air, wound both forelegs around the man's neck, and energetically started humping his russet head. "You bloody bitch!" Randolph howled.

It didn't seem to be Father Earl's day. He struggled valiantly, but the dog was not only large but powerful. The people on the veranda, including all the members of Randolph's family except his wife, sat and laughed. Between bursts of merriment, Alexis told Miss Sanderson, "Emily's in heat but . . . she must be really desperate to have a go at . . . at our Randolph."

Miss Sanderson was roaring with laughter. All she could see was Randolph's rear end bobbing as he struggled to extricate himself from the amorous bitch. His wife jumped up, thumped baby on her chair, and bounded to her mate's rescue. "Bad Emily!" she reproved. With no discernible effort, she lifted the bitch clear of her husband. She held it firmly by the chawed length of rope.

Randolph struggled to his feet. His hair was mussed and his natty shirt and jacket were covered with muddy paw prints. He was raving at the top of his lungs but all he managed to say was four-letter words.

"Remember the children," Millie urged. "Such language. And you know Emily is part of our big family."

"That fucking bitch," he told her succinctly, "is no relative of mine!"

"How right you are," Alexis drawled. "Emily had an impeccable bloodline."

"What is going on out here?" The soft, musical voice spoke from the direction of the door. "Oh, Emily. She's broken loose again. Floyd, take her back. Don't tie her, put her in the run. The rest of you, stop this commotion. What will Miss Sanderson think of us?"

Miss Sanderson knew exactly what she thought of them. With a sigh, she turned to meet the other members of this happy family.

CHAPTER FIVE

FOUR PEOPLE HAD JOINED THE GROUP—TWO MEN, A small boy, a woman. Miss Sanderson knew she should be studying Harriet Pulos, the matriarch of this unlikely clan, but after one glance at the tall young man beside Harriet, she couldn't tear her eyes away from him. Rebecca Holly had mentioned that Dmitri Pulos was handsome, Judy had called him good-looking, but both women had underrated his looks. Shades of the days of the noble Greeks, the secretary thought.

Dmitri was taller than his brother and had golden skin and dark eyes and dark hair. There was a resemblance to Mariana and Alexis but Dmitri's eyes weren't just nice, they were magnificent. The contours of his head and the luxuriant curls brought to mind heads minted on ancient coins, busts of heroes of Athens in the days of its glory. Not handsome, Miss Sanderson thought, but beautiful in the full, romantic, masculine sense. Wrenching her eyes from Dmitri, she rose and took his wife's extended hand.

"I'm Harriet Pulos," the woman told her, quite unnecessarily. "I shall be candid with you, Miss Sanderson. This is far from pleasant for us but I know it must be a disagreeable duty for you, too. I assure you we'll do our best to make it as brief as possible." Without looking away from the secretary, she said, "A chair, please."

Randolph Earl **and** Alexis scrambled for chairs. Harriet

chose the one Alexis offered, directly opposite her visitor, and sank gracefully onto it. Dmitri and his brother hovered over her. "A martini?" Alexis asked solicitously. "Or would you prefer Agathe to make up some hot chocolate?"

"I'm tempted to have chocolate but Leander loves it and it does make his skin break out. No, Alexis, nothing."

At the mention of chocolate, the boy trotted eagerly over to his mother. With a gentle hand, she fondled his dark curls. At three, Leander gave every promise of looking exactly like his father. He smiled and dimples indented his chubby cheeks. "Chowat?" he asked eagerly.

"No, dear. Dmitri, please get Leander his toy box."

Dmitri returned to the house and Miss Sanderson looked inquiringly at the older man. "Oh," Harriet said. "Sorry. Miss Sanderson, Brice Stevens-Parkes. An old friend and my solicitor. Brice, Miss Sanderson."

Brice gravely shook her hand. His was hard and dry. A gray man, the secretary thought, probably looking older than he actually was. Gray eyes, a full gray mustache, a fringe of graying hair around a shiny bald skull. Impeccably dressed in a three-piece suit, gray, of course, and looking like a Cardin. The flinty eyes coldly examined her before he took a seat. Blimey! At Holly House, she seemed about as popular as a rabid male chauvinist would be in the midst of feminists.

Dmitri carried out a gaily painted toy box and set it down near his son. Then he stepped behind his wife's chair and leaned against the wall. At Millie Earl's urging, her younger daughter sullenly joined Leander, and the children began pulling toys from the box.

Looking fondly down at them, Harriet explained, "Traditional toys. No computerized nonsense for my child. A healthy atmosphere for raising a child should be traditional." She glanced at her sister-in-law, who was still cuddled on her boyfriend's lap. "If you need a chair, Mariana, one can be brought out for you."

The girl slid from Fabe's lap and sat on the floor of the veranda. "This will be fine," she said meekly.

Miss Sanderson was amazed. The sound of Harriet's voice

had worked a minor miracle. Alexis had given up his barbed comments and had become quiet and respectful, his spirited sister was now subdued, Suzy and Floyd Earl, who had been slumping back with rather sneering expressions, now sat bolt upright, their faces attentive. Even Millie was no longer thumping baby around but cradled him tenderly in brawny arms. If Miss Sanderson hadn't seen the clan in action, she might now believe they were devoted to each other.

The secretary eyed Harriet Pulos. Her husband's beauty made everyone else look rather nondescript, but even in her youth Harriet couldn't have had any pretensions to beauty. She looked her age. Her figure was garbed in black linen, which should have made her look thinner but didn't. In fact, Harriet was dumpy, not obese but stocky, with heavy hips and thick legs. Topping this solid body was a slender swanlike neck. Her face was an oval; her hair, ash blond and worn parted in the center and drawn into a loose knot on her neck. How, Miss Sanderson wondered, could that gorgeous chunk of man have fallen madly in love with this woman?

"Now," Harriet said, as though calling a meeting to order, "before we begin, I must tell you something else. Much as I respect Mr. Forsythe's reputation, I wouldn't have allowed you to come here for that reason alone. After all, both our tragedies were investigated by the police. There were coroners' inquests."

"I'm aware of that, Mrs. Pulos."

"I consented because of Mother Holly. She's an old woman and she has a severe heart condition. The death of her granddaughter has had a bad effect on her. These unfounded and horrible suspicions are undermining her health and affecting her mind."

Miss Sanderson thought of the coolly rational woman who had faced her in Mark Harmon's library. "Are you saying that Mrs. Holly is unbalanced?"

"Yes, I believe temporarily she is. I've had some experience with this type of mental confusion myself. At the time of my first husband's death, I suffered a mental collapse and then, of course, when Iona . . ."

Her voice trailed off and her husband placed a beautifully shaped hand on her shoulder. "You're not strong enough for this," he told her. "Let me send this woman away."

She touched the shapely hand with her own stubby one. "No, Dmitri, this I must do. For Mother Holly, to put her mind at rest. We certainly have nothing to hide and once Mr. Forsythe explains this to her, I'm sure she'll be easier. Miss Sanderson, I give permission to ask any questions you wish." Her blond head swung toward her sister-in-law. "Mariana, why is Mr. Harcourt here?"

The girl darted an icy look at her younger brother. "Alex said you wanted him."

Fabe started to heave his hirsute body out of the wicker chair. "If you want, I'll leave."

"No, you may stay. But Mr. Harcourt was not here when either of the tragedies occurred. Both were strictly family gatherings."

Apparently Harriet didn't exercise the control on the ex–Lucky Lucifer that she did on her clan. He muttered to the secretary, "Not allowed at family affairs because I'm not good enough."

Harriet ignored him, and Miss Sanderson opened her shoulder bag and took out a notebook and pen. "I wonder if you could outline both these events for me?"

"Certainly. On the day of Iona's death—" Breaking off, Harriet glanced down at her son's curly head. "Dmitri, please call Nurse Yale. Neither Leander nor Edith should be here while we discuss this."

While Dmitri left on the next errand, Miss Sanderson stared down at the notebook. In her own peculiar shorthand, she wrote the date, the names of the people to be interviewed, and the fact that Fabian Harcourt had not been on the estate at the time of either death. She glanced up and saw Dmitri with the children's nurse. Nurse Yale had been there on both days, so Miss Sanderson jotted down her name. The young woman looked more like a disco dancer than a nurse. A pink uniform clung to every curve of a voluptuous body; bright blond hair with obvious coloring from a bottle fell

36

around a flushed, pretty face; large blue eyes were fastened adoringly on the olive face of the man at her side. "Besotted," Rebecca Holly had told Robert Forsythe. "Absolutely infatuated is Nurse Selma Yale."

"Doesn't Dmitri's wife mind?" Forsythe had asked.

Rebecca had shrugged a graceful shoulder. "No reason Harriet should. Every female who meets Dmitri reacts in a similar way and all Dmitri can see is his wife."

It appeared Mrs. Holly had been right about Dmitri. He ignored the pretty nurse, gave Miss Sanderson a daggerlike look, and returned to his post behind his wife's chair. Selma Yale had a more appreciative audience in Alexis and Randolph Earl. Father Earl was surreptitiously eyeing her excellent legs, but Alexis was more overt. His eyes lecherously clung to every curve of the generous figure. He caught Miss Sanderson watching him, lifted a hand so Harriet couldn't see his face, and drew his tongue slowly over his full lower lip.

In a flurry of children's voices, toys being gathered up, and a soft cooing sound from Nurse Yale, Leander and the sullen Edith Earl were shepherded into the house. "Now," Harriet said again. Alexis's hand dropped away from his face and he turned a sober face to his sister-in-law. Remembering his family duties, Randolph bent forward and tickled his youngest child. Little Demmy obliged by blowing bubbles and cooing in much the same way that the nurse had.

"The date of Iona's death," Miss Sanderson prompted.

"Two and a half months ago," Harriet told her. "The first day of May. We have a small ceremony on that day every year. All the family attends and we have a contest for wild-flowers."

"On the estate?"

"Yes. A most scenic spot, a waterfall that drops dramatically into the Nipasagi River. Wildflowers grow in profusion around it. We have notebooks and record the names of as many flowers as we can find. Of course, no flower is touched. The winner receives a prize." Harriet turned her head. "Alexis, will you describe the area?"

"Certainly, Harriet. The water plummets from a high point into a gorge, about two hundred feet down. Above the falls and to one side of it is a lookout point, a shelf of rock. Rather treacherous footing there because of moss growing on the rock. Down the far side of the falls is a series of plateaus, connected to each other by winding paths. Each plateau is set in such a position that a person on any one of them can see none of the others. The only place where a clear view of all the plateaus can be gained is from the lookout point."

Alexis looked at his sister-in-law as though seeking approval. The approval came immediately. "Most clear, Alexis," Harriet told him.

Miss Sanderson had been trying to pin down the woman's manner. For a time, she had thought it merely the articulate speech and composure of a businesswoman. With Harriet's last remark, the light dawned. Much of her earlier profession—the easy, authoritative manner and pedantic speech of a teacher—still clung to her. Harriet had complimented Alexis as though he was a bright student who had given an excellent answer to a question. As she spoke, she smiled at him and he beamed and flushed with what looked like pleasure. Harriet turned her head and Miss Sanderson was the recipient of another smile. As she looked into Harriet's glowing face and blue-gray eyes, she realized what Rebecca Holly had meant when she had tried to explain this woman's charm. Miss Sanderson also sensed why her young, handsome husband was so deeply in love. Feeling the impact of that magnetism, the secretary found she was wishing she had come to Holly House for another reason, that she didn't have to subject this wonderful person to an interrogation about the deaths of a beloved daughter and niece. Miss Sanderson decided that, under more favorable circumstances, Harriet Pulos might have been a new and valued friend. Giving herself a mental shake, the secretary said, "The description of the fall area sounds as though it could be dangerous. Are there guardrails?"

The gray man answered her question. "One has recently

been installed. That was one of the suggestions of the coroner's jury.''

''But there were no guardrails at the time of the accident?''

Harriet shook her head. ''I've had to live with that since my daughter's death. Both Brice and Dmitri urged a number of times that rails be installed and it's my fault it wasn't done. I feared to spoil the beauty of the area. It's also so far from this house—over a mile—that the younger children never go to the falls without adults present. On our annual flower hunt, only the adults and Suzy and Floyd are allowed on the plateaus. The young children are left in the charge of adults on the level area above the falls, and even then they stay well back from the lookout. But''—she took a deep breath—''I accept full responsibility for the lack of guardrails.''

''How did your party get to the falls?''

''Some in the Land Rover with Bert Granger driving,'' Mariana told her. ''Most of us walked. Harriet believes in exercise.''

''I do,'' Harriet said. ''I'm not a health faddist but I do believe in people using their legs. Of course, the ones not able to walk that far rode with Bert in the Rover. The day was beautiful, much nicer than it was last year. Bright and sunny and warm. In the Land-Rover were Nurse Yale, Mother Holly, Demmy and Edith Earl, little Leander, and Iona. The rest of us walked.''

Miss Sanderson glanced up from her notebook and her eyes circled the people being discussed. She tried to imagine that walk. Alexis and Dmitri would probably stride along; Mariana was thin and looked in good shape, as did Brice Stevens-Parkes. Randolph Earl and his son Floyd carried no extra poundage, but Millie and her plump daughter—Miss Sanderson could picture them trudging along, heavy hips rolling, bathed in perspiration.

''The Land Rover arrived before the walkers,'' Harriet continued. ''When we got there the children were playing. Nurse Yale had her hands full. Edith was insisting on joining us on the plateaus and, of course, that started Iona wailing to do the same thing. Mother Holly generally remained with

Nurse Yale to help look after the children, but that day she was feeling quite well and it was such pleasant weather that she decided to join us for our contest. Finally, I agreed that Edith could come with us if she stayed close to her parents. Iona started to cry and Thalia, who was devoted to the children and often looked after them, volunteered to remain with Nurse Yale and look after Iona while the nurse cared for Millie's baby and Leander. We started down toward the path to the first plateau, watching our footing because the spray from the water, which encourages the growth of wildflowers, also makes the soil and rocks moist and in places mossy.''

"Did you stay in groups?" Miss Sanderson asked.

"No," Brice told her. "You must keep in mind this was a contest and there was a strong sense of competition. We spread out through the series of plateaus, much engrossed in locating the flowers and noting them down.''

"How long before the accident occurred?"

Frowning, he fingered his thick mustache. "I really can't say. None of us were paying any attention to time. Perhaps twenty minutes.''

"What alerted you to the child's danger? Was it a sound?"

"These are fairly large falls, Miss Sanderson, and there's no way you can even hear yourself speak that close to them. No, it wasn't a sound. I happened to glance up toward the rocky shelf above the falls and I saw Thalia up there, standing right at the edge of the lookout. She seemed agitated and was waving her arms and her mouth was moving as though she was shouting, but I couldn't hear what she was saying.''

"What about the other people up there, the ones who stayed with the younger children? Could they hear her?"

"Nurse Yale and Bert Granger heard shouting but they couldn't understand what she was saying. You must realize the Land-Rover was parked well back from the lookout for the children's safety. Bert ran toward the lookout but . . . he was too late.''

"And then?" Miss Sanderson prompted.

"Then," Brice told her, "I saw Iona. She'd been attracted by Thalia's cries and she came running up to the edge of the rock to look down and she slipped in the damp moss. I shouted at Thalia and gestured toward the child. Thalia turned her head but she was too late.''

Harriet jumped to her feet. "I saw my child hurtling down. I saw her little body sweep past me. It happened so fast. A few seconds and Iona was gone.'' Her composure had broken and Miss Sanderson saw what was behind it. Pain and grief stared from the woman's ravaged face, from her pale eyes. There was rage, too, rage against the fates who had torn this child from her. "I'd waited so long for a baby," she said brokenly. "Her birth was difficult. Iona was . . ." she paused and then added simply, "she was beloved.''

Dmitri was beside his wife, his arms around her, pressing her face against his shoulder. Both Alexis and the lawyer were on their feet. Millie Earl made a move to go to her cousin, but her husband restrained her. Over his wife's head, Dmitri glared at Miss Sanderson. "That is *enough*. You can see what this is doing to her—to have to relive the whole nightmare again. I *demand* you leave.''

Alexis nodded and Brice said, "I agree with Dmitri.''

There were murmurs of agreement from the rest, but Harriet pulled herself away from her husband's arms and accepted the handkerchief Alexis was pressing on her. "No," she said firmly. "I always taught my students that no matter how hard it is to do something, if it is necessary, it must be done. Do sit down, Brice. You, too, Alexis. Dmitri, please. This is my decision.''

Wiping her eyes, Harriet sat down. Dmitri gazed down at her, shook his noble head, and moved back behind her chair. Harriet looked at Miss Sanderson. "Continue.''

The secretary bit her lip and then asked quietly, "Was Thalia Holly close enough to your daughter to . . .''

"Push her?" Harriet winced and turned toward the lawyer. "Brice?''

"No. Thalia was yards away from the child. I saw that and so did Bert Granger.'' His dry voice warmed into anger. "But Thalia was left in charge of the child and she knew how

41

headstrong Iona could be. It was a case of absolute criminal negligence!''

Harriet shook her blond head. ''At worst, it was a moment of carelessness. But I'm afraid I acted very badly. The men clambered down to the base of the falls and were able to . . . to retrieve my daughter. When they carried her up and I saw . . . when I saw Iona, I turned on Thalia like a fishwife. I cursed her and screamed accusations, and when she tried to explain I . . . I turned my back on her.''

''An understandable reaction,'' Brice told her.

''I'd have done the same if it had been one of my kiddies,'' Millie told her stoutly.

Dmitri leaned over the back of his wife's chair. ''At that moment, I could have strangled Thalia! Our daughter, the child we wanted so much, she was barely seven. We'd celebrated her birthday only two days before.'' He continued more calmly: ''We took Harriet back to the house. She was in a state of collapse. Brice made calls, the doctor arrived, and then Sergeant McBride of the Royal Canadian Police. Harriet was placed under sedation.''

''What about Thalia?'' Miss Sanderson asked.

''She went to pieces. As soon as she made her statement, Rebecca spirited her away.'' Brice shook his bald head. ''None of us was sorry to see her go. We didn't want to see her, to speak to her. Rebecca phoned any number of times, trying to reach Harriet. But Dmitri and Alexis and I made sure none of those calls got through.''

Harriet smiled wanly. ''They were trying to shield me and I suppose they were right. At that time, I was in no shape to worry about Thalia. But two months later, I received a letter from Mother Holly. She told me she considered Thalia's condition dangerous. The girl was wild with remorse and on the brink of a mental collapse. By that time, I was more rational and I realized what I had done to her. My daughter was dead and buried. Nothing could bring her back. But Thalia had to be helped. I phoned Mother Holly and told her to bring Thalia home.'' She glanced around the circle of faces. ''I spoke to everyone about her.''

"That's true," Randolph agreed heartily. "As I told Millie, a Christian gesture. Cousin Harriet told all of us to welcome Thalia, to be gentle. She told us what a state the girl was in." He added, "Harriet's a saint."

"Hardly that." Harriet made a dismissive gesture. "Merely another sinner who'd made a mistake and was trying to make amends. I raised Thalia and I was attached to her."

Flipping a page over, Miss Sanderson asked, "All the family was here when Mrs. Holly and her granddaughter returned?"

"Yes, we were all here. They came to us on a Friday evening, on the second day of July. Mother Holly and Thalia were to spend the weekend and return to Vancouver the following Monday. Thalia was terribly nervous but everyone was nice to her and the weekend started well." Again Harriet's eyes swept over her relatives, and Miss Sanderson had a hunch that they probably had been nice to Thalia Holly. They wouldn't have dared act otherwise. Harriet's hands twisted in her black linen lap and she stared down at them. "On Saturday morning, it happened."

Puzzled, Miss Sanderson jerked up her head. "I understood it was Sunday."

"I didn't mean that. Thalia's body was found on Sunday morning, but it was Saturday when—"

"When *you* killed Thalia!" a young male voice cried.

Every head swiveled toward the source of the agonized cry. It had come from the eldest of the Earl brood. Miss Sanderson was astonished. She'd dismissed Floyd and his sister Suzy as carbon copies of their parents. As she searched the young man's face, she could see she had been mistaken. Despite his coloring, Floyd was not like his father. His mouth was sensitive and vulnerable and his eyes were brimming with tears. Those wet eyes locked with hers. "You never knew Thalia. To you she's a name, a girl who died. She was wonderful. Lovely to look at and when she moved . . . it was like music sounds." Floyd pointed at Harriet. "*She* destroyed Thalia."

Miss Sanderson had time only to decide that Floyd Earl, like Rebecca Holly, was immune to Harriet's charm, when his mother was on her feet. Clutching the baby to her breast, Millie cried, "Floyd! How *dare* you speak to Harriet like that?"

His father took more direct action. He sprang at his son, his arm raised, his hand clenched into a fist. Fabe Harcourt was as fast. One hairy hand grabbed Randolph's arm and wrenched it down. "None of that," he growled.

Suzy flung an arm around her brother's narrow shoulders. "Floyd had a crush on Thalia," she told her parents.

"It wasn't a crush," the boy blurted. "I loved her." Angrily, he dashed tears from his eyes. "Can't any of you understand? Sure, she didn't know I existed, but I loved her. I always will!"

Miss Sanderson no longer was watching the boy. In Dmitri's eyes, she saw understanding. If anyone knew about unrequited love for a woman, she thought, it was probably Dmitri Pulos. Rather gently, Dmitri said, "You'd better take the boy home, Randolph."

"No." Harriet raised her madonna face. "Let him stay. He's right, you know. It *was* my fault."

"It certainly wasn't," Millie said fiercely. "All of us know that. I don't know what gets into that boy. Harriet, dear, I do hope you're not going to take any notice of Floyd. He's so young and—"

"Please Millie," Harriet said. "Let's get this finished. We were talking about Saturday. It was a warm, sunny morning and we decided to spend time outside. Some of the young people were in the pool. The rest of us gathered around the playground, watching the little children play. It isn't a modern playground, Miss Sanderson; in this house we tend to be rather old-fashioned. The swings, teeter-totter, sandbox, and roundabout were built by Bert Granger. On the ground, Bert put down a thick mixture of sand and sawdust so if there are mishaps, the children's falls will be cushioned.

"Thalia seemed in better spirits and I put her in charge of Leander. I thought . . . I decided it would improve her morale and show my trust in her. Floyd''—she jerked her head at the boy, who sat with his face averted—''was swinging Demmy in a baby swing and Edith was playing in the sand-box. Leander has his own little swing but he always begs to use the largest one. I suppose I was feeling indulgent and I allowed this. I suppose . . .''

Her voice trailed off and Brice touched her wrist. ''Would you like me to continue?'' She nodded and he said briskly, ''It was all very peaceful, Miss Sanderson. The children were playing and we were watching them. Thalia lifted Leander onto the swing and he kept calling, 'Higher, higher!' She pushed harder and he was swinging high in the air—far too high for such a small child. Harriet called to Thalia to let the swing slow down and at that moment, when he was way up in the air, the rope broke. Leander fell. Some of the women screamed and I headed to the child. There was blood on his face and one leg. I moved quickly but Harriet got there first—''

''And that's when I did it,'' Harriet said dully. ''All I could think of was my son. My daughter was dead and I believed my son was dying. Again, I turned on Thalia. She tried to kneel beside my child and I . . . I drove her away. I told her to keep her murdering hands off him. I said she'd killed Iona and now she'd killed Leander. What I did is indefensible.''

''That's ridiculous!'' Dmitri said violently. He put a hand on each of his wife's black-clad shoulders. ''You reacted as any mother would have. You were grief-stricken and still overwrought from Iona's death.''

''Was the boy badly hurt?'' Miss Sanderson asked.

Dmitri shook his head. ''He had shallow cuts on his fore-head and one knee. But there was a great deal of blood. At the moment, we all thought he'd been badly injured.''

His wife shrugged away from his hands. ''Nurse Yale was summoned and she examined my son. Dr. Brent was called and there was no sign of concussion. But I went directly to the nursery and spent hours beside Leander's bed, calming him and reading his favorite stories. I had no time or thought for Thalia.''

"And Thalia?"

"She ran up to her room and locked herself in. Even for Mother Holly, she wouldn't open the door. I stayed with my son and had lunch and dinner on trays in the nursery. Toward evening, my husband and Brice persuaded me to go to my room and rest. I was exhausted and did doze for a time. Mother Holly woke me. She was furious. Worried about Thalia, of course. We had rather hot words, but I did agree to go and talk to the girl, see if I could comfort her."

"Thalia allowed you to enter her room?"

"She unlocked her door and we talked for about an hour. I apologized for my behavior and explained to her it was a hysterical reaction."

"What shape was she in?"

"Bad shape. Completely unnerved and close to incoherent. As we talked, she seemed to become a bit calmer, but by then I was as worried about her as Mother Holly was. I persuaded Thalia to go to bed and I rang for Cassie and had her prepare a glass of my own sedative for her. I can't swallow pills and this is in liquid form. It's powerful, but Cassie always measures it carefully—"

"Cassie?" Miss Sanderson interrupted.

"Cassie Beaton, one of our maids. After Thalia was in bed, I tucked her in and kissed her good—" Harriet buried her head in her hands.

"You've had enough," Brice told her gently.

Lifting her from the chair, Dmitri held her close. Her voice was muffled. "I'm not as strong as I thought. I can't go on. But Miss Sanderson—"

"I'll attend to Miss Sanderson," Brice told her. "Dmitri, you take Harriet to her room. Better have Nurse Yale look in on her."

Harriet allowed her husband to lead her into the house. The expressions of her relatives as they regarded Miss Sanderson ranged from the frosty face of Brice Stevens-Parkes to hot resentment from Millie Earl. It was Mariana Pulos who broke the uncomfortable silence. "I've changed my mind about Robert Forsythe. I thought he was a wonderful

46

person. But to send you here, Miss Sanderson, he must be inhuman.''

For once, Millie Earl seemed in agreement with Mariana Pulos. ''He's never known what it is to have a child,'' she muttered. ''Never been a parent.''

Hot color flamed in Miss Sanderson's face. ''I hardly think it necessary to be a parent to understand a mother's grief at the loss of a child.''

''A noble sentiment,'' Brice said caustically. ''But one that has no bearing on this gathering. The sooner you leave Holly House, the better. I'll finish the details myself. The following morning—Sunday—was rather chaotic. None of us rose at our usual times. But, by the time Harriet came down for breakfast, we were all in the dining room—all that is, except for Rebecca and Thalia. Harriet was inquiring about Thalia when we heard a scream from upstairs. It was Rebecca. She'd gone to her granddaughter's room and she found Thalia's body. The girl had hanged herself and she'd been dead for hours. The autopsy placed her death sometime between midnight and one o'clock. I would imagine that Rebecca gave you the details and I won't repeat them. The coroner's jury brought in a verdict of death at her own hands while of unsound mind. And that, Miss Sanderson, is that.''

''Not quite,'' Miss Sanderson said. ''I have questions.''

''Better answer them,'' Alexis told the lawyer. ''Remember what Harriet said.''

Brice caressed his mustache. ''Ask away.''

''When Mrs. Holly found her granddaughter that Sunday morning—was the door locked?''

''In this house, interior doors are seldom locked. Thalia's certainly wasn't.''

''What about the exterior doors? And, are security precautions taken?''

The lawyer moved impatiently. ''Didn't Mrs. Holly fill you in on these details?''

Her expression was as cold as his. ''I'm asking you.''

He shrugged. ''When the household retires, the doors and windows are checked and locked. After this check, a perimeter burglar alarm is activated. Generally, Dmitri attends to this, but that Saturday night he remained with Leander in the nursery and I did it.''

"Were all of you in this house that night?"

"Except for Mr. Harcourt, we were all here. Not the staff. The two maids have their own cottage and so does the cook and gateman. Mariana and Alexis have self-contained suites—Mariana's is in the basement; Alexis's in the attic. These have outside entrances and also have access to the house.''

"The Earl family?"

"They spent the night here. Harriet frequently has the family stay over on special occasions. It's a large house.''

Miss Sanderson was nibbling the end of her pen. "Do sounds travel readily in this house?"

With icy courtesy, he explained, "The house is not only well built but shortly after Iona's birth, Harriet had the second floor soundproofed. The reason we heard Rebecca's screams was because the dining room door was ajar and she was screaming down the stairwell. May I ask what you're driving at?"

"I was wondering if one of you could have entered Thalia Holly's room that night?"

Alexis gave a barking laugh. "Sneaked in, pulled her out of bed, and hanged her? Ridiculous!"

Miss Sanderson pointed out, "She was sedated."

"Sedatives," Randolph said ponderously, "affect people differently. That was brought out at the inquest. What knocks one person out may not another. Thalia was well able to hang herself."

Miss Sanderson flipped back a few pages. "Mrs. Holly told us a length of heavy drape cord had been slashed off. Was a knife found in the room?"

"A pair of scissors," Millie told her. "Harriet's. She always carries her sewing basket with her, you know. A born mother, stitching things for the children. She'd taken it to Thalia's room and remembered the basket but left the scissors on a bed table.''

48

The lawyer got to his feet and looked down at Miss Sanderson. "Harriet made us promise not to mention this to you, but I feel this is one promise I must break. If you had read the transcript of the inquest on Thalia Holly, you wouldn't be making these insinuations. Mr. Forsythe is considering foul play, the possibility of murder. I assure you that not only was there no motive for this but it was proved beyond all doubt that the girl took her own life."

"What do you mean?"

"I mean that Rebecca Holly wasn't honest with you. You and Mr. Forsythe have been used by a vicious old woman to punish Harriet even more than she has punished herself for her attitude toward Thalia. Harriet has suffered *enough*. It's time you know the truth."

"And the truth is?"

"On two earlier occasions, Thalia Holly attempted to take her life. She was talented, dedicated, and beautiful. She was also a hopeless neurotic." He smiled and there was a hint of malice in that smile. "Robert Forsythe is considered brilliant. You can tell him from me that I'm inclined to doubt it. Mrs. Holly victimized both of you."

CHAPTER SIX

LATE-AFTERNOON SUN POURED THROUGH THE GLASS wall of the penthouse library, puddled on a fine old rug, and touched the calf of one of Rebecca Holly's slender legs. The elderly woman sat erect, her shoulders not touching the leather chair back. Miss Sanderson, seated at one end of the desk, was again struck by Rebecca's beauty. Mrs. Holly was wearing a soft, flowing gown and her white hair was framed by a wide-brimmed hat. The color of the gentian eyes was only a shade lighter than the violets pinned to her bodice.

Mrs. Holly wasted no time on preliminaries and spoke directly to Forsythe. "I've been waiting to hear from you. Have you any results on your investigation?"

"The investigation is completed."

She leaned forward. "What have you found?"

"That we were deliberately misled."

"By whom?"

"By you."

Tearing her eyes from the barrister's face, she looked at his secretary. "I didn't think Harriet would tell you."

"Mrs. Pulos did not tell Sandy. Who it was doesn't matter. What does matter is that we were made to look like fools. You swore to us that your granddaughter was not the type to take her life. That is the assumption we went on. Then we discover Thalia Holly had made two previous and unsuccessful attempts to kill herself."

Arching fine brows, Rebecca asked, "How would you have reacted if I'd been wholly truthful about Thalia's past?"

"I'd have refused the case."

"Exactly. Because of a couple of incidents that meant nothing, you'd have refused to look for her murderer."

Miss Sanderson raised her head. "Two suicide attempts are hardly incidents."

"These were. I told you of Thalia's devotion to Harriet. The child had been so starved for affection, so eager to have a mother figure, she was abnormally sensitive to anything that might threaten that relationship. These so-called suicide attempts were simply the efforts of a confused child to gain attention and reassurance. When Thalia found that Harriet was to marry Dmitri Pulos, she panicked, believing he might displace her in Harriet's life. All Thalia did was nick her wrist with a razor blade, a few shallow cuts that hardly bled."

Forsythe's lips were set and when he didn't speak, his secretary said, "The second attempt was when Thalia was told Harriet was expecting her first child, Iona. Mrs. Holly, that *was* a serious attempt."

Mrs. Holly steadily regarded the barrister. "I see you've read the transcript of the inquest. Yes, again Thalia felt threatened. This time by Harriet's own baby. To gain attention, she did a foolish thing."

"She tried to hang herself," Forsythe said flatly.

"By a thin cord that broke. I give you my word my granddaughter did not have any serious desire to end her life. Surely you can see that."

"This is what I see," Forsythe said harshly. "Twice Thalia Holly felt her place in Harriet's life endangered. Once by a husband, then by a baby. Twice she reacted with violence and efforts to destroy herself. The third time, her reason was much more serious. Because of Thalia, Harriet Pulos lost her daughter. Again, because of Thalia's carelessness, Harriet's surviving child was—"

"Nonsense! I was there and saw it. Leander wasn't injured. He had only a couple of scratches."

"Another matter you neglected to mention to us."

"It didn't seem important. And that evening, Harriet went to Thalia and reassured her."

Forsythe bent forward. "How do we know what went through Thalia's mind? Despite Harriet's reassurances, your granddaughter may have felt from that time on she would be an outsider, that Harriet was lost to her. In that frame of mind, the girl could well have cut a piece of curtain cord and ended it all."

Rebecca was on her feet, turning toward Miss Sanderson. "Do you agree? You met these people. You must have sensed what they're like. Harriet? Did she take you in with her charm and that suffering, wonderful saint act she puts on?"

"I'm not saying I care for the people in her household, Mrs. Holly, but Mrs. Pulos is shattered, not only by her daughter's death, but by the death of Thalia. I agree with Robby."

Rebecca stretched imploring hands toward the barrister. "Please, I give you my word—"

"Your word carries no weight with me." Forsythe rose, his expression stony. "You deceived us. You *used* us as instruments of revenge against a grieving mother. Sandy will see you to the elevator. Good day."

Rebecca's shoulders sagged, but at the door she turned, pulled those shoulders erect, and lifted her delicate chin. "Mark Harmon told me how intelligent you are, what a sixth sense you have. He was wrong. You *have* been hoodwinked, but not by me. I make you a promise. I am going to find *proof* that Thalia was murdered. I want you to consider one fact. Thalia was devoted to both Iona and Leander. Many times they were in her charge and she never was careless with them. The day of Iona's accident, Thalia saw something from that lookout point that made her forget her duty. Mr. Forsythe, *what* did Thalia see?"

As the door swung to, Forsythe walked out on the patio and leaned on the parapet, his eyes fixed on the distant mountains. After a time, he felt a touch on his arm and turned. Miss Sanderson said, "Tough job, Robby."

"I ended up feeling like a brute. Do you think I was too hard on her?"

"She had it coming. There's no doubt Thalia Holly committed suicide. Either Rebecca's deluded or out for revenge against Harriet Pulos." Lifting a hand, the secretary started drumming a thumbnail against a front tooth.

Forsythe patiently waited. This habit, annoying as it was, was the signal that his companion was deep in thought. Finally, he said, "Out with it. Something's bothering you."

Her hand fell. "Actually, three things. Dmitri Pulos . . . I have an eerie feeling about that man."

"You're not going fey on me again?"

"I don't go *fey*. I simply get hunches and quite often they're right on target."

"As I have ample reason to know." Forsythe grinned. "Expound hunch-getter."

"I feel I should know him—as though I've met him or someone like him before."

"With a memory like yours, that should be no problem."

"Wrong. I keep trying to track it down and no luck. Irritating!"

"Give it a rest and it will pop up. What else disturbs you?"

"Dmitri's brother." She frowned into the distance. "Alexis has the reputation of being hell on women. When I mentioned the waitress at the hotel coffee shop, Alexis let on he'd been intimate with her. He was also blatantly obvious about his intentions toward the children's nurse, Selma Yale. When I returned to the hotel, I questioned Judy again and also pumped a chambermaid Alexis has dated. Same story. Each time they dated with Alexis's friend, a chap who teaches physical education at the secondary school, and a woman teacher this man takes out occasionally. On every date, Alexis was a perfect gentleman and 'didn't lay a finger' on either of the girls."

"Sounds as though Alexis is acting the role of a lecher. And you think—"

53

"I think he hasn't come out of the closet yet."

"Possible," Forsythe said thoughtfully. "Also understandable. From your description of Harriet's old-fashioned environment for her children, I can see Alexis's reason. What's the third thing?"

"That last remark that Rebecca Holly made. Even Harriet's dreadful relatives agreed that Thalia had never been careless when she was in charge of the children before. I wonder what she *did* see from that lookout point?"

He shrugged. "Probably we'll never know. But one point does interest me. Sandy, did you feel this charm that Rebecca keeps talking about?"

"Full voltage. Harriet smiled at me and I practically melted."

"Charisma?"

"That's such a catchall phrase." Her wide brow furrowed. "What Harriet has is impossible to explain—like quicksilver. For an instant, she makes you feel as though . . . as though you're important to her. That you're her favorite person and she values you. That you want her to approve of you and—"

"Yet she isn't beautiful?"

"Harriet's really rather plain and she has the manner of a spinster schoolteacher." She threw up her hands. "Blimey, you'd have to meet her, Robby!"

"Small chance of that. But let's forget Harriet and enjoy our vacation."

"I second the motion. We're finished with the Hollys and the Stones and the town of Hollystone."

A week later, they were breakfasting at the table on the patio and Miss Sanderson, balancing a coffeepot in one hand, a frosted pitcher of orange juice in the other, stepped out of the kitchen. Forsythe was unfolding the morning paper. She poured juice for both of them and reached for a slice of toast. The barrister made a muffled sound and she glanced across the table. He was staring down at the front page.

Circling the table, she looked over his shoulder. The head-

54

line screamed WEALTHY SOCIALITE FOUND DEAD IN STANLEY PARK.

There was a photograph with the article. It wasn't particularly clear and it was in black and white, but Miss Sanderson knew if it had been in color, the eyes in the fragile face would have been gentian blue.

CHAPTER SEVEN

"**W**E WERE WRONG," FORSYTHE SAID HEAVILY.

"Not so fast," Miss Sanderson said. "Let me read this." Her eyes scanned the article. "It could be a coincidence. Rebecca Holly died from a massive coronary and there were no signs of violence other than the rifled purse. She *could* have been mugged and frightened into a heart attack."

"Better finish reading, Sandy. Look at the time element. An acquaintance of Mrs. Holly was waiting for a bus and saw Mrs. Holly getting out of a cab. They spoke briefly and then Mrs. Holly walked into the park. The time was almost half past nine in the evening. Rebecca Holly wasn't a fool. Can you imagine a woman of that age and evident intelligence going alone into a park notorious for muggings and rapes at that hour unless she had good reason to chance it?" Without waiting for an answer, the barrister said savagely, "I also can't believe three violent deaths taking place in one family in less than three months is coincidental. We'd better try for more information."

He rose and walked into the kitchen with his secretary at his heels. "The police?" she called.

"We'll try that lawyer Mark referred us to."

When they reached the library, Miss Sanderson put the call through while her employer slumped in the chair behind the desk. She spoke for a moment and then nodded at Forsythe. Reaching over, he switched the phone to speaker. "Robert Forsythe, Mr. Barton. I'd like some information."

A mellow baritone told him, "I've been expecting this call, Mr. Forsythe. You've heard about Rebecca Holly?"

"Read about it in the morning newspaper. You knew her well?"

"Really not that well. I am—I should say was—her attorney, and when Mark Harmon mentioned you'd be staying in his suite, I urged Rebecca to consult with you. Rebecca and I didn't socialize that much. She played bridge with my wife and me a few times, I took her to lunch occasionally, and Helen invited her to dine with us a couple of times, but that was about it."

"Could we have her address? And did her granddaughter live with her?"

"Thalia? No, she lived about two blocks from Rebecca's apartment. I've both addresses here." Barton read them off and Miss Sanderson jotted them down. "I take it that Rebecca had been in contact with you?"

"She was."

"I wouldn't be too upset by this, Mr. Forsythe. I was in touch with the police in the capacity of her attorney and it was definitely a heart attack touched off by a mugging. Rebecca had a serious heart condition for many years."

"I'm aware of that. Could you arrange for us to check out Rebecca's apartment? What about Thalia's? Has it been rented?"

"No. There's a year lease on it. I advised Rebecca to clear out her granddaughter's belongings so it could be sublet, but she hadn't gotten around to it. I can phone the manager . . . one moment. Yes, her name is Mrs. Luxton. I'll have her let you in."

"Rebecca Holly's?"

"Sorry, can't help you there. Not until the police are through."

Forsythe moved restlessly. "Did Rebecca confide in you or your wife?"

57

"Certainly not in me—except about her doubts about her granddaughter's death."

"How did you feel about that, Mr. Barton?"

There was a pause and then Barton said slowly, "Rebecca couldn't seem to accept the fact that the last Holly was dead. Frankly, I didn't take her suspicions seriously."

"Could your wife help us?"

"Heavens, no. Helen and Rebecca chatted about the weather, clothes, that sort of thing. Ballet, of course. Helen is interested in ballet, and with Rebecca it was a consuming passion."

The secretary leaned forward. "Abigail Sanderson, Mr. Barton. Mark Harmon mentioned his mother was a friend of Rebecca's. Could we speak with her?"

"Mark's mother has been dead for several years."

"Did Rebecca ever mention a friend she might have confided in?"

"Rebecca was never forthcoming, Miss Sanderson. Bit of a loner. Just a moment . . . there was a woman she mentioned a couple of times. Let me think. I know she lives in the same apartment block that Rebecca lived in. The place is full of widows, well-to-do, because rents in that area are high. Her name is something like Gussie. Anyway, she lives directly across from Rebecca's apartment." Barton hesitated and then asked, "Mr. Forsythe, are you considering Rebecca's death wasn't the result of a mugging?"

"I'm considering that possibility, yes."

"In that case, how may I help?"

"You could check with the police again. Get any detail, no matter how trivial, that hasn't been released to the public. Also, can you recommend a good private investigation agency?"

"I deal with one on occasion that's competent. If you like I can handle this for you. What do you want to know?"

Forsythe said grimly, "Every bit of information they can dig out about the people who live on the Holly estate and a couple more who live in Hollystone. Sandy will give you the names."

"Give me that list and I'll get right on it."

"Thanks. We'll be speaking later. Sandy . . ."

While his secretary gave George Barton the list of names, the barrister sprang up and started pacing the length of the library. She finished, said good-bye, and hung up. Then she swung around and asked, "Which shall I take—Gussie or Mrs. Luxton?"

"You take Rebecca's friend and I'll have a look through Thalia's apartment."

"Seems a forlorn hope. I shouldn't imagine there would be anything to help among Thalia's effects. And from what George Barton said about Rebecca, it doesn't sound as though she would confide in anyone."

"One never knows," Forsythe said. "Anyway, we must start somewhere."

She rose. "So let's start digging."

When Forsythe tapped at the manager's door, it was opened by a youngish, pleasant-faced woman. He gave her his name and mentioned George Barton's. He also gave her a reassuring smile. Mrs. Luxton didn't appear reassured. Rather dubiously, she eyed the tall young man. "You're prompt. Just took the call from Mr. Barton. You don't look like a private eye."

I wonder, Forsythe thought, what she would say if I told her I'm actually a barrister? Aloud, he asked, "What does a private eye look like?"

Her face relaxed and she smiled. "Search me. Never met one before. I guess it's okay for me to let you into Miss Holly's suite, but I'll have to stay there with you. Just a sec, I'll get the master key and take a peek at the baby. Should be okay to leave. He's having a nap."

"Could I see him?"

"Sure. This way."

The room was cluttered. An ironing board with a basket of clothes beside it was set up near the crib. Mrs. Luxton pointed at it. "Should be twenty-six hours in the day. Never seem to catch the work up." She bent over the crib. "This

59

is my youngest, a boy. I've got two girls but they're in school now.''

He gazed down at the rosy face. ''Fine-looking chap. What's his name?''

''Arnie. Named after his dad. I'm thinking of calling him by his second name. Arnie Senior ran out on me right after this little guy was born. Left me high and dry with three kids to support.''

''It must be difficult.''

''It sure isn't easy. But this job's been a godsend. Keeps me hopping, but I can look after the kids and earn a living at the same time. It was either this or welfare and I never was one for charity. But everyone's got problems. Come along, Mr. Forsythe, Miss Holly's suite is on this floor.''

The manager led the way down the hall and stopped before a door near the end of it. ''I felt real bad when I heard about Miss Holly. Then I pick up the paper this morning and see her grandmother is dead, too. Bad world.''

''It most certainly is. Did you know Thalia Holly well?''

''Only nodded to her once in a while when we passed in the hall. The rent was paid in advance and she never come down to my suite for anything. Sure was a pretty little thing. Good tenant, too. Never complained or threw parties.'' Unlocking the door, she stood aside. ''Sorry I have to hang around but it's company rules.''

''No problem.'' Forsythe's attention was on the suite. The living room was airy and uncluttered. The furniture was good, there were few ornaments, and a lovely antique lady's desk. A coating of dust covered all the surfaces except that of the desk. It looked as though it had recently been dusted. ''Was Miss Holly's grandmother here in the last week?''

''Not that I know about. I used to see the old lady once in a while when she visited Miss Holly, but I think Mrs. Holly had her own key to this apartment. She could have been here, but I didn't see her.''

Sitting down at the desk, Forsythe rapidly went through the drawers. There was nothing of interest in them. Some receipted bills, a couple of postcards, writing paper, envelopes, stamps, a checkbook. Pulling the drawers out, he felt behind them. Then he turned them over so he could see their undersides.

"If you tell me what you're looking for, maybe I can help," Mrs. Luxton volunteered.

"I've no idea."

"Funny, Mr. Forsythe. Look at all those pictures and they're all of the same people—a lady and two kids."

The top of the long table was covered with framed photographs. The lady Mrs. Luxton had mentioned he recognized from Miss Sanderson's description as Harriet Pulos. One of the children was Leander. Picking up a double frame, he gazed down at one side of it. A professional shot of Leander. Deep dimples showed in the smile he was beaming at the camera.

"Cute kid," the manager said. "Wonder who the girl is?"

"Probably his sister—Iona."

"Nice name. Never heard it before. She isn't as good-looking as her brother."

Iona Pulos hadn't had her brother's dark good looks. She had an oval face, wide-spaced eyes, long blond braids. A younger edition of Harriet Pulos, Forsythe thought.

He checked out the kitchenette and then the bathroom. Both had been cleared out. "One bedroom or two?" he asked Mrs. Luxton.

"One. Across the hall."

Thalia Holly's bedroom showed more character than the rest of the apartment. The narrow bed was covered in fluffy pink and white and in front of the window was a chaise lounge upholstered in pale blue. On the bed table were a clock radio and a studio picture of two women. Harriet Pulos smiled from the frame and at her side was Thalia Holly. On the wall over the bed was an enlargement of the same photo Rebecca Holly had left with him. In it, Thalia's image reached with graceful arms for the unattainable.

Forsythe turned his attention to the chest of drawers and the dressing table. Underclothes, panty hose, blouses, several sweaters, a few pieces of costume jewelry. On top of the

61

chest sat a doll, not one of the adult dolls loved by contemporary children, but a baby doll, complete with ringlets, bonnet, and ruffled dress. Traditional, the barrister told himself, probably a gift from Harriet Pulos to a young Thalia. The doll, propped carefully on the chest, brought Thalia closer than she had been. With gentle fingers, he touched a glossy ringlet. Then he checked out the clothes closet.

"Find anything?" Mrs. Luxton asked.

Forsythe shook his head. There was nothing here. Except for the photos and the doll, the place was strangely impersonal, feeling like a motel or hotel suite. He turned to tell the manager he was finished and found her standing beside the bed, her hands clasped behind her, staring up at the ballet shot of Thalia.

"I saw her dance once," she said softly. "Don't know anything about ballet, but I was kind of proud having her as a tenant. She was in something called *Swan Lake*. Amateur performance and didn't cost much or I wouldn't have been there. She kind of floated, you know, looked just like a dancing doll. For a while I forgot about the kids, and this place, and Arnie walking out on me. Went into another world." Mrs. Luxton turned to face the barrister. "Don't know how to say it, but it's not just another person dying. Lots of people die but that girl . . . it don't seem right she should be gone."

"A dancing doll," Forsythe said softly. "I know exactly what you mean."

A couple of blocks away, a different type of woman was putting in different words Mrs. Luxton's sentiments. Gussie, now identified as Mrs. Augustine Spencer, handed Miss Sanderson a Spode cup, replaced the silver teapot on its tray, and said, "Of the two deaths, I believe I was most upset by Thalia's. I'm not saying Rebecca's loss isn't a severe blow, but one rather expects people of our age to pass on. But that beautiful child, that wonderful talent . . . the world is the loser by Thalia's death."

"You knew her well?" Miss Sanderson asked.

"I saw her a number of times when she was visiting her

grandmother. I can't say I was well acquainted with the child but I found her delightful. Such nice manners, such a respectful attitude toward her elders. Quite refreshing. And the way she moved! With such grace and poise, she made one feel rather awkward.''

"You must have known Mrs. Holly well."

"Quite well. We met when I moved in here four . . . no, five years ago this December. Shortly after my husband's death. Rebecca and I had much in common. Both widows, both a bit lonely, trying to fill long hours. Our backgrounds are also not dissimilar.''

The secretary put her cup and saucer carefully on the Queen Anne table so as not to mar the lustrous finish. Rebecca Holly and Mrs. Spencer must have had qualities in common—both well dressed, wearing valuable rings and watches, able to afford many of the creature comforts. She glanced around Mrs. Spencer's living room: fine old furniture beautifully cared for and tastefully arranged. Augustine Spencer was also beautifully cared for and tastefully dressed. She didn't have Rebecca's fragile, timeless beauty, but Miss Sanderson sensed this woman was the nicer, warmer person of the two. Her face was round and pink-skinned and the iron gray hair was stylishly coiffed. Her small eyes were unexpectedly shrewd.

"Were you Mrs. Holly's confidante?" the secretary asked.

"To a degree. More tea?" Miss Sanderson shook her head and the older woman continued. "I believe I was the closest to a friend that Rebecca had. Oh, she had many acquaintances. This building is mainly tenanted by widows. But Rebecca was most reticent. I should imagine the reason she did confide in me was because she knew I'm not a person who gossips. Which forces me to make a blunt statement to you. Although Rebecca is dead, I don't feel I can betray her confidences. The manner of her death leaves me in doubt that anything she told me has a bearing on it.''

Her lips, lightly touched with pale pink lipstick, closed firmly. With a feeling of dismay, Miss Sanderson regarded her. If Mrs. Spencer decided to say no more, there was no way she could be forced to. She asked slowly, "May I ask you a question?"

"Of course. But I can't guarantee an answer."

"Was Mrs. Holly in the habit of entering the park in the evening?"

"Rebecca had too much sense for that. The park is within walking distance of this building, which is the reason many of us live here. Many of the women stroll down to the park in the morning or the afternoon, but even then we are careful to stay in the populated areas that the police patrol. It's a wonderful place to walk but, like many other areas these days, it can be dangerous for older people." She considered for a moment and then added, "And younger ones, too. It was less than a month ago when that poor young girl was raped and beaten near Lost Lagoon." The shrewd eyes swept over her guest's attentive face. "I see your point, Miss Sanderson. There must have been an urgent reason for Rebecca to do such a foolish thing. Do you believe she was to meet someone in the park?"

Miss Sanderson decided the only course was a degree of honesty. "That's the theory Mr. Forsythe is working on."

"And Mr. Forsythe feels this person might have been implicated in Rebecca's death?"

"What do you think?"

"It is a possibility. It might explain . . . yes, I will answer your questions."

"Could you tell me about Mrs. Holly's daily life."

"She lived quietly. Her heart wasn't in good condition, but Rebecca was accustomed to this and was most sensible in her habits. I wouldn't say she was constantly unwell, but she had to be careful with her diet and she had to have extra rest. Her social life was limited. She was fond of bridge and belonged to the same bridge club that I do. Other than that, I'd say her main interests were classical music and her granddaughter, or, to be specific, in her granddaughter's ballet career."

Taking out her cigarette case, Miss Sanderson waited for

the other woman's nod and then lit one. "Were Mrs. Holly and Thalia close?"

"You mean were they fond of each other? No, I wouldn't say that. Thalia was dutiful to her grandmother. She visited Rebecca and was always polite and attentive to her, but I didn't sense any real affection between them. They seemed bound together by three things—their relationship, the fact that they were the only survivors of their family, and a mutual interest in Thalia becoming a prima ballerina."

"Did you feel Mrs. Holly was driving the girl in this career?"

"Certainly not. Thalia had quite enough drive of her own. If she had lived, I think she would have attained her goal. I saw her in two performances. Local, of course, and some of the cast were rather amateurish, but not Thalia. She was a magnificent Snow Queen and made a brilliant Aurora in *The Sleeping Beauty*."

"Back to Mrs. Holly. She did have medication for her heart?"

"Yes. Rebecca was careful to have pills in reach. To my knowledge, she had a supply in her bathroom, more beside her bed, a bottle in her kitchenette, and she carried some with her. She had a seventeenth-century snuffbox she used as a pillbox and she always carried it in her handbag. Chased silver and quite valuable."

"Now the last week, from Tuesday until Mrs. Holly's death last evening—did you see her during this time?"

"Yes." Leaning forward, Mrs. Spencer squeezed lemon into her cup. "Tuesday . . . that was the day she saw Mr. Forsythe the second and final time."

"She told you about consulting Mr. Forsythe?"

"She did. In fact, I was so concerned about her distress over her granddaughter's suicide that I urged her to find someone to look into it. I must admit I felt Rebecca was dramatizing the girl's death. She never liked her daughter-in-law, Harriet Pulos, and I believe she came to resent Harriet a great deal because of Thalia. It was obvious Thalia adored her aunt by marriage. She mentioned Harriet a couple of

65

times in my hearing and her face glowed. She called her aunt Mommy and Rebecca disliked that. I felt that Rebecca was trying to put the blame for Thalia's death on Mrs. Pulos's shoulders. However, I did hope Mr. Forsythe might put Rebecca's mind at rest.'' The pink lips set tightly. ''I do feel Mr. Forsythe behaved badly.''

''Mrs. Holly told you about the interview with Mr. Forsythe on Tuesday?''

''Not then. When she returned home, we spoke only briefly. I was waiting for Rebecca to come home, as I suffer, as many do, from curiosity. When I heard her in the hall, I opened my door. She looked dreadful, her face as white as a sheet. She told me she was going to lie down and rest and I urged her to take one of her pills. The following day, I didn't see her and I didn't wish to disturb her, but shortly after dinner I felt I should check on her. Rebecca was pale and drawn and I asked if she'd had dinner. She said she wasn't hungry, but I insisted on making her mint tea and cutting some pâté sandwiches. She did manage to eat a bit and it was then she told me of her treatment at Mr. Forsythe's hands.''

Miss Sanderson snubbed out her cigarette. ''Mr. Forsythe and I deeply regret that. But I assure you at the time, our conduct seemed justified.''

''Perhaps. But Rebecca was in bad shape. She told me Mr. Forsythe refused to look further into her granddaughter's death and had practically called her a vengeful old woman. Rebecca said she was going to act the role and force your employer to apologize. She said that she 'would have to continue to investigate by herself.' I asked her bluntly what she thought she could do and Rebecca told me she would think of something.''

''Was that the last time you saw her?''

''That was Wednesday. Let me think. I saw her on Saturday afternoon. I persuaded her to come out with me and do a little shopping. Her color was better but she was morose and withdrawn.'' Mrs. Spencer took a deep breath. ''Yesterday, I saw her for the last time.''

Miss Sanderson said gently, "Could you tell me about it?"

The older woman templed her plump, ringed fingers. "I saw her twice. The first time was in the morning, around ten. I was leaving to have my hair done, as I'd been invited out for the afternoon and evening. As I left my apartment, I met Rebecca, who was also going out. We parted in front of the building. Generally, even for short distances, Rebecca took cabs, but that morning she was walking. She seemed . . . I suppose the word would be *excited*."

"Did she say where she was going?"

"No. But she walked away in the direction of Thalia's apartment. The child lived only two blocks from here. As I later found out, that had been her destination. I'd returned from my hairdressing appointment and there was a tap on my door. It was Rebecca—"

"What time was this?"

"Let me see . . . I remember I was taking out salad ingredients for lunch. . . . It must have been a few minutes to one. I'm a creature of habit and always lunch at one. Rebecca was in quite a state. She asked if I would give her a little brandy and I hastened to get some for her. When she first came in, she looked quite drained, but color came flooding back into her face, rather too much color. She reached into her handbag and took out a notebook. She waved it at me and said she'd found her proof, that she was going to show Mr. Forsythe up. She said he considered her actions had made him look like a fool but now he would look like an utter ass. She was so excited, I became nervous and cautioned her about her heart. Then she did quiet down a bit."

"Did she tell you what she had found?" Miss Sanderson asked eagerly.

"Not exactly." Mrs. Spencer smiled faintly. "It wasn't that I didn't try to find out. As I said, I am curious. She would only say that for the last few months of Thalia's life, the girl had started writing bits of verse. Very bad verse, Rebecca said. If anything depressed or upset the girl, she would write it out in verse form. Rebecca had finally remembered this, went to Thalia's apartment, and found the notebook in the desk.''

"I suppose Mrs. Holly was triumphant."

"Oddly enough, I wouldn't say that. She was certainly excited, but she also seemed . . . puzzled. She kept saying, 'It's unbelievable, Gussie, there's no reason for it.' At times, I can be blunt and I asked her directly what her granddaughter had written. All Rebecca would say was a poem. I begged her to take it to Mr. Forsythe but she refused. Then I advised her to go to the police and this she seemed to consider, but she finally shook her head and told me the poem was so allegoric and full of metaphors that she doubted anyone who didn't know the family intimately would understand it. I found it completely mystifying.''

Miss Sanderson shook a baffled head. Exactly what had Thalia Holly written that her grandmother had found unbelievable? "What happened then, Mrs. Spencer?"

"Rebecca had me so concerned that I offered to cancel my plans for the remainder of the day and stay with her, but she said no. I asked what she intended to do and she said she was going to check something out before she made up her mind. She replaced the notebook in her handbag, told me not to worry, and then she left." The shrewd eyes closed and suddenly she looked much older. When she opened her eyes, they were damp and one tear rolled down her cheekbone. "If I'd stayed with her, she might still be alive." She dabbed at her eyes and tried to smile. "Hindsight is wonderful, isn't it?''

"We all have regrets. Mr. Forsythe and I certainly have. You may be able to understand how we feel."

"I think I do. Miss Sanderson, I'm afraid I'm rather upset. Do you have further questions?''

"Only one. Would you describe that notebook? How large was it?''

"Small. Much smaller than yours. The kind of little book one slips into a pocket or a purse, perhaps about four inches by three. It was bound in red leather.''

Miss Sanderson rose and tucked her own notebook into her shoulder bag. Mrs. Spencer got to her feet and wiped at her eyes again. She was short and had to look up at the secretary. "You know, I've never thought that I'm a violent person, but when I heard of Rebecca's death, I prayed the police would find and punish the criminal who took her handbag and left her to die. Now my mind is full of even more horrible thoughts. I wonder if it was a mugger or if it was someone she knew and trusted. I find I *am* bloodthirsty. I hope Mr. Forsythe will find who is responsible and I pray the punishment will fit the crime."

"You may rely on that, Mrs. Spencer. Mr. Forsythe won't rest until he does find out exactly how your friend died." Miss Sanderson added grimly, "And Robert Forsythe is an expert in making punishment fit the crime."

When Miss Sanderson returned from Mrs. Spencer's apartment, she found the barrister in the kitchen, heating water for tea. She threw her jacket over the back of one chair and sat down on another. "Any luck?"

"Zilch." He measured tea leaves into the pot. "I hope you did better."

"One intriguing fact and several points of interest. Like it in full?" He nodded and reached for a cookie tin. His secretary proceeded to demonstrate her amazing memory. Without consulting her notebook, she rapidly recounted her interview with Augustine Spencer. When she had finished, he grinned and said, "Sandy, I have no idea why you bother with that notebook."

She tossed her gray head. "Gives me something to do with my hands."

Forsythe took a piece of paper from his jacket pocket. "After I got back here from Thalia's apartment, George Barton rang up. He'd spoken to the lieutenant in charge of Rebecca Holly's death and came up with a few more items. They've established that the woman who spoke with Rebecca at the entrance to the park was the last person to pinpoint her movements. This woman said she tried to dissuade Rebecca from entering the park alone and was brushed off for her efforts. No one had come forward as witness to Rebecca's movements in the park, but shortly after eleven that evening a young man and his girl were strolling along a path near the zoo area and—''

''Couldn't they give a more exact time?''

''No.'' Forsythe took a sip of tea. ''This couple saw a woman facedown on a bench, her head and shoulders resting on the seat, her body slumped on the ground. At first they thought she was drunk, but when they took a closer look, they realized she was either unconscious or dead. They searched for a policeman, couldn't find one, and ended up having to phone from a public booth. The call came in at eleven-thirty-five. There's no doubt about cause of death—a coronary.''

Miss Sanderson asked, ''Where was her handbag?''

''It was found a few hundred feet from the body, thrown into some bushes. Rebecca's jewelry—two rings and a platinum Cartier watch—were missing. In the handbag were a handkerchief, a compact, lipstick, comb, a vial of perfume, an address book, a pen, and a silver box containing a number of white capsules.''

The secretary nodded. ''That would be the snuffbox that Mrs. Spencer mentioned. What about Rebecca's wallet?''

''It was found in a rubbish bin. The credit cards were in it but the money was gone. No fingerprints, everything wiped clean.''

''Blimey!'' Miss Sanderson reached for the teapot and refilled her cup. ''We have a thief who takes two rings and a watch, and a book of amateur poetry and leaves a valuable antique snuff box.''

''Sandy, we aren't certain Rebecca Holly had that book with her.''

Her jaw set. ''*I'm* certain. How does our legal friend feel about our interest in his client's death?''

''Barton was trying to be tactful, but I gather he feels we're off on a wild-goose chase. How do *you* feel?''

She put down her cup with a thud. ''As though we were

hit in our egos and sent a frail old woman straight into the hands of a killer!''

He bowed his head and for moments they sat silently. Then she asked, ''Did Barton manage to get any of that background info from his competent private inquiry agency?''

''Hardly. They're not miracle workers. I told Barton when he does get their report to try here first, then Hollystone.''

She pushed herself to her feet. ''We're going to Hollystone?''

''To Hollystone,'' he told her. ''And to a funeral.''

CHAPTER EIGHT

As befitted Rebecca Holly's position in Hollystone, her funeral was well attended. The old white church was crowded and people lined up on its steps to listen to the service. The drive to the cemetery was a slow, sedate procession, a long line of cars following the hearse. Mark Harmon's Mercedes swung into last place and by the time it reached the cemetery, the mourners were gathered around the burial plot.

The barrister and his secretary stood well back from the grave site and Miss Sanderson opened her handbag, extracted a tissue, and mopped at her damp face. She had expected it to rain—it always seemed to rain at funerals—but the day was blisteringly hot, the sun pounding relentlessly on Hollystone.

The Hollys' plot was a large area, containing many markers and dominated by a marble angel in its center. The statue wasn't well done. The expression on the marble face showed no compassion; the angel merely looked smug and rather sneering, and the uplifted hands gave the appearance of begging for alms. "Dreadful," Miss Sanderson said, nudging her companion.

Forsythe followed her eyes. "Certainly not a piece of art," he agreed. "Point out the members of the family, Sandy."

"From here, you can't see too clearly, but that short

woman with the veil is Harriet Pulos. Dmitri is on her left and the man on her other side is Brice Stevens-Parkes. That group of people near them is the Earl family. Only the two older children are here, Floyd and Suzy.''

"Mrs. Earl looks as though she's sweltering.''

"She probably is. Millie carries a lot of weight.''

"Where are Alexis and his sister?''

"On the far side of the lawyer. You can't miss Alexis. I can see his teeth from here.''

"Mariana is quite pretty. Is her boyfriend here?''

"I caught a glimpse of Fabe Harcourt at the church, but no, I don't see him. May not have been welcome. As he said, he's not one of the family.''

"Who's the old gentleman near Alexis?''

"The one with white hair?'' Miss Sanderson shook her head. "No idea. I noticed him in church sobbing his heart out. He seems to be a sincere mourner.''

They listened to the drone of the minister's voice. He reached "ashes to ashes'' and bent to fill a small silver tray with soil. He extended it to Harriet Pulos, who moved forward, supported by her tall husband, and sprinkled a few grains on the lavish coffin.

Touching Miss Sanderson's arm, Forsythe turned back to the gates of the cemetery. They walked slowly, listening to the murmur of voices behind them. They had reached the car and Miss Sanderson was sliding behind the wheel when she heard her name called. Mariana Pulos came hurrying up. "Miss Sanderson, wait a sec. Harriet wants you and Mr. Forsythe to come back to the house.''

"We'd be intruding,'' Forsythe told the girl.

"You're intruding simply by being here!'' Mariana's attitude toward her favorite criminologist appeared to have soured. She glared at him. "Harriet wants to talk to you. She says to go directly out and Cassie and Bernice will look after you until we get there.'' Turning on her heel, she strode away.

"You've lost a fan,'' Miss Sanderson said with a smile.

"They consider we're here to snoop and pry, Sandy, and they're right."

"Going to accept the invitation?"

"It sounded more like a royal command. Yes, we'll go to Holly House, but in our own good time."

"Where to now?"

"Back to the hotel. We'll freshen up and have lunch."

She put the key into the ignition. "Mrs. Pulos may be going to order us out of her precious town."

Forsythe shrugged. "Let her try. When we leave Hollystone, it will be *our* idea, not hers."

Forsythe glanced out of the car window at the bulk of Holly House. "Looks like a prosperous estate, Sandy."

She nodded and slanted a smile at him. "How did you like the keeper of the gates?"

The barrister grinned. "Straight out of a vintage Western. All he lacks is a six-gun and a horse. But if Tex enjoys playing cowboy, why not?" He got out of the car. The cul-de-sac was crowded with vehicles, but he was staring at a Harley-Davidson. "I suppose that bike belongs to the ex–Lucky Lucifer."

"Alias Fabian Harcourt."

"Looks as though he wasn't allowed at the cemetery but he's attending the reception. Odd."

"As you'll soon discover, this is a weird household."

The front door was ajar and directly behind it was Stevens-Parkes, attired in a black suit and wearing a lugubrious expression. "The drawing room," he told them in hushed tones. "Mrs. Pulos and her husband are in seclusion but will see you shortly."

Forsythe said, "If she'd prefer to wait . . ."

"No. She made it clear she'd like to speak with you as soon as possible. But she does need time to compose herself."

Leaving the lawyer at his post, they turned to the archway he indicated. The room was large but seemed smaller because of two long tables that had been set up. A sizable crowd

74

was milling about, the air was cool, and the mourners appeared to be eating and drinking in comfort. Behind one of the tables, dispensing coffee, white wine, and fruit juices, was a middle-aged maid. The other table was spread with a lavish buffet and this one was tended by a slightly younger woman. Cassie and Bernice Beaton, Forsythe thought, and accepted two glasses of wine. He handed one to his secretary. "Better circulate, Sandy, while I look the family over. See if you can get a line on that elderly chap we saw at the cemetery. He's near the fireplace with your friends, the Earls."

"Not my friends," she muttered, and moved away.

Forsythe started locating the people he had seen at the graveside. Alexis Pulos was chatting with his sister near the buffet. The huge man beside Mariana had to be Fabian Harcourt. He was munching from a heaped-up plate. The parent Earls were still with the white-haired man, and Miss Sanderson had joined the trio. As Forsythe watched, another woman—this one looking as old as the man—moved over and stood at the old man's side. At the far end of the room, perched on a window seat, were Suzy and Floyd Earl. The boy was staring into space and the girl was devouring food as though she had fasted for a week.

The barrister glanced around, conscious of a covert and curious inspection from the mourners. A small town, he thought, and one where news travels fast. He turned and found Alexis Pulos staring at him. The man smiled and Forsythe could see what his secretary had meant when she had mentioned the man's teeth. Forsythe looked back at the group by the fireplace. The old chap had started to weep again and the older woman took the glass from his trembling hand, putting a comforting arm around his shoulders, and led him from the room. Miss Sanderson watched him leave, then she backed away from Millie and Randolph Earl and strolled toward her employer. She told him, "The old chap was a childhood sweetheart of Rebecca Holly's and once carried her books to school. Rather heartwarming to see one person who cares because she's dead. Most of this crowd are treating this as a social occasion, stuffing themselves with free food and catching up on gossip.''

'' 'Twas ever thus, Sandy. Ah, here comes my fellow member of the bar.''

"He's acting more like the local mortician," Miss Sanderson said morosely.

Brice was crossing the room, pausing occasionally to murmur a few words to the mourners. When he reached Forsythe's side, he whispered, "Mrs. Pulos will receive you now. In the study. Please follow me.''

He led the way back to the hall, made a smart right turn, paused, tapped on a door, and then opened it. "Miss Sanderson and Mr. Forsythe," he announced.

Miss Sanderson preceded Forsythe into the study. It was a pleasant room. French doors stood ajar, opening into a rose garden, and scents from the blooms perfumed the air. The furniture was old, massive, and looked comfortable. A brick-faced fireplace dominated the room. The hearth was banked with potted ferns, and sitting close enough to it that the fronds brushed her black skirt was Harriet Pulos. Near her was Dmitri, one arm draped along the mantel, the dark suit flattering against the golden beauty of his face. On the rug at their feet sprawled the dalmatian, obviously no longer in heat, and playing with the animal was Leander. Neither of the adults smiled, but Leander beamed his delightful dimpled smile at the visitors. "Emwy," he told them.

"She's a lovely dog," Miss Sanderson assured the child. "When I was here before, I saw Emily.''

"She jump on Wamdof. Here." He patted his black curls.

"Yes, I saw Emily jump on Randolph.''

A tap sounded on the door and Selma Yale made her hip-swiveling way into the study. Miss Sanderson glanced at Forsythe and found he was eyeing the nurse appreciatively. "You want me, Mrs. Pulos?" the nurse asked. Her voice was as sexy as her figure.

"Please take Leander outside for a time. The playground, I think. He's been too much in the house today. Don't give

76

him any of that food from the buffet. It's too rich for him. If he'd like a snack, give him milk and cookies.''

Leander raised hopeful eyes. "Chowat?"

"No chocolate," his mother told him firmly.

The boy pouted but he took the hand his nurse was extending and obediently went with her. Before Selma eased the door shut, she cast a languishing look at the man leaning against the mantel. Dmitri was watching his wife.

Harriet's blue-gray eyes were still fixed on the door. "Leander's allergy to chocolate makes it so difficult for us. Both my husband and I are fond of chocolate, but we must be careful to have it when Leander is in bed." Her eyes shifted to Forsythe and she smiled at him. Almost instantly, he felt the attraction that both Rebecca Holly and Sandy had mentioned. Harriet's madonna face was ashen and her eyelids were red and inflamed, but that smile was not only warm but seemed his alone. "But you're not here to discuss a child's allergy," she said. "Please be seated. You must forgive us if we seem a bit disorganized but . . ." Her voice trailed off as they took the chairs she indicated.

"We had no desire to intrude on you at this time," Forsythe told her.

"I understand that. But when I saw you at the service, I decided best to have this over with. I'm acquainted with your reputation, Mr. Forsythe, and I much doubt you came to Hollystone just to attend Mother Holly's funeral."

"You're correct. My secretary and I will be in town for a few days."

"Staying at the hotel. The manager phoned me last evening after you registered."

The barrister arched his brows. "You're not entertaining the idea of having Mr. Weston refuse us shelter, are you?"

"Certainly not! Mother Holly was my first husband's mother, the last link I had with Kenneth. If there are circumstances connected with her death that should be investigated, I'd be the last person in the world to interfere."

"I *would* interfere," Dmitri said harshly. "I advised my

wife against this meeting. I want that made clear, Mr. Forsythe.''

Forsythe looked up at him. ''You have something to conceal, Mr. Pulos?''

For a moment, that face was not as handsome. Dull, unbecoming color surged up under the golden skin. His mouth snapped open, but his wife said quickly, ''That remark is why you're here. My family has suffered enough. Even the children—Leander in particular—are feeling the strain. My son is too young to understand what is going on, but children, like small animals, have instincts.''

''I still think you're wrong,'' her husband said hotly. ''There's no reason to let these people into this house. The police have concluded the investigation into Rebecca's death and are satisfied. We don't have to be pestered by these meddling amateurs.'' He turned to Forsythe, his expression ugly. ''There's no way we can prevent you from staying in town, but we most certainly can arrange that no one will talk to you.''

''I wouldn't advise that, Mr. Pulos. If you do, I warn you that instead of dealing with meddling amateurs you'll be dealing with professionals.''

''I repeat—the police are satisfied. The case is closed!''

''If I reveal an item of information that we've come up with, the case will be reopened.''

Dmitri spun toward his wife. ''This sounds like blackmail!''

''Let me handle this. Mr. Forsythe, exactly what are you hinting at?''

''We have reason to believe that your mother-in-law went into the park to meet someone.'' The barrister shifted in his chair. ''You knew Rebecca Holly much better than we did. Do you feel she was the type of woman to enter that area at that hour?''

''No,'' Harriet Pulos said slowly. ''But through the last weeks of her life—after Thalia's death—Mother Holly was not behaving normally. However, I wish to tell you that

78

I'm going to assist you. The sooner you satisfy your curiosity—''

"Hardly curiosity. I've a personal reason for coming here. After I heard about Thalia Holly's previous attempts to take her life, I was ruthless with your mother-in-law. I may have sent a frail and ill woman into the hands of a killer. I intend to find out exactly what did happen in that park."

Harriet's wide-spaced eyes left the barrister's face and wandered to Miss Sanderson's. "Very well. I'll instruct my relatives to answer any questions you wish to ask—"

"I'd like to speak with your staff, too."

"My relatives and my staff. The people you want to reach are mainly on this estate. It will be more convenient and less disquieting in this area if you arrange to stay here rather than at the hotel."

Forsythe shook his head. "We couldn't stay in this house."

"I wasn't thinking about this house. That would be awkward. There's a small house next to the Earls' home—"

"The gingerbread house," Miss Sanderson murmured.

Harriet's face relaxed in a slight smile. "A good name for it, but we call it the Widows' House. Mother Holly lived there for a time after her husband's death and so did her mother-in-law after she was widowed. It's comfortable and the bath and kitchen have been modernized."

"It would be more convenient than the hotel," Forsythe told her. "We accept your offer. You're very kind."

"Not kind, merely practical. I won't pretend you're welcome guests, but at least this way you may be around for a shorter time. I'll have the house aired and cleaned. A supply of food will be taken down to it. You may move in anytime tomorrow." She took a deep breath. "The other reason I wanted to see you is that if you wish to question my husband and me, I'd prefer to do it now."

Dmitri touched her shoulder. "Surely this can wait."

Impatiently, she waved him away. "Mr. Forsythe?"

The barrister nodded at Miss Sanderson and she took out her notebook. Balancing it on her knee, she waited. Templing his long fingers, Forsythe looked down at them. "We'll start on the day of the wildflower contest. Could you tell me your positions on the plateaus at the time of your daughter's fall?''

Touching her brow with a stubby hand, Harriet said, "I don't really know. I suppose perhaps about halfway down—can you remember, Dmitri?''

''Hardly. These aren't actually plateaus. More like shelves—some of them very small—that follow the waterfall. There're about twenty of them. I can tell you this. My wife was on the one directly above me when our daughter fell.''

''I understand that it's impossible to see from one of these plateaus or shelves to another.''

''That's true. The area has been left in a natural state and the shelves are rimmed with bushes and outcroppings of rock. But when I turned away from the falls, Harriet was on the path behind me. She had mud on her hands and skirt.''

''I'd fallen,'' Harriet said dully. ''My only thought was to get down to my daughter and I slipped and fell.''

''It's the mercy of God my wife wasn't closer to the edge, or I might have lost her, too.''

''Very well, Mr. Pulos. Only one more question. I want to know where both of you were on the day of Mrs. Holly's death. The hours I want covered are from five in the afternoon until one the following morning.''

Dmitri raised scornful brows. ''Alibis! Harriet, I won't tolerate this! There's no—''

''That's enough!'' This time, there was no doubt that Harriet once had been a teacher. She had spoken to her young husband as though he was an unruly student, and he wilted like one. She turned to Forsythe. ''We were both in Vancouver at that time. We frequently have to go to the city on business. Dmitri and I drove in the previous Friday. We'd hoped to be finished in time to return home on Sunday, but we were delayed and had two appointments on that Monday. Mr. and Mrs. Earl and their two older children were also in Vancouver. We all stayed at the same hotel.''

''The name?'' Forsythe asked.

Dmitri supplied the name and added sarcastically, "The hotel is only a short distance from the park, which is why we stay there. When we're in Vancouver, my wife and I often walk down to the park. That Monday, we had appointments with both our stockbroker and our accountants. Harriet had not been well and when we were finished, around four, she was tired and had a headache. We went back to our hotel suite, I tucked her into bed, and then I wanted to order dinner for her. She wasn't hungry, so I mixed a glass of her sedative and went down to the lounge for a drink. I'd planned to have dinner and spend the evening with a friend, but a message was waiting saying he had to cancel. Some problem with one of his children. Illness, I believe."

Dmitri paused, thought for a moment, and then continued. "I went up to our suite, but Harriet was asleep and the glass I'd given her was empty, so I went down to the dining room and had an early dinner. I wasn't tired, so I decided to look in at an art show in the downtown area. I spent a couple of hours there and—"

"Did you meet anyone you knew?" Forsythe asked.

"Except for Roger—the chap I was to dine with—I have no friends in the city. Some acquaintances, of course, but no, I didn't see any of them that evening."

"What time did you leave the art show?"

"I can only guess. After all, I hardly expected to have to account for my movements. Say around nine."

"Did you go directly back to your hotel?"

"No. I wandered around for a time. Walked and went into a bar and had a drink. I got back to the hotel around . . . it might have been midnight. I went up to our suite, looked in on Harriet, who was sleeping soundly, went to my own room, read for a time, and that's it."

"Did you take cabs?"

"I walked. Everything was within walking distance. I did *not* go into the park."

Forsythe nodded. "Mr. Pulos, did you see your wife drink the glass of sedative?"

81

Again, color surged into his face. "Are you insinuating—"

"Answer the question," his wife said.

"No," he said sullenly. "I mixed the drops with water, put the glass on the bed table, and left."

"In other words," Harriet said evenly, "I could have emptied the sedative down the drain, dressed, walked to the park, and met Mother Holly. But why would I want my mother-in-law dead?"

Forsythe rose. "At this point, we're only feeling our way, trying to get a clear picture. We must be going now. Thank you for your courtesy."

The barrister and his secretary moved toward the door. Dmitri called, "I won't bother wishing you luck. You're on a wild-goose chase."

Without turning, Forsythe said, "I've been told that before, Mr. Pulos. But Sandy and I have a habit of catching wild geese."

In the hall, Brice Stevens-Parkes was hurrying toward them. "Mr. Forsythe, one moment. What did Mrs. Pulos want with you? What did she say?"

"I suggest you ask Mrs. Pulos."

Forsythe tried to edge past the other lawyer, but Brice moved to bar the way. "I *demand* to know. In my position as her solicitor, I have every right to know!"

With that, he clamped a hand over Forsythe's wrist. Miss Sanderson stepped back. Blimey, she thought, that's torn it! Robby hates being touched by strangers. Wrenching the older man's hand off his wrist, Forsythe shoved him roughly against the wall. "Never," he said evenly, "lay hands on me again."

"*Well!*" Brice said explosively.

Miss Sanderson and her employer moved down the hall, crossed the veranda, and headed toward the car. "Despicable man," she said hotly. "Almost as bad as the Earls."

"None of them seem to be charmers, Sandy. Except Harriet, that little chap Leander, and his dog."

"Well . . . there's Fabe Harcourt. I took rather a fancy to

him, and Floyd Earl seems a decent boy. Other than that . . . Harriet Pulos is welcome to them.''

This time, Forsythe slid behind the wheel. ''Nevertheless, for the next few days, we're going to be seeing a great deal of Harriet's coterie.''

Miss Sanderson's expression was glum, but as the Mercedes rolled smoothly past the Widows' House, she brightened and pointed at it. ''At least, Robby, there is *one* compensation.''

CHAPTER NINE

THE FOLLOWING MORNING, BERT GRANGER SWUNG OPEN the massive gates of the Holly estate and Forsythe piloted the Mercedes through the gateway. "Hold it a moment," Miss Sanderson said. "I want to say hello to my buddy." She pressed the window control and called in her idea of a western drawl, "Mornin', Tex. How you doin'?"

"Fair to middling." He walked with a bowlegged jaunt over to the car. "Wife ain't too good. Agathe's pretty broke up over Miss Rebecca, so Mrs. Harriet give her a couple of days off. Tried to make Agathe stay in bed, but no way a man can handle darn stubborn women. Says she feels better busy, so's she's cooking up a storm."

"Is the Widows' House ready for us?"

"Sure is. Cassie and Bernice tidied it up last night and Mrs. Harriet made me lug grub down for it." He closed one eye in a devilish wink. "Snuck some fresh-baked bread and an apple pie out of the wife's kitchen for you. Agathe sent over a pot of soup, too."

Forsythe leaned past his secretary. "That was most considerate, Tex."

"Took kinda a fancy to Miss Sanderson here. Likely little filly you got working for you, pardner."

Forsythe grinned and his secretary pinkened. As the car

rolled down the road, she asked, "How did you like my western accent, Robby?"

"It sounded like Margaret Thatcher doing an imitation of Johnny Cash. But I can guess who's first on your western hit parade."

"Listen up, pardner," she drawled, stretching her long frame. "Any hombre who calls me little and likely and filly in one breath is tops with me and—"

"Will you cut that out?"

"Ah, Robby, here we are."

Forsythe pulled the car into the driveway of the Widows' House and his secretary hopped out. While he pulled suitcases and her typewriter case from the trunk, she loped up the two steps, across the shallow veranda, and disappeared into the house. When he carried the luggage in, he found her in a small living room, looking around with delight. The room was cozy, with much chintz and some fine old furniture. "I'd swap Mark Harmon's penthouse straight across for this place, Robby."

He prodded at the ancient sofa. "I hope there are two bedrooms. I hate to think of you sleeping on this thing."

"Me? You're plumb loco, pardner. If either of us was going to sleep there, it would be you. But you're in luck. There are two tiny bedrooms, a bath the size of a broom closet, and a fair-sized kitchen. I noticed Agathe Granger's soup on the stove and some yummy baked goods on the counter. Better get lunch ready."

"After we eat, we'll get to work." He followed her into the kitchen.

She flicked on the burner under the soup pot. "Who do you want me to grill?"

"You chat up the staff, starting with Tex's wife. I'll drive into town and interview the family solicitor."

"Nobody can say you ain't got true grit." She unwrapped a loaf of crusty bread. "After nearly shoving Stevens-Parkes through a wall yesterday, he may throw you out of his office."

He patted her shoulder. "Not to worry, little filly. Harriet

Pulos promised cooperation and I should think that's exactly what we'll get.''

Stevens-Parkes's office was located on Factory Street. The street was well named. The paved road ran only a few yards from the corner of Main Street and then trailed off into gravel. The buildings were frame, shabby, and thickly coated with dust. At the end of the street, a huge building reared, topped by a sign announcing this was the home of Fine Holly Furniture.

The building occupied by the lawyer was two-storied, painted pale green, with window boxes filled with bedraggled geraniums. Faded maroon curtains draped two store-sized windows and a brass plaque indicated discreetly that this was the firm of Messrs. Stevens-Parkes, Stevens-Parkes, and Stevens-Parkes.

As Forsythe opened the door, the chime of a bell over it reminded him again of a store. The temperature of the reception area was as torrid as the street he'd just left, but heat didn't appear to bother the gaunt woman behind the desk. She looked as old as the building she worked in, and Forsythe wondered how many generations of Stevens-Parkes she had served.

She lifted her head, and her eyes, behind silver-rimmed glasses, seemed to have been chipped from ice. ''Mr. Stevens-Parkes does not take casual clients. If you wish to consult with an attorney, you will find several in the Holly Building on Main Street.''

Forsythe's voice was as icy as her eyes. ''Please tell Mr. Stevens-Parkes that Robert Forsythe is here.''

She gave an audible sniff but spoke into the intercom. The door behind her desk opened and Brice appeared. ''Mr. Forsythe,'' he said. ''Mrs. Pulos has asked me to extend any assistance I can to you.''

Brice's office was old-fashioned, stuffy, shabby, and, in Forsythe's opinon, probably with more character than the new business block would ever have. The other lawyer seated

86

him, put an ashtray within reach, and retreated to his own chair behind the cluttered desk. He smiled pleasantly at his guest. "We got off on the wrong foot yesterday and I apologize for my behavior. I've been so concerned about Harriet that I fear I became too forceful." He paused and when Forsythe made no response, he said, "I'm completely at your disposal."

Forsythe took his pipe and leather pouch from a pocket. "I'd like to know the terms of Mrs. Pulos's will."

He waited for a protest, but Brice picked up a manila envelope and said mildly, "I've anticipated that. I have a copy here. Would you like to read it or . . ."

"Just give me the main points."

"Highly irregular, but Harriet instructed me to withhold nothing. Though I fail to see what a mugging in Vancouver has—"

"The main points, please."

"Very well." Brice cleared his throat. "There are a number of minor bequests—some charitable donations, a scholarship in the name of Iona Pulos, a grant to the dancing school in Vancouver that Thalia Holly attended. There is a lifetime tenancy for Agathe and Bert Granger in their cottage on the Holly estate. They also receive an annuity, and the same terms cover the Beaton sisters, Bernice and Cassie."

"Is there provision for the nurse?"

"Miss Yale? Yes. If, at the time of Harriet's death, the nurse is still in her employ, Nurse Yale will receive fifty thousand dollars. Among these minor bequests are also provision for the four Earl children. To each child, one hundred thousand."

"To be held in trust?"

"Only until each child reaches the age of eighteen." Brice frowned. "I did suggest to Harriet that seems rather young, but she was insistent. That covers the minor bequests. The bulk of the estate is to be divided into two equal segments. One segment is again to be divided—half for Dmitri and half for little Leander. The other half originally was to be divided among Thalia and Rebecca Holly, Millicent Earl, and Mariana and Alexis Pulos. Of course, with two of the heirs dead, the shares would now be in thirds.''

Forsythe was loading his pipe. ''Could you give me some idea of the amount of these thirds?''

One well-cared-for hand touched the bald dome of Brice's head, then strayed down to caress the luxuriant mustache. ''That would depend on a number of factors. The price of various stocks and bonds, the general—''

''Roughly.''

''Perhaps eight million each.''

''*Each*?''

''At least that. Dmitri and Leander, of course, would receive much more. Harriet is a wealthy woman.''

Forsythe was looking at a silver-framed portrait on the corner of the desk. ''I see you have a picture of Harriet Pulos and her children.''

With a long forefinger, Brice gently touched the frame. ''I've never disguised my affection for Harriet and her little ones.''

''You've known her for a long time?''

''All her life. I'm somewhat older than she, but my family lived next door to the Stone house, where Harriet was raised.'' He sighed. ''How times change. Now Harriet's home is a museum and my home is a boarding house. Pity. Fine old houses. For many years I hoped Harriet and I would live in one of those houses, raise a family there.''

You'd never guess, Forsythe thought, that under that cool gray exterior beats the heart of a romantic. Leaning back in his chair, Brice continued. ''I can describe Harriet's childhood in one word—miserable. People often wonder at her strong maternal instincts. If they had witnessed that childhood, they'd understand why she wants a warm family home for her own children.''

''I take it her parents didn't give her this.''

''She was an only child and perhaps her parents shouldn't be censored for their treatment of her. When she was born, her mother was nearly fifty and her father in his early sixties. Both of them were self-centered people. Ernest Stone was a professor of medieval history and was completely engrossed in his profession. Her mother had been a beauty in her youth and was petulant and badly spoiled. Mary Anne's health was uncertain and, as she grew older, that was what obsessed her. Neither Mary Anne nor Ernest had time or thought for their daughter. I don't mean Harriet was mistreated or her physical needs weren't looked after, but . . . well, I think you understand.''

Forsythe had no difficulty in understanding. His father also had been a man totally dedicated to his profession. Sandy was the person who had given the young Robert a warm and secure childhood. Without her . . . He nodded at the other lawyer. ''Harriet's birth must have been a shock. Were the Stones wealthy people?''

Brice smiled, and it was an unexpectedly charming smile. ''The Hollys are the money-makers. The Stones were . . . I suppose you might call them unworldly people. Many of them were connected with the arts and education. One of Harriet's uncles was an artist, another a musician. Professor Stone, during his lifetime, provided a decent living for his family, but he died when Harriet was eighteen. All he left was the house and a little insurance. Her mother's health had deteriorated and many people close to the family worried about how Harriet could cope with an invalid to support. I was one of them. At the time, I was a struggling law student, but I proposed to Harriet and promised I'd look after both her and her mother.''

''She refused you?''

''Her excuse was that she couldn't burden a young man with her mother's support. Actually, the real reason was that Harriet didn't return my love. She regards me as a good friend, that's all. But she used the insurance money to secure a teaching degree and she cared for Mary Anne until her death, when Harriet was twenty-seven. By that time, Harriet had turned down many proposals besides mine. All her suitors, including me, hoped she might change her mind about us, but within a few months of her mother's death she married Kenneth Holly.''

"Rebecca Holly told us something about her son. What was your opinion of him?"

Brice grimaced. "My grandfather would have called him a bounder, and my father a rogue. Harriet deserved a man who would cherish her, who would have given her the children she longed for. Instead, she got a perpetual adolescent, a man who cared nothing for her. Kenneth was a large, good-looking chap. When he was sober, he could even display a boyish charm. But when he was in his cups, he was completely brutal, bordering on being mad."

"Rebecca said that Harriet loved him."

"That I could never understand, Mr. Forsythe. No matter what Kenneth did, she adored him. He never stopped abusing her. Rebecca urged Harriet to divorce her son. I urged the same course of action. So did Tom Brent, who is Harriet's physician and was once another suitor. But she wouldn't listen to any of us."

Forsythe's eyes wandered back to Harriet's pictured face. "Her daughter looked much like her mother."

"Only in looks. Iona was nothing like Harriet. There's only one Harriet."

"Would you tell me about Kenneth's death?"

"This is rather painful." Brice shielded his eyes with one hand. "I hold myself partially responsible for Kenneth's death. For a time, Harriet blamed me, too. I know she's forgiven but she'll never forget."

"This might be important."

"I fail to see how, but I suppose you're looking for background. You did know that Kenneth suffered from diabetes?"

"Yes."

"At times, he drank heavily and this was dangerous. He'd gone on one of his sprees and early one morning I received a call from Harriet and I hardly recognized her voice. She asked me to drive her and Thalia to Vancouver to stay with Rebecca Holly. I went to Holly House and when I got there, I could easily have killed Kenneth. Harriet was a pitiful sight. Kenneth had attacked her. Her nose had been broken, her eyes blackened, and she could talk and move only with difficulty. She'd intervened when Kenneth tried to use his fists on little Thalia and she paid for it.

"When I arrived, Tom Brent was upstairs trying to calm Kenneth down. I could hear them from the veranda. There was the sound of furniture being thrown around and Kenneth was ranting and raving. Tom came running down the stairs and he was enraged. He told Harriet he washed his hands of Kenneth and he went storming out to his car. Even then, I doubt Harriet would have left her husband if she hadn't feared for Thalia's safety."

Brice pulled a crisp handkerchief from his pocket and wiped at the beads of sweat on his brow. "Sorry, but just remembering works me up. I drove Harriet and the child to Vancouver and left them with Rebecca. I'd only just gotten back to this office when Bert Granger phoned. Harriet had made the servants promise to stay with Kenneth and see he got his insulin shots, but Kenneth had threatened the cook and maids with physical violence and driven them from the house. I was afraid that Kenneth might injure the women, so I told Bert to take the women and leave at once. I assured him I would see Kenneth was cared for." He mopped his brow again. "I'll admit, I had no idea how to do that. There was no use in appealing to Dr. Brent. He was so upset about Harriet, he didn't give a damn about—"

"An odd way for a doctor to behave," Forsythe said.

"You must realize that Tom loves Harriet as much as I do. True, he's married and has a son, but he still loves her. In this case, I'm afraid Tom acted as a man first, a doctor second. Anyway, I didn't dare go to Holly House. I was younger and in fairly good shape, but I was no match for a maniac."

"What did you do?"

"Nothing. Oh, I did phone Rebecca—"

"Not Harriet?"

"No! Harriet would have come directly back and Kenneth might have killed her. Rebecca and I agreed that Harriet should not return until Kenneth came to his senses. So . . . I did nothing and Kenneth Holly died."

"How did Harriet take it?"

"She was the one who found him. Three days later, she left Thalia with her grandmother and returned to her husband. The bedroom and adjoining bath were a shambles. Kenneth was sprawled fully clothed across the bed. He'd been dead for over thirty hours." The lawyer's gray eyes looked into the past—anguished eyes, reliving an old guilt. "Harriet blamed Rebecca and me. It was months before she'd even see us. In time, I think she came to the realization that Kenneth's death was inevitable, that the combination of his ailment and alcohol would eventually have taken him from her. I even began to hope that there might be a chance for me, that after a period of time Harriet might consent to be my wife. Then, with no warning, the announcement of her marriage to Dmitri Pulos came."

Forsythe was lighting his pipe. It finally caught and he puffed out a cloud of blue smoke. "This came as a surprise to you?"

"It was a shock. It set the entire town on its ear. I'd been dismayed by Harriet's first marriage, but this one . . . at first I thought there'd been a dreadful mistake and it couldn't be true."

"How well did you know Dmitri Pulos at that time?"

"I didn't. It may sound snobbish, but we belonged to different worlds. I knew *of* him, of course. This isn't a large town and I knew he'd taken over the store after his father's death and was trying to support his mother and his younger brother and sister. During Harriet's marriage to Kenneth, I'd seen the boy occasionally at Holly House. Dmitri is a handsome man and he was a beautiful youth, but his crush on Harriet was merely pathetic."

"Kenneth Holly didn't object to the boy's attachment for his wife?"

"It amused him. In fact, Kenneth liked the lad and often urged drinks on him. And it wasn't only Dmitri who went to see Harriet. Many of her former students hung around her. She inspired a type of hero worship. Generally, Dmitri went with a group of other boys, and his brother, Alexis, often tagged along. Kenneth used to laugh about Dmitri. He called him Adonis and teased his wife about being another Helen of Troy. An unlikely combination.''

"So you didn't approve of Harriet's second marriage?''

"No, I most certainly did not. Dmitri was barely twenty and Harriet was thirty-five. Their backgrounds were so different, too.'' The lips beneath the thick mustache curved briefly upward. "Love can be an unselfish emotion at times. If I couldn't make Harriet happy, I hoped another man could. As it happened, I was wrong about the boy. Dmitri has proved to be a devoted husband and father. He's given Harriet everything she ever wanted. Now Dmitri and I are on good terms. Our regard for Harriet has given us a common goal.''

"Is it possible Dmitri's interest in Harriet was for monetary reasons?''

"Or to put it baldly—that he married her for her money? I doubt it. Dmitri loved her long before she had money, when she was an impoverished teacher. No, he married her for love. Harriet is a forthright person and she's never pretended to love him. She wanted children, a father for those children, a settled home for them. Dmitri gives her all that and he seems to expect nothing in return.''

Forsythe put his pipe into the ashtray. "We come to the present. I'd like you to cast your mind back to the first day of May and the wildflower contest.''

Brice's expression showed a hint of impatience. "I recounted that in full to Miss Sanderson.''

"What I want to know is what your position was on that series of plateaus.''

"Hmm . . . let me think. There're so many of them and I was absorbed in flowers, I really can't pinpoint the exact plateau, but it was near the center of the falls. I do remember this. After I saw Iona plunge off the lookout, I hurried up the path to the next plateau. My only thought was to get to Harriet. I knew nothing could be done for the child but I was afraid . . .''

After a moment, Forsythe asked, "What were you afraid of?"

"It's such a treacherous area. I knew Harriet would be wild with shock and I was afraid she might slip and fall into the water. When I reached the next plateau, I found I'd been right. Harriet was struggling with her husband. Dmitri was trying to restrain her and her hands were muddy from a fall she'd taken moments before I arrived. Dmitri was wearing a cream-colored shirt and there were muddy marks on it from her hands. I went to his assistance. The sound from the waterfalls was so loud, we had to shout at each other. Harriet wanted to go down to the base of the falls; she wanted to get to her daughter. As Dmitri and I tried to reason with her, Millie Earl appeared. She lifted Harriet in her arms and literally carried her toward the top of the falls. Millie is incredibly strong. Then Alexis came racing down the path and the three of us made our way to the bottom of the gorge." He paused and then asked, "Does that answer your question?"

"Very comprehensive, Mr. Stevens-Parkes. Could you tell me where you were the day of Rebecca Holly's death? The hours I want covered are from five in the afternoon until one the following morning."

Brice nodded his bald head. "I remember clearly. Dmitri and Harriet were in Vancouver and I was working to ready a number of documents for her signature. I knew she would be exhausted and I was trying to make it as easy as possible for her. I worked through the day without stopping for lunch. My secretary generally leaves the office at four. Miss Webster worked for my father and she's no longer able to handle long hours. However, her sense of duty is strong, and unless I remind her, she frequently works later.

"Shortly after four I went to the outer office and sent Miss Webster home. Then I returned to this one and continued to work. Around five, I realized I was hungry and so I packed up the documents I hadn't finished and took them upstairs—"

"You live on the premises?" Forsythe asked.

Brice pointed at the door behind Forsythe's chair. "The

stairs leading to my apartment are there. After my parents' deaths, I sold our home. It was much too large for a bachelor. At the time, the upper floor here was used for storage, but I had quite comfortable quarters installed.''

''Do you have a cook or housekeeper?''

''Mrs. Aston is a combination of both. I make my own breakfast and usually take lunch at the hotel. Mrs. Aston comes in daily at one and she cleans and does the laundry. She also makes dinner for me and tucks it into the oven. On that Monday when I went up to my living quarters, she was preparing to leave. We exchanged a few words and then she left and I had dinner. I put the dishes in the dishwasher and tidied the kitchen. Then I took my briefcase and retired to a little room I use as a den. I worked until . . . it must have been close to midnight. I went to bed but I couldn't get to sleep. I hate barbiturates, so I went to the kitchen and heated some milk. I've picked that habit up from Harriet. She suffers from insomnia and although she occasionally takes sleeping medication, more often she takes hot milk flavored with chocolate. Quite often Dmitri shares it with her—''

''Does her husband suffer from insomnia, too?''

''He says he sleeps like a log. But Dmitri is fond of chocolate and because of his son's allergy to it, he, like Harriet, only has it when his son is in the nursery for the night.''

''Yes, Mrs. Pulos did mention that to us.''

The other lawyer nodded. ''Anyway, Mr. Forsythe, hot milk does help me sleep on occasion and that night it did. I went to sleep after I drank a glass and had a good night.''

Forsythe knocked out his pipe and tucked it into a pocket. ''Where do you park your car?''

''At the rear of this building. There's a garage back there that has access to the lane.''

''Did you receive any phone calls or have any visitors that evening?''

''No.'' Brice smiled. ''I can see I'm shaping up as a perfect suspect. It would have been simple to slip down the rear steps, jump into my car, and drive to Vancouver with no one the wiser. However, as an attorney yourself, don't you find people with perfect alibis rare? So often the innocent can't produce witnesses to swear they didn't commit a crime."

"That's true. But these questions do have to be asked." Forsythe rose. "By the way, who is the executor of Mrs. Pulos's will?"

"I am."

"There is an executor's fee?"

"A generous one." Brice's geniality vanished and his expression was frosty. "I also receive a bequest. Would you care to know the amount?"

"That won't be necessary. Thank you for your time."

As Forsythe returned to the hot, dusty street, he was grinning. Nothing like asking questions about a possible inheritance to bring a sudden chill on. But, as he made a U-turn and pointed the hood of the Mercedes toward Main Street, he wasn't thinking about Brice Stevens-Parkes. He stopped at the corner for a traffic light and glanced toward the Hollystone Hotel. Judy, the friendly waitress from the coffee shop, came out of the hotel door, spotted the Mercedes, and gave Forsythe a beaming smile and a wave. He waved back.

As he drove back to the Holly estate, his mind wandered away from the terms of Harriet's will to the woman herself. Not a young or even attractive woman, but the devotion she inspired—devotion from her students, from her handsome second husband, from her solicitor, even from Dr. Tom Brent. And yet the only people Forsythe had learned that she felt affection for were her brutish first husband, her daughter, Iona, and her tiny son.

"Harriet Pulos is a dangerous woman. Not in herself but in the effect she has on the people around her."

After a moment, Robert Forsythe realized he had said the words aloud.

CHAPTER TEN

Long before Forsythe located Stevens-Parkes's office on Factory Street, his secretary was finding out more about the effect Harriet Pulos had on the people around her. She had gained entry to the Granger cottage, was warmly welcomed by Agathe, and seated in a rocking chair in the sunny kitchen. Miss Sanderson was consuming excellent coffee and freshly baked coffee cake. As she told the cook, both coffee and cake were delicious.

Agathe Granger showed no false modesty. "They should be. I've cooked most of my life."

Miss Sanderson was surprised that this trim woman with a faded rose prettiness was the old cowpoke's wife. Her diction was precise and she spoke in the monotone of the deaf. Miss Sanderson, with her clear, high voice had no difficulty in making her hear. Now, the secretary thought, to get her talking. There proved to be no necessity. Agathe was a self-starter. "Bert and I have been fortunate, Miss Sanderson—"

"Abigail, please. You were saying?"

"Bert and I came here to work when Miss Rebecca was a bride and here we've been ever since. We worked for Miss Rebecca and her husband, Mr. Reginald, and then, after he passed on, we stayed to look after Miss Harriet and Mr. Kenneth."

"How did you like working for Rebecca Holly?"

"She was a good mistress. Strict but fair." Agathe dabbed at her reddened eyelids. "When I heard about her death, I just broke down. Miss Rebecca was frail all her life and such a dainty lady. Well . . . I can't stand the thought of her dying all alone on a park bench. Miss Harriet saw what shape I was in and she sent me home. I couldn't even go to Miss Rebecca's funeral. I did offer to prepare food for the reception, but Miss Harriet said Cassie and Bernice could cope." She lifted damp eyes. "You say you were there yesterday. Was the food all right?"

Miss Sanderson gave her a reassuring smile. "I didn't have any, but the buffet looked most appetizing."

"That's good." Agathe pointed at the counter. "Do you mind if I work while we chat? Working helps."

"By all means. That looks like a mulligan you're preparing."

"Bert loves a good stew." The cook picked up a paring knife and started to scrape a carrot. "Mr. Kenneth was a great one for stews, too."

"Mrs. Holly said her son could be difficult at times."

"To be honest, Abigail, I doubt we would have stayed on at the Holly House after Miss Rebecca moved to Vancouver if Mr. Kenneth hadn't married Miss Harriet. He was difficult all right. I was here when he was born and watched him grow up. Miss Rebecca couldn't abide him. Took one look after the boy was born and she told her husband, 'Reginald, this baby is the image of your father.' Sometimes I wonder if she didn't force Mr. Kenneth into bad behavior."

Miss Sanderson took an appreciative sip of coffee. "Give a dog a bad name?"

"Exactly. Miss Rebecca kept telling the boy he was exactly like his granddad and that's exactly what he acted like. Scandalous behavior! Drinking and chasing after anything in skirts. I couldn't believe my ears when I heard he was to marry Miss Harriet. She's such a nice quiet lady."

"There are times when a good woman changes a man."

"Not Kenneth Holly." Dropping the knife, she turned to face her visitor. "This isn't a Christian thing to say but I'm plain spoken. It was the mercy of the dear Lord when He took Mr. Kenneth. If he'd lived, I swear he'd have ended up killing someone. Toward the last, he seemed to go right out of his mind when he drank. He hurt Miss Harriet badly and even tried to beat little Thalia. I remember the day she took the child and went to Miss Rebecca in Vancouver. Mr. Kenneth was raving like a madman, breaking up furniture and yelling and cursing. The Beaton girls and I were so frightened, we ran out of the house and went to Bert.''

"It must have been dreadful, Agathe. What did your husband do?"

"He phoned Mr. Brice and he told Bert to get us out of there. We took Bernice and Cassie to their aunt in Salmondale and Bert and I stayed with our son in town. Eddie has a house there and he does the gardening on this estate now that his father can't cope anymore." Agathe's face glowed. "Miss Harriet is a wonderful woman! When Bert couldn't do the work, I thought, well, this is where we leave our nice cottage. But she said, 'No, Eddie can garden and you and Bert stay right where you are.' Miss Harriet says this cottage is ours for as long as we need it and she said not to worry, as we get older, she'll look after us."

Miss Sanderson asked, "Do you remember the day of the wildflower contest?"

"How could I forget it?" Agathe shook her head. "That poor child. And Miss Harriet. Wild, Abigail, simply wild that poor lady was. She dotes on her children. Care for more cake?"

"Please. I'd really like the recipe for this cake." Agathe flushed with pleasure and Miss Sanderson decided when this woman was younger she must have been a beauty. She asked the cook, "I wonder if you would tell me about that day?"

"Where will I start?"

"In the morning."

"It was a nice day." Sinking down opposite her guest, Agathe folded her hands in her lap and frowned down at them. "Much better than contest day last year. Those poor people had to climb around those falls in the pouring rain then. I can remember how Mariana complained about having to go out last year. Miss Harriet always insists they go regardless of weather. But this year it was sunny and warm enough that morning that nearly everyone was out at the pool. Some of the young ones—Mariana and the two older Earl children—were having a swim, their first this year. I was in the kitchen preparing the picnic lunch they take to the falls and Cassie and Bernice were upstairs tidying the bedrooms. Mr. Dmitri and Alexis were in the study. I had to go past the study to call one of the maids down to give me a hand and I heard them really going at it—''

"Fighting?"

"Yes. Nothing unusual. Mr. Dmitri quite often takes his brother to task. Quite right, too. Miss Harriet has enough on her mind without worrying about Alexis and his gambling. But this time those men must have been shouting, because I'm hard of hearing and I could hear sounds right through the study door. Cassie came down to help me and when she got to the kitchen, she was white as a sheet. Cassie's nervy. Ever since Mr. Kenneth, she gets real upset. She said, 'They're really going at it, Agathe. Do you think they'll start hitting each other?'

"Now, I didn't like to bother Miss Harriet but I thought maybe she should know. So I went out to the patio and she was sitting there with Leander in her lap and I whispered to her about Mr. Dmitri and his brother. She told me to calm down, that she'd see to it. I went back to the kitchen and about half an hour later, I took some lemonade out and she was still in her chair. I asked her if everything was all right and Miss Harriet told me she'd decided not to interfere, that they were brothers and had to learn to settle their own differences.'' Agathe stood up and returned to her stew pot. "I guess they did work it out, because Cassie said nothing more about shouting. For Miss Harriet's sake, I was glad. She sets such store by that contest.''

Miss Sanderson said thoughtfully, "And Dmitri and Alexis quarrel often.''

"It's not my place to say it, but yes. Always about Alexis's

100

gambling. As I said, I don't hear well, but you can't stop the maids from gossiping. Mr. Dmitri tries to shield his wife and I guess he always ends up paying—what do you call those men who take bets?''

"Bookies."

"Yes. Paying the bookies off." The cook glanced out of the small window over the sink. "Here comes Bert. He'll be glad to see you."

Bert did seem glad to see Miss Sanderson. He grinned down at her and thumped down at the table. "How about a cup of that java? I'm plumb dried out and my throat's like rawhide."

"No doubt from herding all those cows." She gave him a good-natured smile, a cup of coffee, and a poke at his Stetson. "Bert Granger, you come into my kitchen, you take that hat off. And mind you answer Abigail's questions. Remember what Miss Harriet told us."

He patted her trim rump. "Likely little heifer, ain't she?"

His wife flushed crimson and jumped out of his reach. "I swear you've reached your second childhood. What a way to behave!"

"Maybe I have, sweetie, but tell you this. My first childhood wasn't much fun, but I'm making up for it this time around." He turned a smiling face to Miss Sanderson. "What can I tell you, pardner?"

The secretary's forehead wrinkled in thought and then she drawled, "More what you can do, Tex. How's about you and me going out and having a look at them falls?"

Bert looked dubious. "Could do that but it's a mighty rough ride. Might be tough on you."

"I'll take a chance on it."

"Okay. I'll mosey up to the main house and get the Rover. Won't be long."

He was as good as his word. In a short time, he pulled up a dilapidated Land Rover to the kitchen door. His wife had the last word. As Miss Sanderson climbed onto the passenger seat, Agathe leaned around the door and called, "You drive carefully, Bert. None of that wild West stuff with Abigail."

101

Bert waved his Stetson at her, rammed it back on his head, and circled behind the cottage. "The wife's taken a fancy to you. Hang tight there. You're going to enjoy this. Ride's pretty dull till we reach the woods and then it gets more exciting."

The first part of the ride was quite smooth. They rolled over even ground until they neared Holly House. Miss Sanderson caught a glimpse of the rear of it, a patio and the deep blue of a swimming pool. Then they entered the woods. Bert hadn't exaggerated—this *was* exciting. He bucketed the vehicle around trees with wild abandonment. Miss Sanderson clung to the seat and wished she'd never gotten the idea that she had to see the falls. Bert grinned and told her, "Can drive this blindfolded. Done it often enough."

"Is this the way you drive when you take people out on contest day?"

"No way. Miss Harriet would have my scalp. But knew you'd like a real ride. Pretty country, ain't it?"

Miss Sanderson wasn't interested in scenery. She grunted, "How much farther?"

"Nearly to the place where we park on contest days. Bit of a walk from there to the falls. Want me to drive right up to them?"

"Stop as soon as you can."

He pulled the Rover to a stop in a clearing and Miss Sanderson thankfully got down and looked around. Bert was right—this was pretty country. The glade was surrounded by tall, majestic giants of fir and cedar. The grass was lush and in the middle of the clearing were a long picnic table, benches, and a brick barbecue. "Where're the falls, Tex?"

He nimbly hopped down and pointed. "That way."

He led the way through the trees and Miss Sanderson followed him more slowly. A fairly smooth path led to an open area. She could hear the rumble of falling water. The grass became sparser and they stepped onto a stone ledge. Moss covered it and it was dampish. Along the edge, a heavy link fence was erected.

"Watch your step," Bert shouted. "Pretty slippery." He

patted the railing of the fence. "This should have been put up years ago."

Leaning over the fence, Miss Sanderson peered down. A good-sized waterfall sliced through the rocky edge and plummeted dizzily until it foamed into white over jagged rocks far below. Spray moistened her face. "God!" she muttered. "What a terrible fall that poor child had."

Bert moved closer, cupping an ear with one hand. "What's that?"

She shouted, "I said, what a fall that child took."

"Sure was. Guess you want to know where we all was. Thalia was standing right where you are. Iona came running up and went over about here." He moved several yards and bellowed, "Those are the plateaus the other folks was on."

Her eyes moved down the series of rocky ledges. A heavy link fence now ran along each of the ledges. She tried to imagine what they had been like before that fence was installed, deciding no prize could have gotten her down there. She shuddered, took a last look at the jagged rocks far below, and touched her companion's arm. "Let's get back to the picnic area. Okay, tell me about it."

Bert waited until she sank on one of the benches. "I was right here, helping with the two youngest kids. Nurse Yale was sitting in the Rover with Demmy in her lap and I was playing catch with Leander. I looked around for Thalia and Iona and was surprised to see they weren't in this clearing—"

"Why surprised?"

"Miss Harriet's pretty strict with the young kids. Wants the people left to look out for them to stay right here. So, when I didn't see Thalia and the little girl, I went looking for them. Was partway down that path to the lookout when I heard someone yelling. Broke into a run and got clear of the trees just in time to see Iona racing hell-bent for leather toward that rock ledge. Thalia was waving her arms around and screeching and—"

"Could you hear what she was shouting?"

Bert gave her a disgusted look. "Couldn't make out a word. You been there. How much could you hear? But I saw

103

Iona racing toward the edge and I ran as fast as I could. Couldn't make it. She slipped on the moss and skidded right off the edge. I looked to see if Thalia was okay and she was standing with her hands over her face. Then I headed down those ledges to get to Miss Rebecca. She had a wonky heart and shouldn't have been down there at all. Anyway, I got her and helped her up. Funny, she was pretty calm. Better'n some of those folks was.''

He paused to catch his breath. ''Mr. and Mrs. Earl brought Miss Harriet up, the two of them half-carrying her. Miss Rebecca went to look after Thalia and the Earls were holding tight to Miss Harriet, so I went back to the lookout to see if I could help get the kid's body out. Mr. Brice and Mr. Dmitri and Alexis were down at the bottom of the gulch. The two Earl kids, Floyd and Suzy, were with them. They'd formed kinda a chain, holding on to each other, and Mr. Dmitri was fishing the kid off some rocks that had snagged her. They carried her up—'' He broke off and muttered, ''Don't want to talk about that. Never liked the kid much, but God she was broke up!''

Miss Sanderson waited a few moments and then she asked, ''You didn't like Iona?''

''Don't mind telling you that to your face. No one, except her mom and dad, liked her. She looked like Miss Harriet but she took after Mr. Dmitri's mother. What a battle-ax that woman was! Sly kid, sweet as pie when her parents were around and nasty as could be when they weren't. Had nicknames for us all. Called Mrs. Earl 'Fatso' and Alexis 'Baldy' and me 'The Old Fool.' ''

''Her little brother seems like a charming child.''

''Everyone loves Leander. A real nice kid. Hope he stays that way. Trouble is, when kids are made as much of as them two, they get to know they're boss. Get to thinking the whole world runs around them. What that Iona needed was a good tanning on her backside.'' He gave his companion a small smile. ''Don't say nothing to the wife about this. Agathe always says we shouldn't speak ill of the dead, but Iona was a holy terror.''

Miss Sanderson shifted on the hard bench and rubbed her hip. "Do you think anyone could have had a hand in the child's death?"

He shook his head. "I saw it and that was an accident. Sure felt sorry for Thalia. Nobody'd say a word to her. Miss Rebecca took Thalia to that place you're in, the Widows' House, and kept her there till the inquest was over. Then she took Thalia back to Vancouver."

She nodded and changed tactics. "What about the Earl family? How do you feel about them?"

The old man chuckled. "With Miss Harriet, butter wouldn't melt in their mouths, but when they're home you should hear them go at it. Hammer and tongs. At those kids or each other all the time. Keep telling the wife she's lucky she's hard of hearing. Leastways she don't have to listen to the hollering."

"How long have the maids been here?"

"They came after us, come to think of it quite a time. Miss Rebecca hired them just before Mr. Reginald died. Her husband, I mean. They had a son by the same name. Reggie's dead, too. He looked like his mom. Had her eyes. Awful pretty eyes Miss Rebecca had."

"What are they like?"

"Those girls—" Bert laughed. "Always call them girls and they must be nearly fifty now. Well, Cassie and Bernice are good women, hard workers. Kinda mousy and scared of their own shadows but decent enough."

Putting both hands on the bench, Miss Sanderson heaved herself to her feet. Bert walked back over to the Land Rover and sprang up behind the wheel. "That all you want, pardner?"

"One other thing bothering me, old buddy."

"What's that?"

"You're hiding something."

"I don't know what you're getting at."

She looked searchingly at him. "You most certainly do."

"If that don't beat all. You're sharp as a tack!" Bert pounded his knee with a fist. "Okay, so there's something I

105

haven't spilled. Don't intend to, either. Agathe and me, we got a nice comfortable thing here. For life, too. I tell you and you tell Mr. Forsythe and he blabs—''

"Tex," Miss Sanderson warned softly. "Robby doesn't *blab*." Bert's bristly chin jutted stubbornly and she asked, "How did you like Thalia Holly?"

"Fine. Knew her ever since she was a little girl."

"From the way you talk about Rebecca Holly . . . I feel you liked her, too."

"The wife and me thought the world of her."

She touched his arm. "Tex, there's a possibility that someone killed both of them."

"But Miss Rebecca was mugged and Thalia—" He broke off. "You sure about that?"

"No," she admitted. "But there's no way we'll know for sure unless people tell us the truth. And that means you, too, old buddy."

Taking his Stetson off, Bert rubbed a hand over thick white hair. "You win. Here it is. You heard about Leander's fall from the swing?" She bobbed her head and he continued. "That was no accident. After they carried the boy in the house, I started to fix it. The rope had been cut almost through. Couple of good swings and it broke. I didn't bother Miss Harriet because she was so upset, and what the hell! Enough sawdust under those swings that the kid couldn't do more than bruise himself."

Miss Sanderson was staring at him. "Have you told Mrs. Pulos since?"

He squirmed. "No. Figure she'd give me hell for not telling her at the time. Anyway, I figured it might have been intended for Iona. She was the one who always used that swing. Always fighting over it with Edith Earl. Figured someone might have wanted to give Iona a good tumble, take her down a peg or two. Mighta been one of them Earl kids. Iona was holy hell on them."

For a time, she was deep in thought. Then she climbed up beside him.

"Let's get back now," Miss Sanderson muttered.

On the ride back, Miss Sanderson didn't notice the scenery. She was haunted by two pictures: a small body hurtling off a ledge of mossy rock and a smaller body falling from a broken swing.

CHAPTER ELEVEN

Forsythe had returned from Hollystone long before his secretary put in an appearance. He had carried a couple of chairs and a small table from the Widows' House, brought out a drink tray, and was relaxing on the veranda when he saw her walking down the road from the direction of Holly House. She wasn't loping along as she generally did but seemed to be moving stiffly. As she mounted the steps, he waved at the table. "Help yourself to a drink and have a chair."

"The drink, yes. The chair, no." Gingerly, she rubbed the seat of her trim slacks.

"Don't tell me that Tex took you horseback riding?"

"Worse than a bucking bronco, Robby. He took me out to the waterfalls in his trusty Land Rover. And Tex drives as though he's in training for the Grand Prix."

Forsythe reached for the bottle and spilled whiskey into his glass. "You anticipated me, Sandy. I was planning to go there myself."

"Which is exactly why I went. That ride would have wrecked your gimpy knee."

He smiled up at her. "Is that why you didn't have Tex drive you back here?"

She smiled back. "By that time, I was so numb it wouldn't

have made much difference. I wanted to chat up the rest of the staff—the Beaton sisters and the sexy nurse.''

''Did you track them down?''

She took a sip of whiskey and leaned against the railing. ''When we came roaring out of the woods in that ruddy Land Rover, I spotted Cassie and Bernice setting up a buffet dinner beside the pool behind Holly House. At first, they were a bit nervous because of me, but we ended up getting along well.'' She paused and considered. ''Perhaps I'd better tell you what I learned from Agathe and her husband—only the pertinent points for now. Some of what they said ties in with what I heard from the Beaton sisters.'' Rapidly, she gave some details of her conversations with the cook and Bert Granger.

When she had finished and was reaching for the bottle again, Forsythe said slowly, ''Interesting. Could Cassie Beaton tell you anything further about the argument between the Pulos brothers the day that Iona was killed?''

''She only caught a few words but she said they fight often—about Alexis's gambling debts. It seems he's a steady loser and Dmitri has to pick up the tabs. She thought that was the cause of the fight that day. The only thing is, she had never heard them shouting so much. Cassie is a timid little woman.''

''What did she hear, Sandy?''

''She said she heard Dmitri yell, 'I won't let you do this to my wife!' And Alexis yelled back, 'I'll damn well do what I want, big brother, and you won't stop me!' Then Cassie ran to the kitchen and told Agathe. Cassie didn't go near the study for a time and when she did, she said they'd quieted down.''

''That's all the maids could tell you?''

''That's it. They raved on about Miss Harriet and how wonderful she is and what a nice child Leander is, and Bernice—she's not quite as timid as her sister—did say the nurse is a disgrace.'' Miss Sanderson smiled widely. ''I had a little talk with Sexy Selma.''

''Perhaps you should have left that interview to me.''

"Blimey! You'd have been so busy looking at those gorgeous legs, you'd have missed half what she said."

"Was it worth hearing?"

"I'll let you be the judge of that. After I left the Beaton sisters, I wandered up a brick path that leads to that rose garden we caught a glimpse of from the study yesterday. It's a lovely spot. It has a high hedge all around it with a little gate and it's full of bush roses and some climbers. Well kept, too. In the middle of the garden is a small fountain centered with a marble statue of Poseidon. Right beside the fountain was Selma Yale and the dalmatian. She really is a good-looking girl, Robby, but she has a cold and her nose was red and raw. She said that Leander has a cold, too, and he's spending the day in bed. Other than that, all I got was chit-chat."

"Nothing interesting?"

She shook her gray head. "Selma was a nurse at the hospital where Leander was born and Mrs. Pulos took a fancy to her and brought her to Holly House to care for the two children. She said Iona was a 'handful' and Leander a 'living doll.' She mentioned Alexis is all hands and kept grabbing her until she threatened to tell Mrs. Pulos. Since then, he's only looked." She chuckled. "Selma says that Dmitri is 'a beautiful man' and is wasted on his wife. She described Harriet as 'a cold fish with about as much sex appeal as a set of encyclopedias.' She talked a blue streak but that's the gist of it. I've a hunch the only reason she sticks around is that she hopes to have a chance with Dmitri."

The barrister shook his head. "Nurse Yale has another reason, Sandy. She's mentioned in Harriet Pulos's will. Quite generously."

"Ah, so Brice Stevens-Parkes *did* cooperate. Tell all."

He pulled himself from his chair and stretched his long frame. "I'll fill you in while I get dinner. You made lunch and it's my turn."

"Lunch was courtesy of Agathe Granger. All I did was heat up that marvelous soup." She followed him into the

110

house. "Anyway, you're better off that knee and I'm more comfortable on my feet. I'll cook and you talk."

He sat down at the kitchen table and pulled a notebook from his jacket pocket. "I'll have to refer to the notes I made when I got back here. My memory is fair but not in your league. Here goes . . ."

She worked automatically, her mind more on her employer's voice than on cooking. Finally, she turned to Forsythe. "There's a great deal of money involved."

"For everyone, including the family solicitor and even the staff."

"And we know how money affects even nearest and dearest." She lifted a steak from a marinade. "What do we do tomorrow?"

"We'll interview the Earl family and Alexis and Mariana Pulos."

"I've a horrible feeling who's going to get stuck with the Earls."

"You can have them, Sandy. I'll take the young Puloses."

"Thanks heaps! What about Fabe Harcourt?" She dropped the steak into a hot skillet and it started sizzling.

He sniffed the odor hungrily. "We should speak with him. Even if he wasn't there when Thalia Holly died, we must learn about his movements the day that Rebecca died. Why are you looking so worried, Sandy? The Earls?"

"No." She placed a bowl of salad on the table. "I was thinking about that broken swing. But Bert said that one of the Earl children could have done it to spite Iona Pulos. She was the one who used the big swing."

Forsythe's face was drawn with concentration. "Time element again. Iona was killed two months before that rope broke. The weather was good and the playground must have been in use. Surely another child played on that swing."

"That's what making me feel chilled. I asked Selma about the swing and she said the other children played on it often after Iona's death. Edith Earl took it over and once in a while Harriet would let the nurse swing Leander on it. Selma remembered the Friday night that Thalia and Rebecca Holly

111

came for the reunion and the children were in the playground. Edith Earl was using the big swing and it was all right then.''

"Sandy, the rope had to be cut that night.''

Despite the heat, his secretary shivered. "Senseless violence directed against children. Robby, do you think someone is trying to kill that little boy?''

"I don't know. All I know is that we'd better find out.'' He added grimly, "And fast, Sandy, very fast.''

CHAPTER TWELVE

Miss Sanderson jotted a final note in her book, thanked George Barton, and put down the receiver. As she did, Forsythe stuck his head around the door of the living room. "Got it all down, Sandy?"

"For what it's worth. Mainly trivia."

"While we lunch, you can regale me with it. I've set up on the patio behind the house. Did Barton have any trouble tracking us down?"

"Not really." She followed him through the kitchen and onto a redwood patio. The sun beamed down on a rather dilapidated table and two old wooden chairs. "Barton rang up the Vancouver Harmony Hotel and, Mr. Malone referred him to the Hollystone Hotel and, of course, Weasel Weston gave him this number." She dubiously examined one of the chairs. "Where did you come up with this furniture?"

Forsythe was dishing up scrambled eggs. "I found them in that shed back there. They look about the same age as this house but they're solid." He poured coffee. "Eat first, talk later."

When they'd finished their lunches, Miss Sanderson lit a cigarette, pushed back her chair, and stretched long, shapely legs. "Now for the trivia. Barton's firm of investigators do seem competent. Nothing of interest on Mariana Pulos. She graduated from high school with top grades. Only black mark

113

is her association with Fabian Harcourt. And that's not so black. The only record he has is a juvenile offense. Three months in a correctional institute for car theft. Other than that, he's clean. Fabe's been trying to raise money for a motorcycle repair shop and he was in Vancouver the weekend of Thalia Holly's death. No possible way he could have killed the girl."

Forsythe drummed long fingers against the table. "We've decided he's in the clear. Brice Stevens-Parkes?"

"The Stevens-Parkeses have lived off the Hollys since Brice's grandfather took over the family's business affairs. Brice's entire practice is involved with Mrs. Pulos and her various concerns. Brice lives quietly but well, drives an expensive imported car. Impeccable record."

"What about the Earl family?"

His secretary grimaced. "Not exactly solid citizens. Nothing criminal, but Randolph's skated close to the edge once or twice. Seems ever since Millicent met him and they decided not to spoil two houses, they've had nothing but trouble. Randolph likes to be his own boss. He's been involved with about a dozen small businesses and gone broke on all of them. The trouble is that he has no ethics and as much business sense as a child. He went bankrupt right across Canada—Quebec City, Hamilton, Niagara Falls, and Calgary to name a few spots. Worked his way steadily westward until he reached Salmondale."

Miss Sanderson ground out her cigarette and continued. "Randolph pulled his family along with him and in Salmondale finally had a stroke of luck. It seems Millie's mother and Harriet's were distant cousins. The Earls heard about the wealthy Mrs. Pulos in Hollystone and Randolph decided it was time Harriet was apprised about her cousin Millie. They came to Holly House and found Harriet pregnant with her first child. She was trying to build a family on this estate. Harriet warmly welcomed the Earls, gave Randolph a job in the office of her lumber mill, and had a house built for them. To show proper gratitude, in time Millie and Randolph produced yet another little Earl."

The barrister smiled. "Charming family."

A fleeting smile lighted Miss Sanderson's austere face and pale blue eyes. "Now for the interesting part. Remember that educated guess I made about brother Alexis?"

"I take it you were on target."

"Bull's-eye! Alexis's best friend in Hollystone, William O'Day, known as Billy, is overtly homosexual. When Billy was teaching in Vancouver, he became involved with a teenage boy in one of his classes and was asked to resign his position. The boy's parents and the school wanted no publicity, so it was hushed up. At that time, Alexis was a steady visitor to Billy O'Day. Alexis has a great deal of pull in Hollystone and he managed to get his friend a position at the Ernest Stone Secondary School and—"

"Hold it!" Forsythe jerked forward. "What about Harriet's reaction?"

His secretary lifted her head and sunlight glinted on the soft waves of her gray hair. "She knows nothing about Billy's past. As a matter of fact, O'Day has an excellent record in Hollystone. No one in town has an inkling he's a homosexual." She waved a hand. "And that's the lot."

"Anything about Dmitri?"

"Absolutely clean. Industrious young man who worked hard before his marriage to support an aged mother and his younger brother and sister. He doesn't smoke, rarely takes a drink, no gambling, and has never shown an interest in any woman except his wife. As I said, a bunch of trivia."

"One never knows." He started piling dishes on a tray. "I'll stick these in the dishwasher. Then I'm off to see Alexis and Mariana."

She gave him a gloomy look. "And I'm off to interview the ruddy Earls."

"Don't take anything from them, Sandy. If they give any trouble, mention Harriet's name. That should do the trick."

Before Miss Sanderson went over to the Earl house, she took time for a shower and change of clothes. When she'd run out of excuses to delay further, she walked up the driveway, passed the blue Cadillac, and headed for their door. Near that door was the youngest Earl, playing with an assortment of toys in a playpen. Demmy was clad only in a sodden diaper, and when she paused to pat his head, he responded by blowing bubbles and chuckling. As she bent over the playpen, the front door flew open and his mother appeared on the step. Millie's grooming was much better than the last time the secretary had seen her. She was wearing flowered chiffon, stiletto heels, and her hair was fussily arranged. Her manner also had changed. Haughtily, she looked down at Miss Sanderson.

"Cousin Harriet told me to expect one of you," she told the other woman. "But I thought Mr. Forsythe would be speaking with us."

Lady of the manor, Miss Sanderson thought. Aloud, she said, "Mr. Forsythe has other interviews, Mrs. Earl, so he sent me."

Millie sniffed. "You might as well come in."

She teetered into the house and Miss Sanderson followed her. The old English theme had been faithfully reproduced inside as well as on the exterior. Fake beams ran along a low ceiling and the walls were paneled. Millie opened a door and gestured her guest into a large, messy sitting room. Her husband, dwarfed by the high-backed chair he was perched on, nodded but didn't bother getting up. He looked disappointed. "Oh, Miss Sanderson. I was looking forward to meeting your celebrated employer."

"So your wife told me." Miss Sanderson sank on a Regency chair with a striped, slightly soiled covering.

Still speaking in the affected way, Millie asked, "Would you care for tea or perhaps a drink?"

"Thank you, no. But I would like to have your two older children here."

"Certainly not! Suzy and Floyd are far too young to be forced to answer questions on a matter like this. Anything you wish to know, I will answer."

Snapping her shoulder bag open, Miss Sanderson said firmly, "I must insist they are present."

116

"Get them, love," Randolph instructed.

Tossing her head, Millie teetered back into the hall, where she promptly lost her aristocratic manner. "Floyd, Suzy!" she bellowed. "Get down here on the double."

Without waiting for an answer, she returned to the sitting room and sank on a sofa matching the Regency chair. In front of it, a coffee table was piled with magazines and books. An open box of chocolates and a bowl of salted nuts perched precariously on several paperback books. "I fail," Millie said loftily, "to see what my family has to do with a mugging in Stanley Park. I must also tell you that none of us will answer a question we find distasteful."

Miss Sanderson said coldly, "You'd better ring up Mrs. Pulos. She told us that our questions would be answered fully."

Randolph ran a finger along his hairline mustache. "Don't be difficult, love. Cousin Harriet was clear in her instructions."

Millie pouted but consoled herself with a handful of nuts. She was munching when Suzy and Floyd, followed by Edith, entered the room. Millie pointed a commanding finger at the younger girl and said in a muffled voice, "Not you, Edith. You either go back upstairs or get out and watch little Demmy."

"I wanta stay," the child whined.

Her mother flourished a ham-sized hand and the child headed for the door. Before she left, she stuck out a pink tongue at her mother. Millie coughed, swallowed, and said, "Randolph, that girl is getting out of hand." She told the other young people, "Sit down and keep your mouths shut. No smart remarks, hear? Speak only when spoken to."

Their expression sullen, Floyd and his sister perched on a love seat. Randolph said impatiently, "Let's get this started, Miss Sanderson."

"I'd like some background information. How long have you been living here?"

"We came before dear Iona was born. Millie and I were

117

in the neighborhood looking for a good investment and we remembered she had a close relation in Hollystone so—''

''How close? First cousin?''

Floyd grinned. ''More like fifth or sixth. And if I remember correctly, we were flat broke when we got here.''

''Your mother told you to keep that trap shut,'' his father reminded him. ''Start yapping again and I'll ram my fist down your throat.''

His son's grin didn't waver. ''I think I can take you now. Want to find out?''

Balling up a meaty fist, his mother waved it. ''Like to try me, sonny boy?''

''Rather take on King Kong,'' her son muttered.

''Can we get on with this?'' Miss Sanderson asked. ''Mr. Earl, I understand you hold a position in one of Mrs. Pulos's concerns.''

''In the office of her lumber mill. Managerial, of course. I'm in charge of the accounting department. Harriet realized immediately how wide my experience is in business.''

''You'd better believe it,'' Suzy murmured.

''That is enough out of you, young lady. As I started to say, Miss Sanderson, I've an excellent position but I don't feel I'm working up to my full potential. I work much better when I'm owner of a concern. Still, Harriet has been most kind and generous. She had this house built to our plans. Millie was tickled pink with it, weren't you, love?''

Millie was working on more nuts. Rather thickly, she replied, ''In seventh heaven, but I didn't realize I'd have to look after the place myself. It's a big house and with four kiddies and one's an infant, well . . .'' She looked resentfully around the untidy room. ''You'd think Harriet would allow me at least one servant. *She* has a good-sized staff.''

''Your own fault,'' her son told her. ''You put on such a heavy act about being big mother and how you love your kids and so on. Harriet agreed a woman's place was in the home and she did give you the home.''

''That's right, Mom,'' Suzy chimed in.

118

"A fat lot of help I get from you two," Millie snarled. "I feel like a bloody slave!"

Hastily, Miss Sanderson asked Floyd. "Do you work in one of the concerns, too?"

He grimaced. "Learning the business from the ground up. I spend seven hours a day at the mill pulling wood off the green chain. Some job!"

"Look who's talking!" his mother chuckled. "Bone lazy, both you and Suzy."

Floyd winked at Miss Sanderson. "Guess who we inherit that laziness from?"

She heartily wished Robby was handling the Earl family. It was like refereeing a cat fight. She raised her voice. "That's enough background information. Mrs. Earl, I'd like to know your position on the plateaus the day of Iona Pulos's death."

"I really can't say. I was so busy locating the flowers and writing down the names. All of us wanted to win this year. Cousin Harriet gives such lovely prizes. I have never won. Last year, that Mariana won and she got a diamond-studded watch. I've always suspected she cheated. This year, I was determined I would be the winner. Just before we left Holly House that morning, Harriet told us she'd decided to make the prize extraspecial. All of us were simply agog!"

Floyd chuckled. "Mom was probably hoping for three maids."

This time, his mother ignored him. Her brow was furrowed in thought. "I do know I was on one of the higher plateaus. When Iona fell, I hurried downward—my first impulse was to get to the bottom of the gorge. I ran down two or three plateaus and I found Brice and Dmitri struggling to control Harriet. She'd gone completely hysterical, poor dear. I had to use force to take her up. On the way, I found Randolph still engrossed in flowers, but he can tell you himself."

"Quite so, love." Randolph cleared his throat. "I'd found a particularly charming specimen of grandiflorum—that's a trillium, Miss Sanderson—"

"Randolph's so smart," his wife said admiringly.

"And near it was a clump of odorata, a pink violet. Quite

119

rare. I confess I was so intent, I didn't even know the child had fallen until Millie appeared dragging Harriet. Harriet was struggling and Millie shouted that Brice and the Pulos brothers were on their way down to the base of the falls. I was torn two ways, thinking I should help them with Iona and also feeling Harriet needed me.''

"I told him to lend a hand and he did,'' his wife finished up succinctly.

Miss Sanderson lifted her eyes from her notebook. "I understand Edith was to stay with you. Which one was she with?''

"Edith?'' Millie raised her brows. "Not with me. Randolph?''

"I thought she was with you, love.''

Millie shrugged heavy shoulders. "She was somewhere on the plateaus.''

Really loving parents, Miss Sanderson thought. Leaving a child that age to roam a dangerous area. She looked at Floyd. "Was she with you?''

"I didn't see Edith. Suzy and me were trying for that prize, too. We headed down to the lower plateaus and then we split up. When Iona fell, I hustled down to the gorge and Suzy was already there. Iona's body was caught on a rock and we waded in, but the current was so strong we couldn't reach her. Then her dad and Alexis and Brice came running down and we formed a chain, hanging on to the guy in front of us, and Dmitri caught hold of her dress and we hauled her in.'' Floyd looked sick. "She was a mess. She must have fallen headfirst onto those rocks and her face was . . . mangled.''

"Don't,'' his mother moaned. "It was awful. They carried the poor child up and her mother went crazy. We tried to hold her, but she fought like a lioness trying to get to her cub. Harriet pulled herself free and flung herself on the girl's body and we had to pull . . .'' Millie covered her face with both hands. "I can't talk about it anymore.''

Turning a page, Miss Sanderson said, "Let's go on to the
120

evening of Thalia Holly's death. After Harriet left her, did any of you go to her room?"

"Are you accusing one of us of murder?" Randolph demanded. "I can tell you none of us went near that girl's room—"

"Wrong, Dad," Floyd interrupted. "I saw her for a moment." He turned to Miss Sanderson and his eyes were agonized. "I felt so bad about Thalia, that swing breaking and Harriet raving like a maniac at her. I was hanging around in the hall trying to get guts enough to knock at her door when Harriet came out of her room. I could see Thalia sitting on the edge of her bed and I called to her and she looked at me. But Harriet shut the door and ordered me to leave Thalia alone. She said she'd given Thalia something to make her sleep and I wasn't to bother her. I wish I *had* gone in to see her. Maybe . . . maybe she'd still be alive."

"You're a very foolish boy," his father said sternly. "Mr. Forsythe will think you had something to do with the girl's death."

Suzy leaned forward. "Mr. Forsythe is *smart*, Dad. He'll know Floyd didn't hurt her. He loved Thalia."

Randolph scowled and Miss Sanderson intervened. "The day of Rebecca Holly's death. Mrs. Pulos told us you were in Vancouver."

"That's right." Millie had recovered from the emotional storm over Iona's death and was consuming nuts at a great rate. "Cousin Harriet and Dmitri were there on business and we went along for a little holiday. Nurse Yale was looking after Edith and little Demmy, and much as I love those kids I was glad to have time away. All the work, you know. Randolph and I even took separate rooms. Not that I approve of married people sleeping separate but—"

"Harriet and Dmitri have separate rooms," Suzy pointed out.

"That's *their* business, young lady," her mother reproved.

Randolph nodded sagely, "It was my idea we take two rooms. It gave us a chance to relax and not be bothered with the other one coming and going. We had a pleasant time,

121

too, didn't we, love? Shopping and going to the theater and dining out. A real treat.''

"The hours we want covered are from five in the afternoon to one in the morning," Miss Sanderson told them.

"Let's see.'' Millie reached for the nut bowl, found it empty, and selected a chocolate. "That was Monday. That day, I shopped and by three in the afternoon my ankles were swollen something fierce. So I told Randolph I was going to have a nice lazy evening. I took a hot bath and ordered my dinner from room service—that was around five. I stuck the tray in the hall and went to bed. I read for a time.'' She pointed at the pile of paperbacks. "I'm a great one to read. About eleven, I turned off the light and went to sleep. It was so nice. I'm not one to complain, but with four kids and this house and meals to get, I'm kept hopping. Randolph went out for the evening. Went to one of those Ingmar Bergman films. You love those films, don't you?''

"I really do, love. But that night, I wasn't able to see the film I'd have liked to.''

There was an uneasy note in the man's voice and Miss Sanderson looked closely at him. "What did you do, Mr. Earl?''

"There was a lineup for that film and I didn't feel like standing around, so I went to another theater and saw a double feature. It got out around eleven.''

Floyd was wearing a knowing grin. "Bet it was porn.''

Color flooded into his father's face and Miss Sanderson decided she wouldn't bet against it. Randolph looked positively guilty. His wife was watching him narrowly. "Did you come directly back to the hotel?'' Abigail asked.

"Well . . . no. Men like to get out by themselves once in a while. I dropped into a couple of bars and had some drinks. Nothing harmful. Just talked to a few chaps and told some jokes and laughed it up.''

Millie asked softly, "What time *did* you get back?''

He squirmed around in the high-backed chair. "It was fairly late—Maybe two or three.''

122

Millie was looking baleful and Miss Sanderson hastened to ask, "Did you know any of these men?"

"You mean, can I prove it? No, they were strangers and we were all drinking." He gave his wife a placating smile. "Harmless fun, love."

Miss Sanderson had a suspicion whatever Randolph had been doing on his night on the town hadn't been in the company of the boys. Floyd was leering at his father but he said nothing. "Now," Miss Sanderson said briskly, "it's your turn, Floyd."

Millie tore her eyes from her husband's flushed face and answered for her son. "Floyd and Suzy went to a disco together. They were back by midnight. I told them midnight and to stay together and my children always obey."

"Wrong on three counts, Mom," Floyd told her. "We don't obey and we didn't stay together and neither of us went to a disco."

"What did you do?" Miss Sanderson asked.

"As soon as we left the hotel, we split up," Suzy said. "I went to a roller-skating rink and I don't know what Floyd did. The place wasn't far from the hotel and I walked back after one. I skated with a nice boy and he wanted to walk me back, but I knew if Mom or Dad saw us they'd have a fit. And no, I don't know his full name or his address. He said to call him Ted and he had wonderful eyes and that's all I know."

Randolph jumped up. "I think this has gone far enough! It's one thing to interrogate my wife and me, but a couple of children . . . that's outrageous!"

"Don't take on so," Floyd said mildly. "In case you haven't noticed, neither Suzy nor me are kids anymore. She's nearly eighteen and I'll soon be twenty. Lots old enough to kill an old woman. Now, for my alibi, and both you and Mom are going to love this. I spent the entire evening in the park."

"Floyd!" his father gasped.

The secretary asked, "Stanley Park?"

"That's right. As soon as I left Suzy, I walked down and

123

wandered around. I went to the aquarium and over to watch the seals and polar bears at the zoo.''

His mother moaned. ''Rebecca died only a short distance from the zoo.''

Her son shrugged. ''That's where I was at . . . I guess it was about eight. Then I stopped at a hamburger stand and had a couple of cheeseburgers and a milk shake. I ate them and wandered around Beaver Lake and Lost Lagoon. It was after midnight when I got back to the hotel.''

''Son,'' Randolph said solemnly, ''you may just have fitted a rope around your neck. Admitting you were hanging around Thalia's room the night she died and now this. You are a *fool.*''

''At least I'm not a *liar.* I wouldn't have touched a hair of Thalia's head and I didn't even see Rebecca in the park.''

Randolph, his face twisted with rage, leaped to his feet. ''Are you calling me a liar?''

''What do you think? God, but I'm sick of you and this place!''

''Get out then. If you're old enough to talk to your father like this, you're old enough to clear out!''

Floyd gave his father a bitter grin. ''I just talk. Same as you and Mom, too. Complain all the time but hang around to inherit a hunk of Harriet's loot. Ever think she might last another forty years?''

Randolph sprang at the boy, but Suzy jumped in between them. ''No!'' she screamed, her big hands knotting into fists. ''You aren't beating him again!''

Millie shoved the chocolate box away and kicked off her shoes. She lunged at her daughter. Miss Sanderson had just time enough to note that the female Earls were about the same height and build before Millie took a swing at her daughter. At the same moment, Randolph leaped between them. His wife's huge fist connected solidly with his face. Uttering an anguished howl, he folded at his wife's feet. ''Dear God,'' Millie moaned. ''Look what I did. Randolph, dear, speak to me!''

Floyd bent over his father. ''I'll get some ice for that eye.''

124

The boy beat a hasty retreat while Suzy joined her mother beside the recumbent form of Randolph Earl. Shaking her head, Miss Sanderson stuck her notebook back in the shoulder bag and rose to take her leave. The older Earls paid no attention, but when she opened the door she found Edith crouching in the hall.

"Eavesdropping?" she asked the child.

Edith sneered. "I'm a snoop. Mom says that all the time."

The girl backed away and Miss Sanderson called, "Just a moment, Edith. That day of the wildflower contest—where were you on the plateaus?"

Edith crossed her eyes and stuck out her tongue. "That's for me to know and you to find out." She leaped up the staircase and disappeared from view.

Feeling as though she were escaping, Miss Sanderson swung open the front door. In the playpen, Demmy was curled into a ball, chubby arms hugging a big stuffed dog. Looking down at the sleeping baby, she whispered, "You poor little devil."

Then she retraced her steps to the Widows' House to find out how Forsythe had made out with Alexis and Mariana Pulos.

CHAPTER THIRTEEN

FORSYTHE WALKED UP TO HOLLY HOUSE, LOCATED THE side door to Mariana's suite, and rang the bell. Mariana, attractively dressed in designer jeans and a white silk shirt, admitted him. "Watch the steps," the girl warned. "Fabe always forgets and stumbles down them. This way."

He followed her through the basement, along a dim corridor, past a furnace room and a laundry. At the end of the corridor was another door, this one painted Chinese red. "Home, sweet home," Mariana said, and opened the door.

The room beyond was sizable and on the dark side, but the shag carpeting, carelessly tossed pillows, beanbag chairs, and bright posters made it gay and attractive. Switching on a lamp, Mariana said, "Wait a sec and I'll get another chair. You probably don't like those." She went through a doorway and returned with a fan-backed rattan chair. "Try this one." She waited until the barrister was seated and then she sat down cross-legged on the other side of a low table painted cobalt blue. "I've been waiting for you, and before you say anything, there's something I want to tell you. At the funeral, I was rude. I'm sorry. It really wasn't you. It was just . . . I guess I was looking for a scapegoat. Since Iona died, it's been simply rotten around here."

He opened his mouth but the girl rushed on. "I guess you

figure we're a spineless bunch. And you're right. All of us hanging around, scared stiff of offending Harriet—''

"Miss Pulos, I'm not here to form any opinions except those that have a bearing on the deaths of Thalia and Rebecca Holly. Your life is your own business.''

She pushed thick hair away from her face and lifted large brown eyes. "Fabe keeps telling me I'm spineless. He wants me to chuck the whole thing and go away with him. It isn't that easy. You see, Mr. Forsythe, before Dmitri married Harriet, my family was just . . . just nothing in this town.''

"The townspeople were hostile?''

"Something worse—indifferent. We were 'those Greeks who ran the store.' The house I grew up in you wouldn't believe. Five of us crammed in three dinky rooms. There was only one bedroom and Mama and Papa had that. Dmitri and Alexis slept on a fold-down couch in the living room and I had a cot in the pantry off the kitchen. Know where I kept my clothes? In a potato bin!

"Papa was a sweetheart but Mama ran everything. To be honest, Mama was something else. The store wasn't making us rich but we could have lived better than that. But Mama was saving every penny for Dmitri's education. She kept telling us that the eldest son must be educated so he could take care of his parents in their old age. So she bought our clothes at secondhand stores and we lived in that dreadful house.

"At school, I looked like a scarecrow. All the kids laughed at me. Funny thing is, after all Mama's scrimping she never got any good out of it. A week after Dmitri graduated from high school, Papa had a stroke and died and my brother couldn't go to university because he had to take over the store.''

"Is your mother still alive?''

"That's what I meant about Mama never getting any good out of it. Dmitri married Harriet Stone Holly and Mama was thrilled. Figured she had her old age made. But she died a couple of months after they were married, and Alex and I were the ones who benefited from that marriage.''

The girl's lips twisted. "When I was about ten and Thalia

Holly came to live with Kenneth and Harriet Holly, she was sent to public school in town. Thalia was a grade ahead of me and I thought she was so lucky. Harriet had parties for her on her birthday and at Christmas and that sort of thing. The mayor's daughters and the principal's and bank manager's were invited to them. I never was. Thalia didn't even know I was alive. I used to walk past the gates of this estate and look in. I thought anyone who lived at Holly House lived in heaven.''

''You've found it isn't heaven?'' the barrister asked.

Mariana shrugged. ''On this earth, there is no heaven. But for a time I thought I was in paradise. This suite, all that stuff''—she waved at shelves lined with sound components—''when I got my driver's license a Jaguar was leased for me. Credit cards and a good job in the office of the furniture factory.'' The girl pulled up her knees and rested her chin on them. ''The people in town who had looked down on my family and me suddenly so nice and polite. Yes, for a while it seemed like paradise.''

''Then you met Mr. Harcourt.''

''And woke up and smelled the coffee. Harriet is prepared to give me anything my heart desires except what I want most—Fabe. Fabe is furious with her, but I keep telling him what a tremendous person she really is and how much she likes me. Harriet's only trying to get rid of Fabe because she doesn't feel I'd be happy with him.''

Forsythe raised his brows. ''So you don't object to what she's doing to Mr. Harcourt?''

''Of *course* I object! Sometimes I get so angry, I hate her. Once in a while, I feel we're all puppets with Harriet jerking our strings.''

''You could leave.''

''Sure I could. And leave everything behind me. I poke fun at the Earls because they're so greedy and fawning, and I'm no better than they are.''

Forsythe studied the girl's animated face. He had a hunch that Harriet's charm was wearing thin with Mariana. ''Do you know the terms of your sister-in-law's will?''

128

"All of us do. Millions! Could *you* give that up?"

"I've no idea. I've never faced that temptation. If you loved Fabian Harcourt, I suppose you could."

"I do love him!" Jumping to her feet, Mariana paced restlessly back and forth. "He's wonderful. Fabe loves children and he plays with Leander. He worships that boy. When Harriet isn't around, he lets the boy ride on his shoulders and plays catch with him."

"How do you feel about Leander?"

Mariana looked surprised. "The way everyone does. He's lovable."

"And Iona?"

She made a face. "Iona reminded me of Mama. She was a nasty brat. She called Fabe 'the bum' and Alex 'Baldy.' " Her lips relaxed into a wide smile. "Alex is going bald and he's sensitive about it. In fact, Alex is very sensitive. He puts on a tough act, but underneath he really is insecure."

"I want to speak with your brother later. His apartment is in the attic, isn't it?"

"Yes. Much nicer than this one, bigger and brighter. But, if you want to see Alex, you'll have to go into town. After the funeral, he went into Hollystone to stay a few days. Said he couldn't bear being here another moment."

"Where is he staying?"

"With a friend—Billy O'Day. He's Alex's best friend. He teaches at the secondary school and his house is on Vine Street. The second one down from the corner of Main Street. It's a nice house, painted gray and blue."

"Have Alexis and Mr. O'Day been friends for long?" Forsythe's voice was casual but he was watching the girl closely.

"For a number of years. Alex met Billy in Vancouver and they've been chums ever since. Double-date all the time." Mariana giggled. "Alex is quite a man with the girls."

Hasn't a clue, Forsythe thought. He said briskly, "Now, Miss Pulos, I'll make this as brief as possible. The day Iona died—can you remember which plateau you were on?"

The girl's dark brows drew together. "I don't know what

this has to do with Thalia or Rebecca but let me think. I was trying to win the contest and I wasn't thinking of anything but that. Last year, I won and Millie Earl was livid. She had her heart set on winning this year and damned if I'd let her. Last year, the prize was a watch, and Harriet promised it would be even nicer this year. I must have been on one of the lower plateaus. When Iona fell, I remember Alex and Dmitri and Brice rushing down toward me.''

He made a note. "The day of Rebecca Holly's death. The hours between five in the afternoon and one the following morning. Could you tell me your movements?''

She nibbled at her lower lip. "Harriet and Dmitri were in Vancouver, so I was playing hooky from work. I phoned in sick. I was right here.''

"Alone?''

Sinking down on the shag again, Mariana said, "That morning Fabe and I had a row. The usual reason—Harriet had been making life hell for him and he was at me again to throw in the towel and go away with him. He told me even for me he couldn't stay around much longer and I fired back at him. Fabe stormed out of here and for a while I considered driving into town and making up. Then I thought, no, let him come to me. I was in a rotten mood. I made supper— I've a kitchenette—and then I spent the evening playing cassettes and watching a video. I kept waiting, hoping Fabe would come back, but he didn't. About half past ten, I went to bed and cried myself to sleep.''

"If you had left, would anyone have known about it? The Grangers or the Beaton sisters?''

"They weren't on the estate that night.''

Forsythe raised his head. "They weren't in their cottages?''

"Harriet gave them a few days off. Selma Yale was taking care of Leander and the Earl brats and she was making meals for them. I think the Beaton sisters went to Salmondale. They've an aunt they visit there. Bert and Agathe were in town at their son's house. I can't prove I didn't leave the estate.''

"How did you get on with Thalia and her grandmother?"

"Rebecca despised Alex and me. Thalia? I admired her and would have liked to have been her friend. Thalia wasn't snobbish but she was . . . I suppose you'd call it remote. All wrapped in ballet, and when she was here, the only person she could see was Harriet."

Forsythe put his notebook in his pocket and followed Mariana down the shadowed corridor to the outside door. "Watch those steps," she warned again. Admiring brown eyes stared up at him. "It must be interesting to be a criminologist."

"At times. Most of the time, it's merely hard work. Thank you, Miss Pulos."

Forsythe paused to allow his eyes to adjust to the glare of sunlight. After the cool basement, it felt like stepping into a furnace. He could feel beads of sweat breaking out on his brow and upper lip. Then he forgot about the heat. A girl in a pink uniform was walking across the lawn. She was holding the hand of the little boy who had been very much on the barrister's mind. At the child's side, the dalmatian paced. With long strides, Forsythe caught up with them.

The girl turned her head and smiled. The end of her nose was pink and her voice was husky. "Mr. Forsythe? I'm Selma Yale. I saw you for a moment in the library the other day."

"Yes. How's your cold?"

"Much better. Leander's feeling quite well again, too. Aren't you, dear?"

"Better." The boy dimpled up at Forsythe and patted his dog. "This is Emwy."

Emily lifted her head and nuzzled at the barrister's hand. He patted a smooth ear. "I have two dogs at home, Leander."

"Like Emwy?"

"Emily is much prettier than my dogs."

Flinging back her blond hair, the nurse said, "I enjoyed meeting your secretary. Miss Sanderson is a pleasant woman." She stopped and glanced at her watch. "Must get back to the nursery, Leander. Time for din-din."

"Cookies?" he asked.

131

"If you eat all your veggies. Nice meeting you, Mr. Forsythe."

The barrister gently rumpled the boy's glossy curls. "Take good care of him, Miss Yale."

"I always do." The nurse tinkled a laugh. "That's what I'm paid for."

Forsythe watched them walking toward Holly House. Leander's short legs pumped along trying to keep up with his nurse's. The dog bounded along in front of them and the boy was calling its name. When they were out of sight, Forsythe turned back to the road leading to the Widows' House. He found his secretary in the living room, slumped on the sofa, a glass in one hand.

After helping himself to Glenlivet, Forsythe sat down beside her. "How did it go?"

"Later, Robby. I'd rather not talk about it now. I can tell you this. It was like trying to interview a family of baboons. Ended up with the parent Earls and Suzy and Floyd bashing away at each other."

The barrister laughed. "Who won?"

"Looked like a draw. Father Earl stepped in at the wrong moment and got a dandy roundhouse Mother Earl was aiming at Suzy." She looked faintly pleased. "It connected with his eye."

"Whose turn is it to get dinner?"

"Mine. You got lunch."

He asked plaintively, "Why do I always get stuck with lunch?"

"Because I value my stomach and you can't do too much harm with scrambled eggs and tinned soup."

"So what elaborate meal are you cooking?"

"Bangers and mash."

"Amazing." He glanced at his watch. "How long before that gourmet fare is ready?"

"Don't be snide. About ten minutes. Why the rush?"

"We have to go into town tonight. Alexis is staying with Billy O'Day. You can drop me off at O'Day's house and then you can locate Fabe Harcourt."

132

"At least Fabe will be a pleasant change from the Earl menagerie." She put down her glass. "After we get back from Hollystone, we can fill each other in, but there's one item I want to tell you now."

"Fire when ready."

"Edith Earl. She's a self-confessed snoop and eavesdropper. Unpleasant brat. But she was on one of the plateaus when Iona Pulos fell. I'm wondering if she could have seen anything."

"Did you question her?"

"I tried to, but she stuck out her tongue and ran."

Forsythe said slowly, "In that case, we'd better not waste time. There may be two children in danger."

CHAPTER FOURTEEN

THEY LOCATED BILLY O'DAY'S HOUSE WITH NO TROUBLE. On a street of small, attractive houses it stood out. It was the neatest house with the prettiest garden on Vine Street. Parked in front of the gate was the red Alfa-Romeo that had been at Holly House.

Miss Sanderson said, "If you're finished here before I come back, walk to the hotel and I'll pick you up there." She gave the blue and gray house an approving look. "Billy O'Day's house certainly looks pleasant."

So did the young man who opened the door. He was slender and tall and under carefully groomed hair he had a frank, open face. His voice was pleasant, too. "Sorry," he said with a glance at Forsythe's briefcase. "If you're selling magazines, I have my quota."

"I'm Robert Forsythe. I was told that Alexis Pulos is here."

"He is, but Al isn't feeling well. Mrs. Holly's death and the funeral have upset him. Would it be possible to delay this until tomorrow?"

"No."

"If you insist. Please step in. Would you wait here for a moment while I prepare Al."

The barrister waited in the tiny hall. The walls were washed with pale yellow and a table bore a pottery bowl of daisies. After a few moments, the door opened and Billy ushered his

134

guest into his living room. Alexis was seated in the depths of a huge leather chair, but he rose, hesitantly extended a hand to Forsythe, and darted a look at his friend.

"Do be seated," Billy said cheerfully. "We don't stand on formality. Call me Billy and I know Al would prefer his first name used. May I call you Robert?"

"If you wish." Forsythe opened his briefcase and took out a notebook.

"Do sit down, Al, and relax. I'm sure Robert isn't going to bite you."

"There's no need to be nervous, Mr.—Alexis. I'm only going to ask a few questions."

Alexis retreated to his chair but he didn't look reassured. Pulling over a hassock, Billy sat down beside him. "Do you mind if I remain?"

"Not at all. Now, Alexis—"

"One moment," Billy interrupted. "I'm going to level with you."

"Billy!" Alexis protested. "You promised you wouldn't."

"I promised I'd be discreet with the townspeople. But take a good look at Robert Forsythe. He's a man of wide experience. Do you think he hasn't checked on my background?" Billy's intelligent eyes questioned the barrister.

"You're correct. I'm aware of your life in Vancouver and of the nature of Alexis's relationship with you."

Alexis jerked forward. "Have you told Harriet?"

"No. If this has no bearing on the case I'm investigating, I have no intention of telling anyone. My purpose is to find the truth about Thalia and Rebecca Holly's deaths, not to expose innocent people. However, and this I warn you, if your relationship does have a bearing on this case, I *will* expose you."

"You could be ruthless," Billy said.

"Murder is hardly gentle."

"I'm not aware there has been a murder. Thalia Holly was a suicide and her grandmother the victim of a mugging."

Forsythe made an impatient gesture. "I'm not here to argue with you—"

"We're not criminals. Al and I hurt no one. I hate this

135

deception. I've argued and argued with Al about it. Leave this town, I keep telling him, come with me, let's live openly together. We love each other. Is that a crime?''

Forsythe opened his mouth, but Alexis said hotly, "In Harriet's eyes, it is. It's fine for Alexis to chase girls and even to gamble. But this . . . Harriet would throw me out faster than you can say *gay.*''

"What do you care if she does?" Billy fired back. "She doesn't own you. I told you I can make our living. I can't give you an Alfa-Romeo or all the expensive toys you have now, but I can give you a decent life. Right now, you're nothing but Harriet's vassal. Tugging your forelock and toadying to her!''

"*Billy.*" Color surged into Alexis's face. "I've warned you repeatedly not to speak about Harriet like that. She's a fine woman and she thinks the world of me.''

"You utter ass! All that woman cares about is herself and her son. I promise you, one of these days you'll open your eyes and you won't like what you—''

Forsythe rapped his knuckles sharply against the chair arm. "Billy, if you want to stay, sit down. Alexis, the day of Iona's death, where were you on the plateaus?''

Billy sank back on the hassock and Alexis's face became thoughtful. This man, Forsythe thought, was wholly different from the Alexis Pulos Sandy had met on the veranda of Holly House. The brash young chap was gone and in his place was a softer, less assured man. Alexis's big teeth hadn't flashed once since Forsythe had entered the room, and for this the barrister was thankful.

"That's not an easy question to answer," Alexis said. "I was genuinely competing in the contest this year. A couple of years ago, I won and Harriet gave me a lovely cigarette case. That morning, she told us this year's prize would be even better.'' He turned brown eyes on the man at his side. "I was hoping to surprise you by giving you the prize.''

Billy was over his fit of temper. "How thoughtful," he murmured.

"The plateau?" Forsythe reminded.

"It was higher than the ones Dmitri and Harriet were on.

I saw Dmitri and also Brice on the path in front of me as I went down. When Iona fell, I ran down the path and met Millie dragging Harriet up. Millie shouted that my brother and Brice had started down to the base of the falls, and I followed them. The two Earl children were already there. Suzy and Floyd were soaked to the waist from trying to get to the child. We formed a line and Dmitri managed to pull her body loose. Iona was—'' He buried his face in his hands.

Billy patted the other man's shoulder. ''Must you, Robert?''

''I must. Alexis, did you like your niece?''

His hands dropped and color surged up under the olive skin. ''No one could *like* that child. Iona was dreadful. Cruel!'' Tenderly, a hand caressed the bald spot on his head.

''Leander?''

''The direct opposite of Iona. A charming little fellow.''

''Let's return to the morning of that day. I understand you had a quarrel with your brother in the study.''

''Who told you that? Oh, don't bother answering. Servants will gossip. Yes, Dmitri and I had words. Nothing unusual. Dmitri gets upset simply because I lay an occasional bet.''

''And this quarrel concerned your gambling debts?''

''Yes.''

Billy stirred. ''Al, you mustn't lie. Tell Robert the truth.''

Doubtfully, Alexis bit his lower lip. ''Very well. But this has nothing to do with Thalia or Rebecca.''

''The truth,'' Billy ordered.

Alexis gazed down at his clasped hands. ''Dmitri had received an anonymous letter about Billy and me. One of those nasty—''

''It wasn't nasty,'' Billy said airily. ''I thought it was rather tastefully phrased.''

''*You* sent it.'' Alexis whirled on his friend. ''After giving me your solemn word you would say nothing to Harriet.''

''I didn't say it, I wrote it. And it wasn't to Harriet. It was to her husband.'' He tried to take Alexis's hand. ''We can't go on like this. I'd do anything to free you from that woman's bondage; this life is destroying both of us.''

Wrenching his hand loose, Alexis turned away from his

friend. Forsythe again rapped sharply. "Please! Alexis, continue."

"My brother said dreadful things to me and I lost my temper. We shouted at each other. Dmitri said unless I broke off immediately with Billy, he'd tell his wife."

Forsythe nodded. "According to a witness you shouted . . ." Flipping pages, Forsythe located Miss Sanderson's interview with Cassie Beaton. "Dmitri Pulos shouted, 'I won't let you do this to my wife!' and Alexis shouted back, 'I'll damn well do what I want, big brother, and you won't stop me!' " Forsythe glanced up. "Alexis, would you explain that?"

"The part about his wife is clear. All Dmitri ever thinks about is Harriet. Not for a minute did he worry about me. What I said to him . . . well, that's simple, too. Dmitri has always looked after Mariana and me. After Papa died, he acted like a father for us. Even feeling about Harriet the way he does doesn't change that. Dmitri threatened me, but I knew he wouldn't tell Harriet and have me kicked out."

Forsythe raised his brows. "So you settled the matter amicably?"

"Hardly. Dmitri was enraged. But he didn't tell Harriet and he didn't take it out on me. He went after Billy."

"He most certainly did," Billy said. "In June, at the end of the school term, I was told my services would no longer be required. He had me fired."

The barrister cleared his throat. "Alexis, your movements on the day of Rebecca Holly's death."

"In the morning—"

"From five in the afternoon on."

"Let me see. I came in here to see Billy about . . ."

Billy nodded. "It was around two. You see, Robert, with Al's brother and his wife away, Al was free to come and go as he liked."

"What about your job, Alexis?"

"What job?" Alexis's unfortunate teeth gleamed briefly. "It's a tailor-made position. I'm supposed to be head of the sales department at the furniture factory, but my assistant does all the work. I merely turn up, put my feet on the desk, and ogle the steno pool. That Monday, Billy was planning to cook dinner for us—he's a marvelous cook—and we were to spend the afternoon and evening together. Shortly after I got here, he picked a fight with—''

"I certainly didn't pick a fight. I delivered an ultimatum.'' Billy turned candid eyes on Forsythe. "I told Al I was returning to the coast in September and if he wouldn't go with me, he could stay and rot. He flew into a frenzy and went storming out.''

Alexis nodded his dark head. "I went down to the hotel and into the coffee shop. I was toying with the idea of asking Judy out on a date—to spite Billy. I decided not to. Judy was so coy, so eager. I drove back here to make up and I tapped on the door—''

"Tapped? You tried to break it down.''

"Billy wouldn't let me in, so—''

Forsythe interrupted. "What time was this?''

"I've no idea.''

Billy smiled at the barrister. "I can tell you to the minute. While Al was battering at the door, the oven timer started to ring. Al was here at twenty minutes to four.''

"What did you do then, Alexis?''

"I was even angrier with Billy and I decided to drive to Salmondale and have dinner and go to a disco. I was nearly there when I realized I couldn't face food or dancing. So I turned around and headed back to Hollystone. Then I thought of a place where Billy and I sometimes go. You drive down this lane and come out on a level spot above the Nipasagi River. The view is spectacular.''

The barrister glanced up. "Were any other cars there? Would anyone have noticed you?''

"I was all alone. I took a rug and a bottle of rye I keep in the glove compartment and I sat on the rug and drank. I drank nearly half the bottle. Then I went to sleep or passed out and when I came to, I was chilled and had a splitting headache and my mouth tasted like a sewer. I hauled myself

139

into the car and drove back to town. This house was dark, so I went back to Holly House."

"Have you any idea what the time was?"

"Late. I can't tell you how late. I was so sick, I just fell into bed."

Forsythe rose. "Can you hazard a guess, Billy?"

He stood up, too. "It had to be after one. That was when I turned off the lights. I take it that's all you want to ask."

"That's it. Thank you for your patience."

Alexis started to rise, but Billy pushed him back. "Relax. I'll see Robert out." He escorted Forsythe to the door and walked with him to the gate. Looking back at his house, he sighed. "I'll hate to leave this house. I've put a lot of work into it."

"You did a fine job."

Billy shrugged. "It's only a house. People are what really matter."

"You're definitely leaving town?"

"I don't make idle threats. Yes, I'll be going and I hope Al has sense enough to come with me." Billy hesitated and then looked earnestly at the barrister. "I'm well aware that Al can't prove he didn't go to Vancouver the evening of Mrs. Holly's death. I also know he was at Holly House when Thalia died. But he's absolutely incapable of violence."

Forsythe met his eyes. "And you?"

"I'm entirely different. If there was a good reason . . . yes, I could be violent. But I don't count, do I?"

"No, you don't count."

There was no sign of Miss Sanderson or the Mercedes, so Forsythe said good-bye to Billy O'Day and walked up Vine Street, turned on to Main, and headed toward the Hollystone Hotel.

Miss Sanderson had problems locating her own quarry. Finding Fabe Harcourt's boardinghouse wasn't difficult. Directions from an aged man walking an aged terrier sent her to a shabby house in the mill area on the outskirts of town. The woman who opened the door looked as sordid as the house did. Hard eyes swept from Miss Sanderson's neatly coiffed hair, over the elegantly tailored suit and Hermès scarf, down to the Italian sandals. "Well?" she asked.

"Is Mr. Harcourt here?"

"You got to be that English woman Fabe was talking about. Said he met you out to Holly House." Her lips curled unpleasantly. "How should I know where he's at, and even if I do, why should I tell you? What's the likes of you want with a bike bum? Fabe was really messing this place up with those bikes. Told him straight out he had to stop it."

Blimey, Miss Sanderson thought, how could bikes mess this place up? She opened her shoulder bag, took out a bill, and waved it under the landlady's nose. "Does this answer all your questions?"

She clawed it from the secretary's grasp. "Try the doc's place. Up on the hill. White colonial."

The colonial house on the hill was an improvement. In fact, the whole district was an improvement. Large houses were set well back from the street on lush lawns shaded by huge trees.

She knocked at the imposing front door of the white colonial. There was no answer. She wandered along a walk bordered with trim shrubs toward the rear of the house. Beyond a beautifully kept garden was a double garage. Light spilled from the open doors and inside Fabe Harcourt and a boy were working on a Honda bike. The boy saw her and stepped out of the garage. He looked in his late teens and was a rangy lad with carroty hair and the white skin and freckles that generally go with that coloring.

"Can I help you?" he asked politely.

"I'm looking for Mr. Harcourt."

Fabe dropped a wrench, grabbed a cloth, and wiped grease from his hands. "What can I do—oh, if it isn't Miss Sanderson."

She looked up at him. A strip of red flannel held long hair away from his face and he had a golden brown beard. With those clear eyes, he could have passed as a Viking. "I'd like to ask you a few questions, Mr. Harcourt."

"Fabe."

"Wow!" The boy was excited. "You work for Robert Forsythe? Dad's got a magazine with an article about you two in it. I knew you both were in town. In this place if anyone sneezes, the whole town knows about it."

"Meet Tom Brent, Junior." Fabe ruffled the boy's flaming hair. "Not a bad brat and nuts about bikes. How'd you find me, Miss Sanderson?"

"Your charming landlady. After I bribed her."

"Libby's not a bad person. Used to be fairly decent to me, but that dump she calls home belongs to the Puloses. Either she jumps when they tell her or she gets turfed out." Fabe gave his hands a last swipe. "Some questions, eh? Don't know what I can tell you but ask away."

"Hey," the boy said eagerly, "why don't you talk in the kitchen? Dad's out on a call and Mom's playing bridge. Got some beer in the fridge."

Fabe nodded. "Sounds good, Tommy. Lead the way."

The boy led them through the garden, up a flight of steps, and into a kitchen so clean it gleamed. He switched on lights, waved a hospitable hand at the chairs ringing a plastic-topped table, and produced beer from the fridge. Snapping caps off the bottles, he set two and a glass on the table, and, carrying the third, made for the door.

"Wait up there," Fabe called.

"I thought you'd want me to make myself scarce."

"Nothing I say you can't hear." Fabe's lips split in a warm smile. "Anyway, you're my alibi, aren't you?"

"Sure am. Me and Dad." Tommy pulled out a chair. "Want me to tell her now, Fabe?"

"Tell away. Better make it convincing."

"One moment," Miss Sanderson said. "I haven't asked anything yet."

Fabe took a swig of beer. "Don't have to. I got a pretty fair idea why you and Mr. Forsythe are in town. You think there's something fishy about the old lady's death. I may be a bike bum, but I can put two and two together. So, not to waste your time, here's what I did that Monday—"

Miss Sanderson interrupted to tell him the hours they

142

wanted covered. Tommy thumped his bottle down. "Fabe was here all afternoon. Mom was visiting my aunt in Salmondale—Mom doesn't like Fabe hanging around, thinks he's a bad influence—Hey . . . I shouldn't have said that!"

"No reason not to," Fabe said. "Whole town agrees with your mother."

"Dad doesn't, he likes Fabe. Anyway, Dad and Fabe and I had supper together and Fabe and I worked on my bike until Dad came home about eleven. We had a couple of beers right here and then around midnight Dad told me to get to bed. Fabe was still here when I went upstairs."

"And I stayed here until two in the morning. Dr. Tom and I played rummy and drank beer. That answer your question, Miss Sanderson?"

"Completely." She drained her glass and accepted another bottle from the boy. "You're not a suspect. We know where you were when Thalia Holly died. What I'd like is your impression of the Puloses and the Earls."

He grinned. "Couldn't use words like that in front of a lady. To water it down—they stink. Not Mariana. As I told you before, I'm going to marry that girl. I know what Mariana is. She's a kid who always felt second-rate in this town and all of a sudden she's something else. Mariana loves driving around in that Jag, lording it over the townspeople, but deep down she's someone special. If I could just pry her away from that bunch—but this isn't what you want. Okay, if I had to pick any of them, I guess it would be either Floyd Earl or his sister Suzy. They're nice-enough kids and if they cut loose from their parents, they'd make out fine.

"Floyd had a thing about Thalia Holly. He probably thought it was his secret, but one look at him when she was around and you knew how he felt. Thalia wasn't pretty, she was beautiful. Not just her face but everything about her. I only saw Mrs. Holly a few times and she froze me out. Alexis? He lives off Harriet and doesn't even pretend to work for his keep."

Miss Sanderson asked casually, "What about Leander?"

Fabe's face glowed. "Now that's a *boy!* Sure would like

to have a son like him. When I go out to see Mariana, I play with the little guy if his mother isn't around. Don't know how Harriet ever had a son like Leander.''

"I take it you aren't fond of Mrs. Pulos.''

"Let's put it this way, if I wanted to knock off any of them, I wouldn't have gone after that lovely girl or her grandmother. Harriet Pulos is the one I'd have a go at. That woman does more harm than you'd believe. She's ruining Mariana, has already done a job on Alexis, and the Earls—'' Throwing back his head, Fabe roared with laughter. "The Earls, no one could ruin. Millie and Randolph were born that way.''

Tommy was watching the man with admiring eyes. It was plain that Fabian Harcourt was his idol. "Dad doesn't agree with you about Harriet.'' The boy turned to face Miss Sanderson. "Mom's green-eyed about her. Know's Dad's still sweet on Harriet. Can't see why. Mom's much better-looking than she is.''

Fabe wagged a finger at Tommy. "Better learn the facts of life. With some women, looks don't count. Can't see myself what Harriet's got, but she's got something. Look at Dmitri Pulos. Could pick and choose any female and he's got eyes only for his wife. Same with Stevens-Parkes and your dad. And Thalia worshiped her.'' After pushing his empty bottle aside, Fabe took the one Tommy was offering. "Anything else, Miss Sanderson?''

"How do you feel about the deaths of Thalia and Rebecca Holly?''

"Something weird there.'' The man's wide brow furrowed. "Iona . . . Thalia . . . Mrs. Holly. I don't know why and I don't know who but I do know someone's cracked out at that house. I'd like to get Mariana out of there and as far away as I can.''

"Why?''

Fabe lifted clear eyes and studied Miss Sanderson. "I have a feeling it isn't finished.''

By the time Miss Sanderson picked up her employer at the hotel and they drove back to the Holly estate, it was nearly

144

midnight. The two cottages were dark and there was only a hall light on at the Earl house. "Looks like our neighbors are tucked in bed," Forsythe said.

"And that's where I'd like to be, Robby. But we'd better compare notes."

He made a move toward the front door and she said, "That house is like an oven. Shall we talk out here?"

He sank into a chair and fumbled for his pipe. "You go first with the Earls and Harcourt and then I'll cover Alexis and Mariana Pulos."

They reported in full and when her employer had finished, she said, "So the quarrel between Alexis and Dmitri the day of the contest wasn't about Alexis's gambling."

"It had nothing to do with gambling. Billy O'Day blew the whistle on Alexis with an anonymous letter. You'd like Billy. Nice chap."

"Fabe Harcourt is a fine man, too. Mariana Pulos should grab him while she can. Fabe is definitely in the clear. Airtight alibi for the evening of Rebecca's death. Other than that, all I learned is how he feels about Mariana's relations."

Forsythe puffed on his pipe and blew a cloud of smoke, watching it float away on the warm night air. "Sandy, I've been thinking about Edith Earl. I don't feel she's in any danger."

"Your reasoning?"

"She sounds like a child who would like to look important. She also sounds like her parents—greedy. I'm willing to wager she was so busy trying to find flowers that she didn't notice anything else."

"You could be right. It was the first time Edith had been allowed in the yearly contest and she probably wanted to win the prize." Looking up at the sky, Miss Sanderson heaved a sigh. "Too beautiful a night to be engrossed in this grisly subject. Look at the stars, Robby. Sequins sprinkled across the black velvet."

He followed her gaze. "To say nothing about that full moon. I, too, can wax poetic. 'The moon was a ghostly galleon tossed upon cloudy seas—' "

"Blimey, that's not even appropriate. There isn't a cloud

in that sky. Oh, oh! Looks like the moon and the stars and the night are about to go down the drain. Father Earl just hove into view and he's heading our way.''

"So he is." Hurriedly, Forsythe got to his feet. "I'll be in the house. When he leaves, give me a yell."

"Coward," she muttered, and walked to the top of the steps. "What is it, Mr. Earl?"

"Ssh! Keep your voice down." The little man halted at the foot of the steps. One of his eyes was swollen shut and the left side of his face was a rainbow of colors. His good eye peered up at her. "Sorry to bother you this late, Miss Sanderson, but I felt I should clarify one point. This afternoon, it was difficult with Millie listening but . . ."

"You weren't truthful about the night of Mrs. Holly's death. Is that it?"

"That's it. Now, I don't want to give you the wrong impression. I love my wife and kids and I'm a family man but—"

"Just tell me, Mr. Earl."

He hung his head and his voice was muffled. "I did see a double feature and when I came out of the theater I met this girl—"

"A hooker?"

"I guess you'd call her that. Young and quite attractive. We had a drink together and then we went to a hotel and . . . I guess you know what for."

"Yes," Miss Sanderson said coolly. "I know what for. Can you prove this?"

"How can I? All I know is that her name's Phyllis and she's blond. Not natural because—" He stared at the secretary with his good eye. "What am I supposed to do? Advertise in a paper for her? If Millie finds out, she'll kill me! This is most embarrassing. I swear I was with Phyllis until three in the morning."

Miss Sanderson backed away toward the front door. "Very well, you've told me."

"Do *you* believe me?"

"It makes no difference what I believe," she told him flatly. She watched the man turn and plod away. When he was out of sight, she called, "All clear. You can come out now, Robby."

"You come in. I'm making a little treat for you."

She followed the sound of his voice into the kitchen. The light over the table was on and Forsythe was pouring coffee into pottery mugs. He turned a smiling face toward her. "Was Father Earl straightening up his alibi?"

"He was. But he's still very much in the running. He can't prove this one, either." She glanced down at the mug he was setting in front of her. "Coffee? Some treat!"

"Taste it. I poured a generous dollop of brandy into it. Kind of a reward for valor under Earls' fire. Now, we've both had a chance to digest the information we've garnered. Do you have any ideas you'd like to share?"

"Oodles. One wilder than the other." She lit a cigarette and looked at its glowing end. "But we'd better start at the right place and go on—"

"What place is that?"

"The last words Rebecca Holly said to us. Exactly what did Thalia see from that lookout point on the first day of May? We must assume it was something traumatic. Something riveting enough to take her attention away from Iona. Something serious enough to result in her death and then in her grandmother's."

Forsythe stared into his mug. "I'll say the word, Sandy. Murder. Or, should I say, attempted murder. From what you said, the falls would have been an excellent spot—before those guardrails were put up—for a murder made to look like an accident. But . . . who was the intended victim and who was the unsuccessful murderer?"

His secretary blew a smoke ring and regarded it. "Now, for my wild ideas. Alexis Pulos. His older brother had just been apprised of Alexis's homosexuality. Alexis may have wanted to hold on to Billy O'Day and also not lose his posh life with Harriet Pulos."

"Sandy, Alexis said his brother would never betray him."

"What if Alexis wasn't sure of that? He might have decided to push big brother into the falls and ensure Dmitri's

147

silence. Or it could have been the reverse. Dmitri's devotion to his wife might have inspired him to get rid of his trouble-making younger brother.''

''It's possible. Any further wild ideas?''

She drained her mug and pushed it over to be refilled. ''So many, my head's spinning. Harriet Pulos. She was broken up by the death of her first husband and she blamed both Rebecca and Brice Stevens-Parkes for leaving Kenneth to die. Could Harriet have decided to avenge her dead husband by pushing either Rebecca or Brice, or perhaps both of them, into the falls?''

He handed her the steaming mug. ''Why did she wait for so long? If she had decided to kill them, wouldn't she have moved faster?''

Miss Sanderson rubbed her brow. ''Robby, all we're doing is dancing around the obvious. Of all these people, there's only one whose murder would make sense. And only one theory that would explain the booby-trapped swing.'' For a moment, she looked into space and then she said, ''We both know what Thalia saw from that lookout point, don't we?''

''We know *part* of what she saw.''

''The question is, What do we do about it?''

''There's only one course of action we can take. In the morning—''

''It's morning now.''

He glanced at his watch. ''So it is. Past four. About nine, I want you to ring up Harriet and tell her I want all the interested parties at Holly House by two in the afternoon.''

''What if she refuses?''

''Offer her an enticing reason for agreeing. Tell her we'll be leaving this estate and Hollystone directly after the meeting. She'll jump at that.''

Miss Sanderson arched her brows. ''Will we?''

''We will.'' Forsythe's chin set. ''After that, there'll be nothing to keep us here.''

CHAPTER FIFTEEN

WHEN MISS SANDERSON PULLED HERSELF OUT OF BED to make the call to Holly House, the sky was gray and heavy with cloud. After the call was made, she didn't linger but went back to bed and immediately fell into a heavy sleep. The next time she awoke, it was close to one and rain was slashing against the bedroom window. The rain didn't alleviate the heat, merely made the air damp and steamy and oppressive. Neither of the people in the Widows' House had any appetite. They dressed, packed their cases, and carried them out to the car. A few minutes before two, the Mercedes was moving through a curtain of rain toward Holly House.

As the house loomed up, a motorcycle roared up behind them, splashed the Mercedes with mud as it passed, and raced into the cul-de-sac. "Fabe Harcourt," Miss Sanderson muttered. "Surely he's not an interested party."

"We'll soon know, Sandy."

Forsythe pulled the car level with the Harley-Davidson and his secretary hopped out. "Great day to be riding a bike, Fabe."

"Sure is, Miss Sanderson." Fabe hung his dripping helmet over a handlebar and glanced at the barrister. "This must be your famous employer. How about an introduction?"

As she introduced them, she noticed that although Forsythe was over six foot, he looked like a stripling beside the huge man. Forsythe said, "I'm surprised to see you here today, Mr. Harcourt."

"Make that Fabe. Because it's family weekend, you mean?"

"Family weekend?"

"Haven't you heard about Harriet's famous family weekends?" Fabe waved at the wide veranda. "Better get out of this deluge. Yeah, ever so often the entire clan stays at Holly House. The Earls pack up their litter of kids and Brice comes out from Hollystone. Fun and games. And don't get the idea I've been invited. I came to see Mariana and"—his wet beard jutted—"I'm going to see her." He knocked on the door and asked, "What are you two doing here?"

Before Forsythe could answer, the door swung wide and a middle-aged woman in a neat gray uniform smiled up at the secretary. "Hello, Miss Sanderson."

"Robby, this is Cassie Beaton. We're expected, Cassie."

Brice Stevens-Parkes loomed up behind the maid. "I'll handle this." Cassie ducked her head and backed away. "Mr. Forsythe," Brice said, "you and your secretary may come in. Not you, Mr. Harcourt. You get on that bike and get out of here."

Forsythe and Miss Sanderson stepped into the hall but the lawyer barred the door to Fabe. With no discernible effort, the huge man lifted him out of the way. "I want to see Mariana," Fabe said softly.

"Not today. You know well you aren't allowed here on family weekends. I'd strongly advise you to—"

"If there wasn't a lady present, I'd tell you what to do with your advice. Out of my way, shyster, or I'll plaster this wall with you!"

Brice glared up at Fabe, shrugged, and led the way to the living room. "Harriet," he called, "Miss Sanderson and Mr. Forsythe. Also Mr. Harcourt, who refuses to leave."

Without the long tables that had been arranged the day of Rebecca Holly's funeral, the living room proved to be enormous. Gray light seeping through four long windows fell bleakly over white carpeting, furniture covered with white

150

brocade, a marble fireplace, and the people stiffly seated in a semicircle. Harriet Pulos had arranged a smile on her face, but as she looked at Fabe it faded. Her eyes traveled disdainfully over his sodden denim jacket and jeans. "Mr. Harcourt, I hardly expected you still to be around."

"I'm not easy to discourage. I can be stubborn."

"We have something in common. I, too, can be stubborn. But, as you forced your way in, you may as well remain—if you understand one thing. This has nothing to do with you. It's a family matter."

"Wouldn't have it any other way." Crossing to Mariana, he pulled up a chair and sat down. She held out a hand and he gripped it in one huge hand.

Harriet paid no further attention to the intruder. She turned to Forsythe and gestured. "Over there, please. I had the furniture arranged to make it simpler for your interrogation."

The barrister seated Miss Sanderson and took the chair facing Harriet. "Hardly an interrogation, Mrs. Pulos. That has been concluded. We're here to give you the results."

Miss Sanderson gazed from Harriet Pulos to Robert Forsythe. They had one quality in common—an air of command and assurance. Harriet was looking much better. The black clothes had been replaced by a becoming silk dress, a shade darker than her eyes, the color kind to the ash-blond hair and pale skin. She looked rested and relaxed. The remainder of the family didn't look at all relaxed. They were all there. Millie and Randolph Earl, flanked by Suzy and Floyd, Mariana Pulos, clutching at Fabe's hand, Alexis, sitting near his sister. On Harriet's right, Brice was seated and Dmitri, for once not standing, was on her left. Miss Sanderson's eyes lingered on Dmitri's face. Beautiful features, she thought uneasily, but showing not a trace of emotion.

Under different circumstances, some of the byplays would have been amusing. Alexis's teeth weren't in evidence and his brown eyes were fixed apprehensively on Forsythe. The left side of Randolph's face was even more swollen and discolored than it had been the previous evening and his good eye guiltily avoided Miss Sanderson. Brice seemed to be dividing his attention between Fabe and Forsythe. And why not? One had tried to push him through a wall; the other had offered to plaster him over it.

Harriet shifted restlessly and raised an ironic brow. "Results? I thought you were merely wasting our time and your own."

"I don't waste time," Forsythe told her. "One point I'd like to make clear. I'm not here because of you or your relations but to try and make amends to a woman who might still be alive if I'd treated this matter seriously from the time it was brought to my attention."

"Very well, I, too, will take this seriously. Will you proceed?"

Millie Earl gave a loud, nervous bray of laughter. "Reminds me of an Agatha Christie novel, Harriet. You know where Hercule Poirot gathers all the suspects in the library and unveils the murderer."

Without turning her head, Harriet said, "Please, Millie."

"Mrs. Earl," Forsythe said. "This isn't fiction. I'm not here to unveil a murderer. I'm trying to save a life."

Touching his mustache, Brice said evenly, "We are far from convinced there has been a murder."

"*Two* murders, Mr. Stevens-Parkes. One disguised as suicide, the other as a death from a heart attack. We're dealing with a patient, cold, methodical person who is quite familiar with your strengths and weaknesses and uses them for his own ends."

"*His?*" Alexis asked.

"It's necessary to use some term and it's awkward to keep on saying he or she. I've no idea if this person is male or female."

"Exactly *what* do you know?" Dmitri asked.

"A fair amount, Mr. Pulos." Templing his fingers, Forsythe gazed down at them. "This began the first day of May at the contest for wildflowers. Thalia Holly looked down from the lookout point and witnessed a murder attempt. She tried to warn the victim by shouting and waving her arms. Because of the noise from the waterfall, what she was shouting we don't know. Her attention was riveted on one of the

152

plateaus and your daughter fell to her death. The murderer's attempt was thwarted but—''

''One moment,'' Harriet said imperiously. ''If Thalia had seen anything as shocking as that, why didn't she tell us immediately?''

Forsythe lifted his eyes and looked at Millie Earl. ''Mrs. Earl, what would your reaction have been if Thalia Holly had told you she'd seen one of you trying to shove another person into the falls?''

''Well . . .'' Millie was flustered. ''Thalia was an unusual girl. An artist, and we all know what they're like. Not normal. She'd slit her wrists and tried to hang herself and—'' She raised a finger like a sausage and pointed at her forehead. ''Gaga! I wouldn't have believed a word!''

''She wasn't gaga!'' Floyd glared at his mother. ''I'd have believed her.''

Forsythe told the boy, ''I don't think Thalia would have confided in you. But your mother's reaction is one that would have been common to most of you.''

''No,'' Harriet said. ''Either Mother Holly or I would have listened.''

''Rebecca? I doubt that Thalia would have told her grandmother. I should imagine there was a barrier between Thalia and Rebecca. When the girl was very young, her grandmother left her to the mercy of indifferent parents and servants. She made no effort to care for the child after her parents' deaths. As for you, Mrs. Pulos, what chance did Thalia have to tell you what she'd seen?''

''That is true,'' Harriet admitted. ''At that time, Thalia didn't have a chance. I refused to see her. But when she came home—that Friday—she would have told me.''

''Cast your mind back. Were you alone with Thalia that evening at any time?''

Harriet's wide brow wrinkled in thought. ''That evening, we stayed in a group. I was intent that Thalia be reassured by all of us that she was welcome. But the next day—'' She stopped abruptly.

''Saturday? The swing broke, Thalia was blamed for Leander's fall, and again she was a pariah. Mrs. Pulos, that swing did not break accidentally. The rope was cut almost through."

Harriet sat bolt upright. "Who told you that?"

"When Bert Granger repaired the swing, he examined the rope. It had been booby-trapped."

"Why didn't he tell *me?*"

"You mustn't blame him. You were with your son, worried, anxious. He didn't want to increase your anxiety."

Alexis's teeth flashed in a nervous smile. "Bert is senile, Harriet. Look at that outfit he wears to open and close the gates. I don't believe a word of this."

Forsythe looked sternly at Harriet. "Thalia was 'gaga,' Rebecca was 'unbalanced,' now Bert is 'senile.' Think of your *son.*"

"I am. And I'm getting to the bottom of this. Millie! This sounds like a prank Edith might have played."

The florid color was draining from Millie's face. "No! My little Edith would never do that."

"It wasn't Edith," Forsythe said. "And it wasn't a prank. It was a successful effort to discredit Thalia. Leander was in no real danger. The cushioning of sawdust and sand prevented any serious injury. But Thalia went to her room in disgrace and you, Mrs. Pulos, again closed yourself off from her. For the moment, the murderer was safe."

"But that evening, I went to Thalia. We talked for nearly an hour. Surely, if this was true, she'd have told me then."

"We can only theorize," Forsythe said slowly. "Thalia was still so upset, you insisted on giving her a sedative. Maybe at that point, Thalia felt you would feel she was making it up, trying to excuse herself. Perhaps she couldn't bear to speak of it in her condition. And, she did feel she had Sunday. But she had no further time. Later that night, she died."

Harriet said slowly, "Even if what you say is the truth, why did she have to die? As you pointed out, Thalia wouldn't have been believed. What threat did she pose?"

"As I said earlier, this murderer is patient and relentless. The attempt at the falls hasn't been given up, only postponed. Suppose Thalia had told what she'd seen. Granted,

154

at that time she wouldn't have been believed, but later . . . if the victim she'd named had died, questions would have been raised. The killer didn't want *Thalia* dead. He didn't want to kill *Rebecca*. But both of them had to be silenced.''

"Go on, Mr. Forsythe."

"Thalia was sedated. The murderer waited until the household retired. Then he went to Thalia's room, cut the curtain cord, tied it to the hook in the ceiling, pulled the unconscious girl from bed—''

"Sorry," Brice said. "I don't like to interrupt, but this would take strength. A man could have done it but I doubt any of these ladies could have.''

"How much did Thalia weigh?"

"She was tiny," Floyd blurted. "Less than a hundred pounds.''

"Look at these ladies, Mr. Stevens-Parkes. Mrs. Earl is strong enough to carry Harriet Pulos up a steep slope. Her daughter Suzy has the same build and probably the same strength. It might be more difficult for Mariana Pulos, but she is athletic. If the need is great, amazing things can be done.''

"You haven't mentioned me," Harriet said.

"You aren't large, Mrs. Pulos, but yes, I think you could have handled a girl Thalia's size. We return to my summary. Thalia was silenced, her death looks like suicide, and the murderer could then patiently wait to commit the vital murder. But another factor arises. Mrs. Holly, convinced that her granddaughter was murdered, came to me and I sent Sandy to this house. This didn't frighten the murderer. A good guess again was made at a weakness. In this case—mine. As soon as I heard about Thalia's past, I reacted much as I was expected to. My vanity was offended by what I considered to be Mrs. Holly's deception and I refused to have anything more to do with the case. But the killer misjudged Rebecca Holly's reaction. Instead of being crushed by my disgust and rejection, she took it as a challenge.

"Sandy questioned a friend of Mrs. Holly's who was able to give a clear picture of the week preceding Rebecca's death. It was obvious she intended to find the proof she had prom-

155

ised me and it was just as obvious she had no idea where to start looking. For several days she did nothing, no doubt turning over in her mind everything that had happened on the weekend of her granddaughter's death. Finally she did remember something.

"Thalia, in the last months of her life, had started to write poetry—a type of therapy, I would imagine. Rebecca remembered this and went to Thalia's apartment and in the girl's desk found the girl's notebook, a purse-sized one bound in red leather. Among the poems in this book, she found her proof."

Mariana, still clinging to Fabe's hand, leaned forward. "A poem?"

"A poem so full of allegories and metaphors that, as Rebecca told her friend, only a person connected with this household would understand it. Rebecca certainly wouldn't have brought the book to me and she hesitated to take it to the police. I also feel she found the poem impossible to believe. To her friend she said, 'it's unbelievable . . . there's no reason for it.' She also may have toyed with the same thought Mrs. Earl stated so baldly—that Thalia was hallucinating. Before she went further, she made a fatal mistake. She contacted the murderer and made an appointment to meet him in the park—"

"How?" Dmitri demanded. "If she'd phoned Hollystone, it would have shown a long-distance call on her bill. Was there an item like that?"

"No. But Rebecca could have made the call from a public booth or—" Forsythe looked at Harriet. "Was Rebecca aware that six of you were in Vancouver at that time?"

"Certainly. In the last letter I wrote, I mentioned that Dmitri and I as well as Millie and her family would be in Vancouver that weekend. Mother Holly knew the hotel where we always stay. I'd hoped to visit her but time didn't allow."

"So," Forsythe said, "it might have been a local call."

Millie reddened. "I resent this!"

Harriet said, "Continue, Mr. Forsythe."

"Rebecca went to the park and met this person—which

gives us another fact about the murderer. Neither Thalia nor Rebecca feared this person. Thalia returned to this house knowing the murderer was here and Rebecca went into a dark park to meet him.''

"Rebecca died from a coronary,'' Alexis pointed out.

"An induced one. Cold-blooded, calculated murder. For weeks after her granddaughter's death, Rebecca had been under intense stress. The day of her death, her friend told us she was in an excited state and flushed. Not a good condition for a woman suffering from a heart condition. Then she met the murderer and was frightened into an attack. How, I can only guess. Perhaps a confession and threats against Rebecca. The purse containing her medication was taken away and the murderer watched her die. Then the jewelry was taken from her body, the money from her wallet, and the red leather notebook from her purse. Here the murderer made a mistake. Rebecca carried a valuable antique snuffbox and that was overlooked.''

Looking around at the intent faces, Forsythe said, "Both these women's weaknesses were used against them—Thalia's history of suicide attempts, Rebecca's heart. Clever and cold.''

Brice Stevens-Parkes, who had been sitting bolt upright, now relaxed, sank back in his chair, and toyed with his mustache. "An interesting summary. An intelligent and intricate weaving of events. Completely circumstantial. None of this would hold up in court.''

"I'm aware of that.''

"The only way I could be convinced this nonsense is factual would be if you name the murderer and offer proof of his guilt.''

"Impossible, I told you I haven't the faintest idea of this person's identity, but I do know the motive and the identity of the vital victim.''

Brice gave him an amused, contemptuous smile and Forsythe told the other lawyer, "You know the motives for murder as well as I do—jealousy, hate, fear, revenge, lust, gain. All the deadly sins that humans suffer from. For a time, Sandy

157

and I were off the track. We were searching for an obscure motive and the correct one was staring us in our faces. The motive is financial gain and the victim"—Forsythe pointed a long forefinger—"is Harriet Pulos."

"My wife?" Dmitri was on his feet. "Someone is trying to kill my *wife?*"

"Sit down, Dmitri." Harriet's smile echoed the lawyer's. "This whole discussion is ludicrous, and as for the motive— Mr. Forsythe, don't you realize my family has no need to wish me dead? I've given them everything and if there is anything they lack they need only tell me to get it."

"Everything but one important necessity. You see, Mrs. Pulos, human beings want freedom. Certainly you heap luxuries on them, but if they displease you, all of them are aware what the penalty would be. You'd take that bounty away from them. If you died, not only would they be wealthy but they'd be free to satisfy their own desires." Slowly and deliberately, Forsythe's eyes circled the faces turned to him. "Every person in this room has an avid desire your death would solve."

Harriet's amused smile didn't waver. "Have any of you a wish to see me dead?"

A chorus of denials broke out. Everyone was talking at once. Harriet listened for a moment and then her smile vanished and she held up a hand, quelling the tide of words. She told the barrister curtly, "That should answer your question. My patience has been strained past all limits. I've allowed you to harass my family and stay in the Widows' House while you did it. Your secretary told me you'd leave after you had spoken to us. May I rely on that?"

"I gave my word."

Forsythe rose and Floyd Earl jumped up. "*I* believe Mr. Forsythe," he said.

His mother snarled, "Will you *shut up!*"

Fabe Harcourt dropped Mariana's hand and kissed her cheek. As he passed Harriet, he glanced down at her. "Mrs. Pulos, you're a fool not to listen."

Wrenching her eyes from the barrister, she beamed them at Fabe. "Mr. Harcourt, you are to leave my house and this estate at once! You will not be allowed here again. You're not to see or speak to my sister-in-law. The only time you may enter this house is to tell me you're leaving Hollystone for good. Then I'll allow you to say good-bye to Mariana.''

Fabe's jaw set. "Last chance, Mariana. For God's sake, come with me now!''

The girl made a move, met Harriet's icy eyes, and slumped back on her chair. Mutely, she shook her head.

Forsythe paused in the archway and allowed Miss Sanderson and Fabe to precede him. He glanced back at Harriet Pulos. "I've done all I can. You've been warned.'' He turned on his heels and walked down the hall.

In the shelter of the veranda, Miss Sanderson and Fabe were waiting, staring at the teeming rain. "Let's get out of here,'' Forsythe said.

Grabbing his helmet, Fabe rammed it on his head. He kicked the bike into staccato life and shouted over the racket, "Someone *should* knock that bitch off!''

Miss Sanderson slid behind the wheel and waited for Forsythe to close the door. "Now,'' she said, "we can leave this damn place.''

"After we make a couple of stops, Sandy.''

"Where?''

"First to a florist. Then to the cemetery.'' Forsythe told her.

As they entered the Hollystone Cemetery, Miss Sanderson decided this gray, wet day would be a dandy time for a funeral. She followed Forsythe's tall figure through blowing rain to the Holly plot. He carried a posy of violets and she had an armful of long-stemmed roses. As she passed the Stone plot, she glanced down at an imposing double headstone with the carved names of Professor Ernest Stone and his beloved wife Mary Anne. Harriet's parents, she thought, the people responsible for the woman who refused to listen.

Forsythe stopped abruptly and Miss Sanderson dodged around the angel guarding the dead Hollys. Today, the cupped hands dripped tiny torrents of water and the smug face appeared to leer at the graves. She paused beside her employer, darted a look at his face, and then down at the raw muddy soil at her feet. Rebecca Holly's offerings lay in sodden, decaying heaps on her grave. Conscious of hair wetly plastered against her head and rain seeping down the collar of her raincoat, Miss Sanderson took a few paces to the next grave. This one was still raw, too, but no flowers rested on it.

She gazed down at the resting place of a girl she'd never met. Under this earth, she thought, rests the remains of Thalia Holly, a tiny girl, less than a hundred pounds, a girl whose every movement reminded Floyd Earl of music.

She bent and placed the roses on the mound. Against the mud, they blazed like valiant scarlet beacons. She heard her own voice whispering, "Augustine Spencer is right. The world is the loser by your death, Thalia Holly."

When she backed away, she saw the violets resting on Rebecca's grave. Robert Forsythe was striding toward the gates. Hunching herself into the sodden raincoat, Miss Sanderson followed him.

On the drive through the mountains, Forsythe took the wheel and his secretary didn't argue. She sat silently, her hands loosely folded in her lap, gazing out of the window. On this dismal day, the scenery was not inspiring. Fog clung to the mountainsides and lashing rain limited vision. After a time, she looked straight ahead, at the arcing windshield wipers and the wet black curves of the road.

Her companion glanced at her. "Why so glum? I thought you were glad to leave Hollystone."

"I am. But it seems so . . . so unfinished."

"It is. But at least we alerted Harriet Pulos. We can do no more."

"Do you think we could have frightened off the would-be murderer?"

"Who knows? We can only hope we did. Would you light me a cigarette, please?"

She lit two and handed him one. "At least we can eliminate one suspect."

"Dmitri Pulos?"

Her eyes widened. "Are you reading my mind?"

"I know you well, Sandy, and I know that devious memory of yours. It's been gnawing away trying to recall where you'd met Dmitri's double."

"Not a double in appearance but I think a double in nature."

"When did the light dawn?"

"While you were trying to convince Harriet of her danger. I was watching her husband and wondering about him. He seems so obsessed with her. Either he's touching her or staring at her. Then there's his attitude toward sexy Selma Yale and—"

"Lack of attitude, Sandy. Dmitri doesn't seem to realize she exists. And, no matter how fond a man is of his wife, I assure you he would *see* Nurse Yale."

"Exactly! Then I remembered Raymond Harswood. I know why he was so hard to dig out. It's one of those horrible things one has a tendency to tuck away in a corner of one's mind and draw a curtain across."

"And it frightens you."

"Blimey! Harswood frightened me then; Dmitri terrifies me now."

He butted his cigarette in the ashtray. "Tell me."

"I was young, Robby, and had just taken a position with your father. A solicitor—in fact, it was Willis Sutton—offered your father a brief to defend a young man accused of double murder. An impossible case to defend. There had been an eyewitness and all that could be done was to enter a plea of insanity." She said **grimly,** "And there was no doubt Raymond Harswood was insane and had been for years. The disturbing part was that he seemed so normal. Really an admirable chap. He had many friends and his employer valued him. They couldn't believe it when he . . ."

Forsythe slowed the car for a sharp curve. "Carry on, Sandy."

"He killed his wife and her lover."

"The eternal triangle."

"Not quite. Raymond and Lily had been married for three

161

years at the time of the murders but Raymond had been mad about the girl from their school days—"

"Ah! I begin to see a parallel."

"You'd see even more if you'd stop interrupting," she said tartly. "Even at school, Raymond was several cuts above Lily. He was a good student and an attractive boy. Lily was on the dull side and with the morals of a female alley cat. Raymond was always trying to date her, but she couldn't stand him. She liked flashier boys, more or less delinquents. After they left school, Raymond got an excellent job in sales and Lily became involved with a succession of minor criminals. But Raymond kept tabs on her and never even looked at another woman. His friends couldn't understand it but Raymond was obsessed with the little witch."

She paused to catch her breath and then continued. "Finally, his chance came. Lily's current lover, a man named Jim White, came afoul of the law and received a sentence of three years for drug trafficking. He went off to prison leaving Lily about seven months pregnant. Raymond immediately offered to marry her and to raise her child. They were married and the child was stillborn."

Forsythe said wryly, "Touching love story."

"Perhaps for Raymond Harswood it was. He gave Lily everything he could—a house, nice clothes. His job took him away from home a great deal and in his absences Lily went right back to her earlier lifestyle—making the rounds of the discos and pubs and sleeping with everything in pants. When her husband came home, he spent his time cleaning the house, which, according to friends and neighbors Lily kept like a pigsty, and waiting on his wife hand and foot—"

"And Raymond found his wife was unfaithful and—"

"One more word, Robby!"

"My lips are sealed."

"The appalling thing was that Raymond was well aware of what his wife was up to, but as long as she was waiting for him when he came home, he didn't seem to care. But then Jim White was released from prison and the next time

162

Raymond came home, he found his wife had gone to live with White.

"Raymond immediately went to her and begged her to come home with him. This took place in the yard behind the dump where White and Lily were living. White had been chopping firewood and the ax he'd been using was propped against a shed. A neighbor woman was hanging out wash and she heard and saw everything that happened. Raymond argued with his wife and White was swearing at him. The witness said that Raymond appeared calm and reasonable until his wife screamed not only would she never return to him but that she was getting a divorce. Then Raymond went berserk. He picked up the ax and chopped White and then Lily to pieces."

Forsythe took a deep breath. "And you feel Dmitri is the same type as Raymond Harswood?" She nodded and he asked, "Then how can you say Harriet Pulos is safe with a man who is a double for an ax-wielding maniac?"

She shivered and pulled her damp coat closer to her thin body. "As long as Harriet stays with Dmitri, she's quite safe."

"And if she gets the notion she'd like to leave him?"

"He'll butcher her," Miss Sanderson said flatly. "Not by trying to push her into a waterfall but a hands-on way. He'd use an ax, perhaps a knife."

"You seem convinced of this."

"I am. But, thank God, we're out of it now. Soon you'll be with Jennifer and I'll be on my rounds of duty calls."

He smiled at her. "Not only that but the rain has stopped and I see a break in the clouds. Cheer up, Sandy."

In a short time, the sun struggled clear and the warm light turned the narrow road into a ribbon of gold. Miss Sanderson's face relaxed and she cheered up.

CHAPTER SIXTEEN

O<small>N THE FIFTEENTH DAY OF AUGUST</small>, F<small>ORSYTHE EA</small>-gerly boarded the jet for Los Angeles and Abigail Sanderson enplaned for Idaho. She returned to Vancouver a day later than she'd expected and waited at the luggage carousel for her case. She was tired and slightly hung over and when she plucked off her leather case, it seemed to weigh a ton. Of course, she thought it was weighed down with purchases and souvenirs from Boise, Seattle, and White Horse. As she headed for the exit, the case dragged her shoulder down.

"Hey, lady! Want a porter?" A hand touched her wrist.

Gratefully, she relinquished the case and looked up into Forsythe's smiling face. That face was tanned and relaxed. "No need to ask how your month was, Robby." She fingered the sleeve of his lightweight beige suit. "Did Jennifer pick this out?"

"That she did. Excellent taste in both clothes and men."

"Not modest men though."

She followed him out to the parking area and waited while he unlocked the BMW, tossed her case in the rear seat, and opened the passenger for her. As he reversed the car out of the slot, she sighed and rubbed her brow.

"Headache?" he asked.

"Hangover. Well and truly earned."

"I've some news that will be good medicine—"

"Jennifer agreed to marry you?"

"Sandy! Stop pushing the nuptials. That will come in time. She—"

"Made you promise to have that knee operation."

His head jerked and he stared at his secretary. "Now you're reading *my* mind. Unless—did you have anything to do with this?"

Her lips curled up in a tiny smile. "I did mention in my last letter to the lass that you were having hell with that knee and were having to use a cane often. Also, that you've been taking far too many painkillers and—"

He hit the brakes and waited while a young woman wheeling a pram scurried across the street. "No wonder Jennifer was so insistent."

"Did she make you give a date?"

"I told her when we get back to London I'd have to take over the practice and let Gene and Morley Mertz have some time off. Perhaps early next year."

"Make that definite. Name a date."

Forsythe sighed. "*Women*. Very well, Sandy, January. And before you ask—that's a promise. Scout's honor. Now, what about your duty calls? How did they go?"

"Brother William and Cousin Caroline—disasters. Kay and the Yukon—wonderful. I suppose one out of three are—ah, home, sweet penthouse."

Forsythe parked the BMW in the underground garage of the Vancouver Harmony Hotel and, as the elevator speeded them up to their suite, he squeezed her thin arm. "Hold on, Sandy. You put your feet up and I'll whip up my never-fail remedy for hangovers."

She stepped into the suite and made directly for the patio. Throwing her shoulder bag and jacket on a chair, she took Forsythe at his word and practically fell on a lounge. Putting her head back, she closed her eyes and felt the sun warming her face. When Forsythe appeared, she was almost asleep. Drowsily, she opened an eye and peered at the tray. "Your magic remedy is *tea*?"

"Tea and sympathy. Tell me about your brother."

"For the first couple of days, it went smoothly. William and I reminisced about our parents and brothers and sisters and related tidbits of news about our nieces and nephews and then . . . well, I suppose you could say we ran out of conversation. We hadn't seen each other for years and have nothing in common. After that, it was painful—comments about the weather and long, uneasy silences." She accepted a steaming cup and took a cautious sip. "I know when I left, William must have been as relieved as I was."

"And your cousin?"

"Caroline is in her nineties and the sprightly, intelligent woman I remember is no longer there. She has a companion and her memory is practically gone. I don't think Caroline really knew who I was. She kept confusing me with my mother, one of her sisters, and her own daughter, who has been dead for years. Pitiful."

He patted her shoulder. "Then you went north to the Yukon."

"With some trepidation, Robby. After those ghastly visits, I half-expected Kay to have changed from a bouncy, amusing girl into a sour old hag but—"

"But she hadn't?"

"Kay's the same person I remember from boarding school. She married a great, robust man and they have six great, robust children and a mad mob of grandchildren. Kay and Sid live in a big log house on the outskirts of White Horse and they were the most marvelous hosts. I enjoyed every moment."

Forsythe refilled her cup and offered a plate of biscuits. "So where did the hangover come from? Farewell party?"

She selected a biscuit and gave him her gamine grin. "A real bash at a pub called the Malamute Saloon—Floor covered with sawdust, antlers on the walls, even a player piano. Kay and Sid introduced me to the speciality of the house, namely boilermakers."

"Just what is a boilermaker?"

"A jigger of whiskey and a pint of beer."

"Doesn't sound horrendous."

"You should try it. First you knock back the whiskey and chugalug the pint. Then you have another and another."

"Good Lord!"

"After a number of boilermakers, it seems I put on a floor show—"

"Don't you remember?"

"By that time, I didn't remember my own name. Kay tells me I hopped up on a table and regaled the locals with a spirited rendition of *The Shooting of Dan McGrew*."

He threw back his head and laughed. "How did the locals take to that?"

"According to Kay and Sid, I received a standing ovation. Of course, you must keep in mind many of the audience had been chugalugging, too."

The barrister shook his head and regarded his secretary; the neat gray waves, the cool blue eyes, the long, deceptively austere face. "Sandy," he said gently, "never change."

"I couldn't if I wanted to." She pulled her long frame off the lounge and leaned against the parapet. The mountains against the skyline were a misty shade of violet. "Marvelous weather, Robby. A true Indian summer. I hope it stays for a time."

He joined her and followed her eyes. "Mr. Malone says it might be like this for the next fortnight, maybe into October. But he warned that on this coast it could suddenly change and be winter almost overnight. Have you plans for our last month?"

"Explore this city. Do some shopping and go to the theater. That sort of thing. And you?"

"Tomorrow, I'm taking the ferry to Vancouver Island. There're a couple of art exhibits in Victoria I'd like to attend. There's also another display of jade. After that, I'll tour the island. Drop in and see an old school chum who lives in Nanaimo."

"Robby . . ."

"Yes?"

She had been about to ask if there was any news from Hollystone. She changed her mind. No use of spoiling Indian

167

summer and enjoyment. Instead, she smiled and said, "Come into the library and I'll introduce you to the house speciality from the Malamute Saloon."

"A whiskey, yes. Chugalugging beer? No way, Sandy. Anyway, I'm not about to hop on a table and I haven't memorized any of Service's poems."

The sun continued to shine on the lower mainland of British Columbia and the days were balmy, with a pleasant autumn haze. The nights were cool and Miss Sanderson noticed that some of the trees were flaunting red and gold colors. In the first week of October, Indian summer fled and a less kind weather front moved in. Cold wind whistled in from the north and rain pattered down. Miss Sanderson reluctantly gave up leisurely hours on the patio and switched on the gas fire in the library. The evening of Forsythe's return from the island found her in the kitchen, preparing his favorite food. She heard the front door open and then halting steps down the hall. His knee, she thought, it's giving him hell again.

He limped into the kitchen. "Greetings, Sandy. Why are you slaving over a hot stove when you could have ordered from room service?"

"Because the gourmet kitchen doesn't run to steak and kidney pudding and peach tart." She pecked a kiss at his cheek. "Change of weather giving your leg problems?"

He smiled wryly. "As soon as the weather changed, it started to ache. Strictly a fair-weather knee." He inhaled deeply. "Smells good. How long until dinner?"

"By the time you freshen up, it will be on the table."

She was as good as her word. By the time Forsythe had washed and changed, a hot meal was waiting in the dining room. He paused in the doorway and looked at the table. It was spread with white linen and crystal and silver; the odor of steak and kidney competed with the spicy scent of the pink carnations in the centerpiece. "Is this an occasion, Sandy? Have you run out of traveler's checks and hope to float a loan?"

"Depends on the rate of interest. As a matter of fact, I still have a few checks left. This is in the nature of a welcome-home feast."

"Let's extend that welcome until tomorrow. I'll have kippers for breakfast and—"

"You want kippers, you cook kippers. Now, eat."

She was slicing the peach tart when a phone gave a shrill, demanding summons. "Sit where you are Robby. I'll get it." She headed toward the kitchen and a few words drifted back. "There are phones in all those ruddy baths. You'd think Mark Harmon would have put one in the dining room. Eat your tart before it cools."

Forsythe had only a few bites of tart when his secretary returned. All lightness was gone from her voice as she said, "For you. Sergeant McBride of the Hollystone R.C.M.P."

His fork dropped, spattering the linen with pastry. "Harriet?"

"He wouldn't tell me."

The barrister lunged from his chair but Miss Sanderson didn't follow him. She remained where she was, clutching the back of a chair, gazing with unseeing eyes at the mass of carnations. She could hear the murmur of Forsythe's voice but she didn't strain to hear the words.

He stepped back into the dining room. The fresh color had drained from under his tan, making his skin look muddy. Miss Sanderson said softly, "Is Harriet Pulos . . ."

"No. Brace yourself, Sandy. It's the little boy—"

"*Leander*?" Tears started to her eyes. "We were wrong!"

He put an arm around her shaking shoulders. "Sandy, we were right. Leander's death was an error. Harriet was supposed to die."

She was clinging to him. "Tell me."

"I don't know all the details. What I do know, I'll tell you on the trip to Hollystone."

She pulled away from him and her eyes sought the dark, wet window. "I hate that place! But, we must go back, mustn't we?"

"We must." He added grimly, "Not for Harriet Pulos but for that child."

By the time they reached the garage, Miss Sanderson had steadied and she insisted on driving. As she turned the Mercedes onto the winding road leading through the mountains, the rain turned first to sleet and then to snow. The headlights bored twin tunnels of light through swirling snow, briefly illuminated firs dusted with white, and slid across the guardrail. Under the fine coating of snow, there was ice and, after the heavy car fishtailed across the road, Miss Sanderson slowed it to a crawl. By the time they reached Hollystone a pallid dawn was breaking and she was cramped and exhausted.

She forced her hands to relax on the leather wheel. "The hotel?"

"First stop is to see Sergeant McBride. The R.C.M.P. detachment is near the secondary school."

"I noticed it when I drove you to Billy O'Day's. Looks like a big white cottage with a flagpole in front." She glanced at the stores lining Main Street. "It must be early. Nobody around yet."

"Seven-thirty. But it's Sunday and this town closes up on the Sabbath."

"I'd forgotten. Then Leander . . ."

"He died on Friday night."

"I'd sell my soul for a cup of coffee."

He pointed at a white building. "There it is."

In front of the building, a flag snapped in the wind, the red maple leaf standing out against its white background. In the circular driveway, a heavily bundled officer was sweeping snow away from the door. He moved toward the car, slipped and caught himself, and opened the driver's door. "Miss Sanderson and Mr. Forsythe? Sergeant McBride is expecting you. Down the hall, first door to the left. Watch your footing. Ice under the snow."

They got out of the car, watching their footing. Miss Sanderson said, "I hope you have coffee in there."

170

"The sergeant generally has a pot on." He glanced around. "Beastly weather."

The main office was a bleak place with white walls and a long counter. Behind a counter, a young woman was working at the console of a computer. She glanced up, nodded, and pointed down the hall. The sergeant's office was as unadorned as the outer office, the furnishings consisting of a metal desk, three chairs, and a bank of filing cabinets. On the wall over the desk was the only spot of color. Queen Elizabeth II, a gleaming tiara in her hair, a diamond necklace clasped around her plump neck, smiled from an ornate frame.

The man getting to his feet could easily have posed for a recruiting poster. The glamour of the dress uniform was missing and his tunic was dark blue, but he had the build to carry a uniform to perfection. He had crisp blond hair and a pink boyish face but his eyes were not boyish. They looked as though they'd seen too much. He smiled and completed the picture of an ideal Mountie. His teeth were white and even and perfect.

He shook hands. "Considering the weather, you made good time. I didn't expect to see you so soon."

Miss Sanderson was looking longingly at coffee bubbling in a glass pot, and he poured two steaming mugs. She took a scalding sip and sank into a chair. The sergeant said, "You may be wondering why I phoned—"

"This is a small town." Forsythe hung his Burberry over the back of his chair. "You knew about our previous visit and why we were here."

"And about your warning to Mrs. Pulos. From the entire family following the boy's death. All saying, they should have listened to you." The Mountie smiled again. "But I've also met a friend of yours. Superintendent Kepesake of New Scotland Yard."

Miss Sanderson's eyes widened. "You know Adam?"

"I was in England last year. Extradition case. Kepesake was most hospitable. Gave me a tour of the Yard and dinner at his club. He filled me in on some of your cases. Stressed the fact that you have a talent for difficult cases."

171

Forsythe was fishing for his pipe from the pocket of his tweed jacket. "You only gave me a quick sketch of the boy's death on the phone. Could you fill in the details?"

Templing his fingers, McBride stared down at them. The secretary started. That gesture was exactly like Forsythe's when he was deep in thought. "Mrs. Pulos has what is called a family weekend occasionally. Do you know about these?"

"Mr. Harcourt mentioned them."

"Last Friday, the overnight guests arrived about four in the afternoon. Mr. and Mrs. Randolph Earl and their four children. Brice Stevens-Parkes was already there when the Earls arrived. Mariana Pulos and her brother Alexis have suites in Holly House and Fabian Harcourt—"

"Harcourt?"

"You seem surprised, Mr. Forsythe."

"The last time Sandy and I were at Holly House, Mr. Harcourt was ordered off the estate."

"Mr. Harcourt struck a type of bargain with Mrs. Pulos. She'd promised when he left Hollystone for good, he could enter her house to say good-bye to Mariana Pulos. Mr. Harcourt was leaving town and went to the house to see his girlfriend. Mrs. Pulos decided to be a generous winner and invited him to stay the night."

Forsythe's brow wrinkled. "In Mariana's suite?"

McBride struggled to keep from smiling and failed. "Mrs. Pulos runs an old-fashioned house. Mr. Harcourt was given a room on the second floor." The faint smile vanished. "Apparently, it was a fairly harmonious gathering. They dined and proceeded with the evening entertainments. A bridge game was set up in the living room, a poker game was in progress in Dmitri's study, and in the game room, which opens off the kitchen, two of the guests played snooker."

"Leander?"

"The boy and his nurse both had cases of influenza. Leander was recovering and was kept in bed for precautionary reasons, but Nurse Yale was so ill that when Dr. Brent made a visit that morning, he insisted she remain in bed. With the boy and the nurse ill, it entailed a great deal of running up and down the stairs by the maids, Cassie and Bernice Beaton, and, after they left, by Mrs. Pulos and several of her guests.'' Reaching for the pot, he refilled their mugs. ''Do you know about Mrs. Pulos's habit of taking milk at bedtime, Mr. Forsythe?''

''Mr. Stevens-Parkes mentioned it to me.''

''She doesn't care for plain milk, so it's always flavored with chocolate. The cook, Mrs. Granger, made up the thermos of hot chocolate before she left the house for the night. Mrs. Granger got to her cottage shortly after nine, so it was made up before that time. As soon as she had it ready, she gave it to Bernice Beaton, who carried the thermos to Mrs. Pulos's bedroom and placed it on a table beside the bed. Leander, who had a skin problem when he took chocolate in any form, was never allowed it.''

Miss Sanderson set her mug down on the corner of the desk. ''I remember. The child broke out in spots from it.''

''Did the boy go into his mother's room and take some?'' Forsythe asked.

''I should have made that clear in my phone conversation. His father gave it to him.''

''*Dmitri*?'' Miss Sanderson frowned. ''He'd never do that. Dmitri knew how the child's allergy worried his mother.''

''Nonetheless, that's exactly what Mr. Pulos did. He explained to us that all that evening he'd been more concerned about his wife than his son. Leander was on the mend but Mrs. Pulos was up and down the stairs all evening, tending to the boy. From what I've gathered, Mrs. Pulos became overanxious if the boy was even slightly ill. When Dmitri Pulos checked on the child just after eleven that evening, he found Leander still awake, fretting, and demanding some of his mother's hot chocolate. Mr. Pulos said he weighed his wife's welfare against the boy's and decided this one time to make an exception and give Leander a cup of chocolate. Then he sat by the boy's bed until he dozed off. This didn't take long. The milk was loaded with a powerful barbiturate that Mrs. Pulos used for insomnia.''

The sergeant paused and then continued. ''This sedative

was kept on the top shelf of the medicine cabinet in the bathroom Mrs. Pulos shares with her husband. About eight yesterday morning, the boy's body was discovered. His mother had looked in earlier, assumed the child was still sleeping, and it was Nurse Yale who got out of bed to check on him and realized he was dead.''

Miss Sanderson stared across the desk at the officer. "How much did the thermos contain?"

"A liter. And, to anticipate your next question, Mrs. Pulos didn't drink any of the chocolate. It appears she seldom eats in the evenings, but the sandwiches the cook had prepared for an evening snack were Mrs. Pulos's favorite—roast beef and hot mustard. She consumed several and decided she was too full to have any of her usual chocolate.''

The secretary shivered. "Harriet had a lucky escape."

"So did her husband. While Mrs. Pulos and Mr. Stevens-Parkes were saying good night at her bedroom door, her husband joined them. When he heard his wife didn't care for a hot drink, he took the thermos into his own room, intending to have a cup. He actually poured some milk into a cup and was going to down it when he decided he'd have a shower first. By the time he returned to the bedroom, the milk in the cup had cooled and was skimming and, as he'd left the top off the thermos, the remaining milk was in the same condition. So he put both containers on his bureau and went to bed.''

Forsythe asked, "Did Dmitri tell his wife he'd given Leander some of her milk?"

"No way. He said he intended to tell her the following morning. Said he figured that way both his wife and son would sleep soundly.''

The barrister was frowning. "Suppose Harriet had opened the thermos? Wouldn't she have noticed some milk missing?"

"Of course. But Mr. Pulos was ready to cover for that. He said if she had, he would have told her he took a cup himself. Apparently once in a while he did.''

Forsythe was loading his pipe. "Did she use any of the sedative?"

"No. Mrs. Pulos said, and Dr. Brent backed her up on this, that she'd taken so many drugs at the times of the earlier deaths in the family that she was reluctant to continue. After Mrs. Holly's funeral, she left the barbiturate untouched. Too bad. Perhaps if she'd taken a dose that night, she might have noticed a good share was missing. Who knows? There might have been time to save her son."

"Fingerprints?" Forsythe asked.

"The barbiturate bottle was wiped clean. The thermos had only Mr. Pulos's prints."

"The drug is a liquid?" Miss Sanderson asked.

"Yes. Mrs. Pulos couldn't swallow pills. Made it simple for someone to nip upstairs, take the medicine from the bathroom, empty part of it in the thermos, and replace the bottle in the cabinet."

Forsythe rubbed his aching knee. "How many had the opportunity?"

"All of them," McBride said flatly. "Would you believe it, in a house that size there are no bathrooms on the main floor? So . . . they went up to the bathroom, up to their rooms. The only ones in the clear are the two younger Earl children and that's because one is an infant and the other only eleven."

McBride noticed Miss Sanderson's cup and refilled it. "All the rest are suspects. Each with the motive, the opportunity, the knowledge of the hot chocolate that Mrs. Pulos had nightly, the location of the barbiturate. The burning question is, Which one? That's why I wanted to see you. Can you give me any pointers?"

"I only wish we could. When we left this town in July, we were stymied. But I can give you all the information we came up with." The barrister concisely summed up the results of their investigation.

The Mountie looked morosely at him. "Most of this I have. With the exception of the red leather notebook belonging to Thalia Holly and the broken swing. I agree with your

175

reasoning but Stevens-Parkes was correct. There isn't one shred of evidence. The swing—Edith Earl could have cut that rope. Thalia's notebook? Except for the word of Mrs. Spencer, we can't prove it ever existed. Even if we could, we still have no idea of what it contained. Off the cuff, I'll tell you this. We'll continue to investigate but I doubt we ever uncover the person responsible for these deaths. This murderer doesn't make mistakes.''

''Wrong,'' Forsythe told him. ''He's made two. His knowledge of weaknesses and his use of them failed him on Friday night. Dmitri Pulos had a weakness he didn't take into account—his intense feeling for his wife. To spare Harriet further anxiety about the health of her child, Dmitri gave Leander hot chocolate to calm him down. The murderer never dreamed Leander would get the drugged drink.''

''That's one mistake,'' McBride pointed out.

''He killed a child. You may have to give up. I never will.''

The policeman leaned back in his chair. ''Speaking of weaknesses—Mrs. Pulos can't have many. She did a merciless job on Harcourt.''

Miss Sanderson thought of Fabe's clear, honest eyes. ''She did manage to drive him out of town?''

''By using every trick in the book. Even had Randolph Earl drop a hint to me it wouldn't be taken amiss if I would 'hassle' Harcourt a bit.'' For a moment, it looked as if the sergeant's face were carved from stone. ''In this community, Mrs. Pulos is a powerful woman, but she cuts no ice with me. I told Earl I'm here to enforce the law and Harcourt hasn't broken it.''

''Exactly what did Mrs. Pulos do?'' Forsythe asked.

''She made certain Harcourt couldn't even find a shed to repair bikes in and—''

''We've heard about that,'' Miss Sanderson said.

''He was doing a little work in Dr. Brent's garage, but Mrs. Pulos had the doctor cut that off. Funny, I wouldn't have expected that. The doctor likes Harcourt. Harcourt tried to go around to the homes of boys who wanted work done, but either the boys or their dad's work at one of Mrs. Pulos's

176

concerns and word was put out: Employ Harcourt and lose your jobs. By that time, Harcourt was broke. He tried for a job doing anything. The merchants had been warned off, but a chap who runs a small café near the lumber mill decided to give Harcourt a job as a dishwasher. Seems he owns the building himself.''

"Brave man," Forsythe said.

"He turned cowardly when he found the mill hands stopped coming in for meals, and he had to fire Harcourt. By that time, Harcourt was desperate. He couldn't pay his rent and Libby Mason promptly booted him out of her boardinghouse. He tried to get a room at the hotel but couldn't. In this weather, he couldn't camp out, so he threw in the towel and went to Holly House to say good-bye to his girl.''

Anger flared in Miss Sanderson's eyes. "And *you* sat on your hands!''

"You sound like Tommy Brent when he came in here raving about what this town was doing to his friend. I know Harcourt was hounded and persecuted, but no one would talk. All I had was Tommy. I went up and spoke to his parents. Mrs. Brent insisted it was her idea to bar Harcourt from their property. I could hardly charge a woman for objecting to Harcourt's dismantling bikes in her garage.''

"Dirty!''

"Rotten," Forsythe agreed. He patted his secretary's arm. "But calm down, Sandy. The sergeant was powerless to do anything about it. Sergeant, is Harcourt still in town?''

"At the hotel. He has to stay on here until our investigation is concluded.'' His mouth tightened. "I had a word with Bob Weston.''

Forsythe got to his feet. "We'd better go to the hotel, Sandy, and have breakfast. Then we'll see what we can find out.''

McBride rose. "Mr. and Mrs. Pulos are at Holly House and the Earls are on the estate. Mr. Stevens-Parkes is probably at his office. Mariana Pulos is at the hotel and her brother is staying with Billy O'Day.'' He walked to the door with them. "If you come up with anything, will you let me know?"

"Of course. But we're treading the same ground you've covered."

"They might open up and tell you something they haven't me." McBride showed the perfect teeth in a warm smile. "And you do have a reputation for pulling rabbits out of hats, Mr. Forsythe. At least that's what Adam Kepesake told me."

Forsythe returned the smile but by the time they were in the Mercedes, his expression was somber. His secretary gave him a sidelong look. "Why do you think Mariana is at the hotel? Do you think she's finally broken loose and is going to leave with Fabe?"

"We'll soon know," Forsythe told her. "We'll talk with Mariana first."

Mariana opened the door of the third-floor room. In one corner, a television blared and on one of the unmade beds Fabian Harcourt was sprawled. His hands were clasped behind his head and he was staring at the ceiling. Mariana was dressed in a gay silk shirt and pale stone-washed jeans. Above the shirt, her face was haggard. She gazed from Forsythe to his secretary. "I knew you'd come," she said.

"Will you speak with us?" Forsythe asked.

"Why not?" The girl stood aside and pointed at an armchair near the window. Miss Sanderson crossed beige carpeting to it. Mariana gazed around, pulled out a chair from in front of the desk, tossed a backpack off it, and told Forsythe wryly, "All the comforts of home. Sit down, Mr. Forsythe."

The room was a mess. Two cases were piled on the desk, another was open on the floor, with a froth of lingerie spilling from it. The bed table was cluttered with fast-food wrappings and pop cans. Miss Sanderson picked up an ashtray, emptied it in a wastepaper basket, and lit a cigarette. Harcourt continued to stare at the ceiling and Mariana switched off the television and perched on the edge of the other bed. "I suppose you're wondering why I'm here."

178

"Leaving home?" Miss Sanderson asked.

"Not voluntarily," Harcourt said. "More like thrown out."

"All he'd allow us to take were our clothes," Mariana said shrilly. "His son was dead and you know what he did? After he'd phoned for the doctor and the police, he called the company the cars were leased from. Told them to come out and pick them up. He—"

"He?" Forsythe's voice cut across the girl's.

"My big brother. The brother who once saved money from odd jobs to buy me candy and toys." Tears spangled from Mariana's long lashes. "Dmitri told us he should have gotten rid of us when you were here in July. He said he'd taken what you said seriously and wanted to put all of us off the estate but Harriet overruled him. I asked him what I'd do for money. I only had about ten dollars in my purse." The tears brimmed and trickled down her cheeks. "Dmitri said to pick up my holiday pay from the office. He said that's all I'd ever get from him or his wife." Burying her wet face in her hands, she rocked back and forth.

"For the love of God," Harcourt said gruffly, "stop that whimpering."

He still hadn't moved. With compassionate eyes, Miss Sanderson regarded him. How could a man like this have suffered the abuse he had for this spoiled, selfish girl?

The barrister said, "Fabe would you tell us about Friday?"

Rolling over, he lowered his feet to the floor, staring down at calloused big hands. "Harriet won and I lost. I figured I was big and brave and could take anything she handed out, but I couldn't sleep in the snow and I had to eat. I caved in, went out, and meekly told her I'd come to say good-bye to Mariana. She was . . . I guess you could call her gracious. Said I could stay the night, that she wouldn't turn her dog out in that weather."

"Did you spend the evening with Mariana?" Miss Sanderson asked.

A bitter smile twitched the corners of his wide mouth. "It

179

didn't take long to find out what I wanted to know. I asked Mariana to come with me. She said no."

"I said more than that!" The girl wiped the back of one hand over her eyes. "I told you why I couldn't go."

Miss Sanderson frowned. "Surely you two have talked during the past few weeks."

His bitter smile was echoed in the clear eyes. "Harriet had forbidden Mariana to talk to me. I sent a couple of notes to her by Tommy Brent and a few times I waited outside her office, but she was afraid of being seen with me."

"Harriet," the girl wailed. "She said she'd disinherit me."

"Why didn't you leave town sooner?" Miss Sanderson asked Fabe.

"I loved her."

"You don't!" the girl said fiercely. "You won't even take me with you when Sergeant McBride lets us leave Holly-stone."

"Too late, Mariana. Now you've *got* to go. We're through."

The girl's mouth snapped open but Forsythe said sharply, "Please be quiet, Miss Pulos. Fabe, tell us what happened on Friday evening."

He ran his fingers through long hair. "Harriet had a room made up for me and we had dinner. Afterward, Alexis asked me to join the poker game. At dinner, the Earls looked down their noses at me and Brice was like ice, but Alexis was kind of nice. He staked me to some money to play and Randolph and Floyd played, too. We played poker and drank beer until about two. By the time the game broke up, everyone else was in bed."

"What were the others doing?"

"Harriet and Dmitri and Millie Earl and Brice were play-ing bridge in the living room. Suzy Earl and Mariana were fooling around playing snooker in the game room."

"Where was Edith Earl? In bed?"

"She was hanging around the study watching us for a while."

Mariana nodded. "Edith came in and watched her sister

and me play snooker for a few moments and then her mother told Suzy to put her to bed. I don't know what time that was."

"Very well," Forsythe said. "Did either of you go upstairs after nine that evening?"

Harcourt laughed. "The poker players were guzzling beer and the bathroom is on the second floor. Sure we went up. I was up three times—twice to the bathroom and once to see Leander. Before Bernice left, she came to the study and told me Leander had broken one of his toy soldiers and he wanted me to fix it. I went up to my room, got some contact cement out of my backpack, and fixed it for him."

"What time was that?"

Fabe shook his head. "I wasn't paying any attention to time." He glanced at Mariana. "When I came back to the study, you were bringing in sandwiches."

Mariana bit at her full lower lip. "Suzy and I served sandwiches at eleven, Mr. Forsythe. Agathe had cut them and left them in the fridge and we made coffee and took the snack to the living room and the study."

"When you saw the boy, Fabe, was he all right?"

"Right as rain. Laughing and talking. That dog was on the foot of his bed. Leander tried to make me promise I'd take him for a ride on my bike. He was always begging for a ride. That kid, that poor little kid!" Harcourt's hands opened and closed spasmodically. "I loved that kid! I can't believe—"

"I loved him, too." Mariana moaned and started to cry again. "He was my nephew and I adored him. I told Dmitri that. Who would hurt a child like that?"

"No one," Forsythe said. "Harriet was the one who was supposed to die."

"Harriet!" Mariana cried. "She's making a new will. Dmitri told us that. Not one red cent for any of us. And he's my *brother*."

"So," the barrister said slowly, "Harriet Pulos is drawing a new will. That certainly should remove her from further danger."

"That's what my brother said. None of us would gain from the murder attempt. All Dmitri thinks of is his wife. When his son died, he was like a stone. I feel sorry for Brice, too. Brice said something about drawing up the new will and Dmitri told him no, he wouldn't be handling any more business for Harriet. Dmitri said he was calling in another lawyer."

Forsythe looked at Harcourt. "What about the Earls?"

"They're allowed to stay on in their house until McBride is finished with them. Then they have to clear out. All they can take with them is their personal effects. Dmitri told them if they come near Holly House, he'll shoot them." Harcourt's head sagged. "Dmitri made a clean sweep."

The barrister's eyes wandered to Mariana. "Miss Pulos, did you have occasion to go upstairs after nine that evening?"

"Several times. Once I checked in on Leander and on Demmy, too, and I took tea up to Nurse Yale. I went to the bathroom to freshen up once."

"During these trips to the second floor, did either of you see anyone entering or leaving Harriet's or Dmitri's bedrooms?"

Mariana shook her head. "I saw Randolph Earl but he was going to his own room."

Harcourt considered and then said, "Millie Earl was in the main bathroom. I had to wait for her to come out of it and she took her time. She's the only person I saw."

Forsythe's eyes flickered toward his secretary and Miss Sanderson shut her notebook and got to her feet. The barrister gazed down at Harcourt. "When Sergeant McBride releases you, where do you intend to go?"

"Vancouver, I suppose."

"How will you travel?"

"The only way I can afford—my bike."

"With the roads in this condition, that may prove foolhardy."

"I've no choice. I've exactly fifty bucks. Know where I got that? Tommy Brent forced me to take it. His savings. Taking handouts from a kid!"

182

Forsythe said hesitantly, "I could advance—"

"No handouts! Don't worry, Mr. Forsythe, and thanks for the thought. I'll make out. I'm a good mechanic and finding a job won't be hard."

After jumping to her feet, Mariana stood over Fabe. "Why won't you take me with you? For over a year, you've begged me to go. Now I'm ready."

"Let it go."

"You *don't* love me."

"I did love you. More than you'd believe. But you're right, that's all over."

"I demand you tell me *why*."

His eyes were hard as he stared up at her. "Okay, you're asking for it. When Dmitri came down yesterday morning and told us about Leander, I was watching you. You didn't give a damn that the little guy was dead—"

"I did!"

He continued remorsefully. "All you cared about was losing your lousy Jag and the rest of the goodies. All those millions you'll never inherit now. I've let Harriet Pulos kick my butt around all this time, and for what? For a selfish, shallow little snob who can't even mourn her own nephew."

Mariana Pulos was weeping again. "What will I do?" she wailed.

"Try getting a real job or tag along with Alexis. He won't let you starve. I couldn't care less what does happen to you."

Forsythe jerked his head at his secretary and stepped into the hall. As he closed the door, she took a deep breath. "Blimey, but Fabe's had a narrow escape!"

"That he has. But he's on the right track now."

"Do you think he'll be all right?"

They'd reached the second landing and started down the stairs. "You've really taken a shine to the lad, haven't you?"

"Bet your boots I have. And so have you."

"Fabe will be fine, Sandy. As he said, he's a good mechanic and can find a job. Perhaps in time, he'll get that bike shop he wants."

183

Miss Sanderson gave him a dreamy smile. "And meet a decent girl and have children and—"

"Sandy! Stop anticipating." He gave her an indulgent smile. "You really like happy endings."

"And they lived happily ever after," she agreed.

There were no patrons in the coffee shop but Judy made them welcome, seated them in a booth, and brought coffee. They ordered and Miss Sanderson stifled a yawn. "I feel as though I've a fresh case of jet lag. Do you realize how long it is since we've slept?"

"We'll sleep tonight. We'd better finish off in town this afternoon. You can take Brice Stevens-Parkes and you can drop me off at Billy O'Day's."

She shook her gray head. "You take the car, Robby. I'll walk. I need to stretch my legs. Speaking of legs, I stuck your cane in the trunk with the luggage. Better get it out. Those walks are like skating rinks."

He muttered and she leaned across the table. "What did you say?"

He grinned. "I said, 'Yes, Nanny.' "

CHAPTER SEVENTEEN

On Factory Street, no effort had been made to clear the walks. Snow drifted up against the door of Stevens-Parkes's office. Miss Sanderson rang the bell again and peered around the maroon curtain. A shadow wavered behind that curtain and then the door swung open. As usual, Brice was immaculately groomed. "Ah, Miss Sanderson. Sorry to have kept you waiting. I was upstairs. Do come in."

Miss Sanderson stepped in and brushed the snow off her shoulders. She loosened her coat and shivered. The office seemed as cold as the wind that was clawing with icy fingers at the window behind her. The lawyer gestured. "We'll go up to my living quarters. During the winter, Miss Webster and I use electric heaters down here, but on weekends . . ." He led the way through the inner office and up the narrow staircase. Behind the door at the top was a welcome blast of warm air and a crowded sitting room. He bustled around, taking his guest's coat and scarf.

Miss Sanderson was admiring an elegant rosewood spinet. "This is a fine piece of furniture."

"My grandmother's. The desk belonged to my great-grandfather and the ormolu clock was my mother's. I brought as much furniture as I could crowd in here when my home was sold. Do be seated."

185

She selected a chair and Brice asked, "May I offer brandy or coffee?"

She accepted a thimble-sized glass of brandy and watched her host take a seat, pinch up the sharp crease in his trousers, and then she asked, "Do you mind me coming?"

"On the contrary, I welcome someone to talk to. I should imagine you've heard the steps Dmitri has taken."

"Yes, we've heard."

"I can't find it in my heart to blame him. And, although my dismissal is a disaster for me, I don't blame him for that, either."

Her jaw firmed. "Did you have anything to do with Fabe Harcourt's persecution?"

"No. Harriet used Randolph Earl for that. I've a distaste for that sort of thing."

"But you didn't try to stop it?"

"I made no effort to dissuade Harriet. I believed she was in the right and Harcourt wasn't a suitable man to marry Mariana."

"Why?"

"His background. And he served time in prison, you know."

"In a correctional institution for a juvenile offense. At the time, he was fifteen." She said slowly, "There but for the grace of God . . ."

"Go I. I take your point. Now that I've had a taste of Dmitri Pulos's brand of mercy, I can appreciate Harcourt's treatment. However, as I said, I don't blame Dmitri for my dismissal. After you and Mr. Forsythe left Hollystone in July, I sided with Harriet against her husband. Dmitri thought Mr. Forsythe might be right and his wife was in danger. Harriet refused to listen and I agreed with her. If we had only . . ." His voice trailed away and then he continued more firmly. "But we can't turn back the clock. The child is dead and Dmitri, by ridding himself of all of us and disinheriting us, has safeguarded his wife from further danger. For that, I am thankful."

"Was the decision about the will and the evictions Harriet's idea?"

"Dmitri told us about this shortly after Sergeant McBride arrived at Holly House. Tom Brent was already administering to Harriet, who was in a state of shock. No, Dmitri handled this himself."

"What position does this put you in?"

"My entire practice was connected with Harriet's concerns. My source of livelihood is now cut off. I have two choices—to leave town and begin a practice elsewhere or to retire. I've decided to retire. Hollystone is my home and I can't picture myself anywhere else. Of course, my mode of living will be different. Luckily, my father provided a pension for Miss Webster, so I don't have to worry about her welfare. I've some investments that yield a small income and by practicing economy I'll be able to survive. I'll be forced to get on without domestic help." His lips twisted wryly. "No doubt I'll have a great deal of time for cleaning and cooking. I've no close friends and the townspeople will shun me like a pariah."

"Not unlike Fabe Harcourt," Miss Sanderson said.

"Exactly. Now, how may I help?"

"Friday evening," she told him.

He told her about Friday evening. The bridge game he'd been involved in had been in the living room and all the players left the room at different times. "When we were dummy," he said, "we did wander around. I went upstairs twice—once to get my cigar case from my bedroom and once to the bathroom. Millie Earl was away from the table a number of times and Harriet was continually running up and down stairs. She was concerned about Leander, although Tom Brent had assured her the boy was well enough to get out of bed. It was Harriet who decided the little fellow was not to join us for dinner and I understand he was restless and peevish."

"Dmitri?"

"He went up to the nursery a number of times, too. I don't remember how many times. After eleven, sandwiches and

187

coffee were served by Suzy and Mariana. We played until midnight and then Harriet said she was tired and the game broke up. Dmitri was checking the doors and setting the alarm system and I walked upstairs with Harriet. For a few moments, we stood chatting in the hall. She was looking quite pale and drawn and, frankly, I was concerned about her. She'd been on edge all evening about Leander and she does . . . did have a tendency to get overwrought about the boy even when he wasn't seriously ill. I told her this and chided her and then I advised her to go to bed immediately and remember to take some hot milk to soothe her. She smiled and patted her stomach and said she'd made a pig of herself with the beef sandwiches and she was so full, she wouldn't be able to drink her chocolate. She also said she was so exhausted, she would have no trouble sleeping. At that point, Dmitri joined us. He heard what she said and asked if he could take the thermos into his room and have some milk. She said of course, we said good night, Harriet and Dmitri stepped into her bedroom, and I went to my own room.''

He glanced at Miss Sanderson and his gray eyes glinted. ''You want to know anything I saw in the upper hall that could assist you. When I got my cigar case, I did see Floyd Earl. He was entering the room he shared with this brother, Demmy. The second time I went up, I saw no one.'' He shook his head. ''I don't envy Mr. Forsythe his task. Every one of us had the opportunity to put the drug in Harriet's thermos and, as Mr. Forsythe pointed out, most of us had motives.''

''Except you,'' the secretary said.

''Except me. Perhaps I can't persuade you of my innocence but I have no desire . . . I should say had . . . to inherit from Harriet Pulos. I'd far rather live an impoverished, lonely existence and know she lives than have her dead and inherit her entire estate.''

There seemed nothing more to say. When Miss Sanderson was again on Factory Street, she bent her head, trying vainly to shield her face from the stinging blasts of snow. She trudged toward Main Street and the warmth of the Hollystone Hotel.

On Vine Street, Forsythe didn't encounter the difficulty Miss Sanderson was having on Factory Street. O'Day's walk was not only cleared but had been sanded. Alexis Pulos opened the door and Forsythe was surprised to see him. The barrister had expected to find Alexis crushed and despairing but he looked well and appeared calm and assured. In the cheerful living room, Billy was seated before a table covered with mah-jongg pieces.

Billy seemed pleased to see the barrister. "How nice of you to come, Robert. We heard you were back in town. The news about your arrival was delivered with the paper this morning. Miss Sanderson isn't with you?"

"Sandy's busy elsewhere."

"No doubt grilling another suspect. Al, do make Robert comfortable."

Alexis proceeded to do that. He seated Forsythe, carried over an end table, and offered an ashtray and a choice of drinks. The ashtray was accepted, the drink declined. While Alexis moved around, he watched the man closely, and Billy, watching Forsythe as intently, gave him an understanding smile. "Hardly expected to see our boy looking so well, eh, Robert?"

"Hardly."

Alexis sat down on a chair at the mah-jongg table. "Oddly enough, I find it a relief. The blow has finally fallen and it doesn't hurt as much as I'd imagined. Now that my life here is finished, I realize how right Billy has been. This is an awful town."

"Where do you intend to go?"

"Billy's made that decision for us."

The barrister turned his attention to Billy. "By this time, I thought you'd have left Hollystone."

"I intended to leave early in August, but I found trouble selling this house to anyone but the Puloses. I'd have given it away before I sold to that woman. But early in September

189

it sold, and as soon as Al is free to leave, we'll go to Medicine Hat. My cousin has a business there and he's offered me a position." Billy chuckled. "I can read your thoughts, Robert. You're wondering if it's interior decorating or hairdressing. Neither. My cousin runs a contracting firm and, believe it or not, I'll fit in well. I put myself through university by working for him in the summer."

Alexis smiled. "People do tend to look for stereotypes."

"Always," Billy agreed. "Take Robert Forsythe here. Before I met him, I had a mental picture of a wizened bachelor with stooping shoulders and bifocals. What a shock when this handsome young man appeared."

Forsythe said dryly, "You might do well in public relations, too."

"I might, but I know you're not here for small talk. Proceed with the grilling."

Alexis leaned forward. "This time, I know exactly what you want. Friday night. It seems impossible that was only a couple of days ago. You know who was at Holly House, don't you?"

"Yes."

"Harcourt was a surprise. I'd no idea Harriet would invite him for dinner and the night. Through dinner, he was quiet. He also paid no attention to Mariana. Later, I organized a poker game in the study and invited Fabe to play. To be truthful, I felt badly about him. He'd been shabbily treated by Harriet. He was broke, so I lent him some money and we started to play. I was a bit nervous about Fabe and Randolph. Thought there might be angry words, but Fabe was subdued and polite to all of us. We started the game at eight and played until—"

"You did leave the study that evening?"

"All of us did. We were drinking beer and you know what that does to bladders. That house is barbaric. All those floors and hardly any bathrooms. Not one on the main floor."

The barrister glanced up from his notebook. "How many bathrooms are there?"

"Five. Which may sound sufficient, but one is in Mariana's

suite in the basement and another is in the attic in my suite. Both inaccessible. Harriet and Dmitri have one that's between their rooms but has no door to the hall. You have to go through one of their rooms to get to it, and Harriet won't stand for that. There's another in the nursery wing, but one doesn't like using it for fear of disturbing the children and the nurse. The only other is the main one near the head of the stairs. It's quite posh, two toilet stalls and an island with mirrors and hand basins.''

''How many times did you go upstairs?'' Forsythe asked.

''I suppose maybe four or five times. Yes, it must have been five. I visited the main bathroom four times and I went up to my quarters for a case of beer. We'd drunk all there was in the fridge in the kitchen.'' Alexis's low brow furrowed. ''This is difficult. I was interested in the game and my mind was on that. I know what you want. An accounting of the movements of the family in the upper hall. Yes, I did see Suzy. She was pushing her sister, Edith, into the room they were sharing. Millie had told Suzy to put the brat to bed and Edith was howling at the top of her lungs. Later, I met Floyd Earl as he came up the stairs. When I went down from the attic, Fabe was waiting in front of the main bathroom. He told me Millie was locked in it and had been for some time. I was glad I'd used my own bathroom when I was up in my suite. I told Fabe to bang on the door and tell her to hurry up, and, as I went downstairs, that's what he was doing.'' Alexis flung out an expressive hand. ''That's all I can tell you.''

''You saw no one either entering or leaving Harriet's room? Or Dmitri's?''

''Heaven, *no!* That's strictly forbidden.''

Billy raised his brows. ''Someone put the drug into the thermos, Al; someone had to go into their rooms.''

''I realize that, but that's all I saw. Mariana brought us sandwiches and coffee and she tried to cozy up to Fabe, but he ignored her. Around two, our game broke up and Randolph, Floyd, and Fabe went to bed. I stayed behind to straighten up the study. Dmitri hates a mess. I was the last to go to bed.''

"The following morning?" Forsythe prompted.

"Shortly after eight, Bernice came up and routed me out of bed. She told me Dmitri had ordered all of us down to the living room but she had no idea why. I'd a dreadful hangover but I took some aspirin, pulled on a robe, and went down. All the adults, except Harriet and Dmitri, were already there. Fabe was the only one who had dressed. All he had with him was a backpack, and he probably didn't have a robe or slippers.

"For a time, we speculated and then Randolph hazarded a guess something might have happened to Harriet. Tom Brent came to the door and he ran up the stairs. Shortly afterward, Sergeant McBride and a constable came and they went directly upstairs, too. We stopped talking and I could tell what they all were doing—practically counting their inheritances if Harriet was dead.''

"Including you," Billy said unexpectedly.

"Including me. She should have died. It would be much better—''

"Careful!" his friend warned.

"I don't care!" Alexis flushed to the roots of his curly hair. "You were right all along, Billy. She cares nothing about me and she is a despot! When we heard about Leander, I was shattered. I find I must look at it this way. When Iona was Leander's age, she was rather a nice child, and look what she developed into. A horror! Leander was a sweet kid but maybe if he'd lived . . .''

Forsythe said sharply, "A callous way to look at the murder of a three-year-old child.''

Billy's intelligent eyes studied his friend. "Al is simply trying to rationalize his grief.''

Tears started to form in Alexis's eyes and he put his head into his hands. "I'm not callous. I adored the child. I can't stand the thought that he'll never grow up. . . . Yes, I can understand a person wanting to kill Harriet, but the boy—no!''

192

"The murderer was a bungling *idiot*," Billy said flatly. Forsythe's pen stopped abruptly and Billy looked at the barrister. "Is something wrong?"

"No. Alexis, I realize this must be painful, but would you finish the details of Saturday morning?"

Alexis lifted wet eyes. "After the police arrived, we sat around for about an hour. Then Dmitri came down and told us Leander was dead, killed by an overdose of Harriet's sleeping medicine, and the victim was supposed to have been his wife. Dmitri was . . . he was unbelievable. He phoned the rental agency the cars were leased from and arranged to have our cars picked up. The Earls' Caddy, Mariana's Jag, and my Alfa-Romeo. He told us we had to wait until the police questioned us and after that he ordered us to leave the house, leave the estate."

Alexis stared into space. "I reminded him that Mariana is his sister, that he's my brother. He said he disowned us and never wanted to see us again. He said either Mariana or I might have tried to kill his wife. Then Dmitri told all of us that Harriet's will would be changed and we'd be cut out of it, and Brice said he'd draw the necessary papers. Dmitri promptly lit into *him*. It was a nightmare! Millie Earl was blubbering and Randolph was whimpering and about then Edith came in and started to howl. Fabe sat there looking like death and Mariana was having hysterics. She tried to throw herself in Fabe's arms but he pushed her away. As soon as the police had taken my statement, I left." He took a deep breath. "I'll *never* return."

Billy put a protective arm around the smaller man's shoulders. "No, you'll never return to that house." He said to Forsythe, "I drove out to Holly House and picked him up. He was in terrible shape and so was his sister. We brought Mariana back to the hotel and I gave her some money to tide her over. I tried to get Harcourt to ride in with us but he insisted on riding his bike. How he ever got into town on those roads, I've no idea. I tried to lend him some money but he refused it. He's a proud man."

Yes, Forsythe thought, Fabe is a proud man. He remembered Fabe's reaction to Mariana, and he asked Billy, "Are you willing to have Alexis under these conditions?"

"Because now he has no other choice? When it comes to him, I'm not proud." His arm tightened around Alexis. "I'd take Al under *any* conditions."

"It's as well you weren't at Holly House that night."

"I certainly had a motive, didn't I?" Billy smiled grimly. "But if I had done it, I assure you Harriet Pulos would be dead, not the boy. Any further questions?"

Forsythe rose. "That's it."

"I hope we helped, Robert."

"You've tried."

Alexis remained where he was and Billy handed the barrister his coat in the pleasant hall. As Forsythe opened the door, he told the other man, "If you ever come to London, Billy, look me up. We'll have dinner."

"Are you serious?"

"Completely."

This time, Billy's smile was ironic. "Not even going to ask about the student I was supposed to seduce?"

"No."

"In that case, I'll tell you. The boy was a complete male Lolita. He seduced *me*. When I told him I was a one-man man and loved Al, the little devil ran to his parents. Revenge, Robert."

The barrister scanned Billy's face. "How will you feel if I nail Alexis as the murderer?"

"Murderous. But you must do what is necessary, and I'll still regard you highly."

Forsythe laughed and walked down the path. Over his shoulder he called, "Better try public relations, Billy. You're a natural for it."

He was opening the gate when his name was called. He turned and saw Alexis standing with Billy in the doorway. "Robert, I've been struggling with my conscience. There's something I really should tell you."

After retracing his steps, Forsythe looked up at Alexis. "Yes?"

His lips trembled and he looked up at Billy. "Dmitri's my brother."

"We know that," Billy told him patiently.

"Even if he disowned *me*, it doesn't change how I feel about *him*." Alexis paused and although the wind was buffeting Forsythe, reaching icy fingers down his collar and driving snow against his face, he didn't try to hurry Alexis. Finally, the man's thick lips firmed and he said slowly, "When he came into the living room and told us we all had to get out . . . he was happy. I swear he was delighted. Leander was dead and Dmitri was happy."

Billy frowned. "Al, what is this supposed to mean?"

"I don't know." Alexis Pulos stared down at Forsythe. "And I don't think I want to know."

195

CHAPTER EIGHTEEN

ABIGAIL SANDERSON GOT BACK TO THE HOLLYSTONE Hotel before Forsythe returned from Billy O'Day's house. When he stepped into the lobby, he spotted his secretary sitting on one of the angular chairs, watching a couple of elderly men playing checkers. Generally, there were few people in the lobby, but Forsythe noticed that there was now a number wandering aimlessly around.

Miss Sanderson glanced up and rose. As she did, a man and woman came out of the Stone Lounge and two men and another woman stepped out of the Holly Room. The men's eyes flickered over Forsythe but the women were staring at him. He noticed that only the checker players seemed to be indifferent to his arrival. Even the youth with the undershot jaw was leaning forward behind the desk, his mouth slightly ajar.

"What's the attraction, Sandy?"

"You are." She grinned. "The news has traveled and the locals are rushing in to see the contemporary Sherlock Holmes. Nothing like a murder to stir interest. I swear everyone in town is trying to crowd into the dining room to ogle us as we eat. Wonder why there aren't swarms of media in town?"

"Dmitri Pulos has a great deal of clout here and he's probably keeping the lid on. The media will eventually hear, but let's hope we're out of here by then.'' He sighed. ''I'm starved. Shall we crowd into the dining room, too?''

''Not necessary. Judy volunteered to bring chow up to your room.''

''Bless her!'' He took his secretary's arm. ''Exit left, Sandy, and a couple of whiskeys before that chow.''

They hadn't finished their first drink when the door opened and Judy wheeled in a trolley. She lifted covered dishes and set them on the table in front of a window. ''Those gawkers!'' she said wrathfully. ''No decency. That poor little boy dead and folks are acting like it's a circus.''

''The public is like that.'' Forsythe put down his glass. ''It was thoughtful of you to allow us to dine in private.''

''Least I can do. Leander was such a handsome little guy.'' Tears started in Judy's eyes and she fumbled for a hankie. ''Mrs. Pulos brought him in here a few times and he was so cute. Always talking about his dog. Who would do that to . . .''

Miss Sanderson patted the girl's arm and Judy blew her nose and tried to smile. ''Anyway, you people better eat. Our cook, Pete, is fair at some things and lousy at others. His meat loaf is like dog meat, so I brought prime ribs. And that 'home-baked' pie on the menu comes from the bakery down the street and has a crust like cardboard. So I decided on the cheesecake. Is that okay?''

Forsythe chuckled. ''Judy, if you ever change jobs, promise you won't go into sales. You're too honest for it.''

''My granny always preached honesty was the best policy. Drilled it into us kids. Come to think of it, she never got one thing from being honest. Found a wallet with a wad of money on the street once and handed it over to the cops. The owner never even gave Granny a thank-you.''

She took a swipe at her nose and headed toward the door. As she opened it, Forsythe caught her and pressed a bill into her hand. She looked at it and her eyes widened. ''Thanks a lot! Sir, maybe honesty *does* pay, Mr. Forsythe.''

The barrister and his secretary devoured their meals and then Forsythe produced a bottle of brandy and poured generous portions. Miss Sanderson reached for her notebook. "Want the interview with Stevens-Parkes in full?"

"Only the highlights. Then I'll do the same with Alexis."

"There are no highlights, Robby. Brice was on the second floor a number of times on Friday evening but says he saw nothing of interest. I still don't like the man but I do feel sorry for him. I had the impression that it wasn't as much the loss of livelihood he regretted as the loss of Harriet Pulos."

"That doesn't surprise me, Sandy. Brice has loved her for years. A different love from her husband's, though. Brice is a male Griselda."

"Then we can forget about him as murderer."

"Not so fast, Sandy. You never truly know what a person is thinking."

"True. Tell me about Alexis."

"Much the same story you got. Mainly a long, dreary tale of people running up and down to the bathroom. That room certainly had a great deal of traffic that evening. He did say something that caught my attention. As I was leaving, Alexis came after me and said something about his brother." He flipped through his notebook. "Ah, here it is. 'When he came into the living room and told us we all had to get out . . . he was happy. I swear he was delighted. Leander was dead and Dmitri was happy.' "

His secretary shuddered. "That man gives me the cold shakes. But I don't think Dmitri's happiness was because of his son's death. He had a golden opportunity to get rid of the people he'd been forced to share his wife with. What do you think?"

"I agree. But the point is, I sensed Alexis changed his mind about what he really was going to tell me."

She raised her brows. "You think Alexis lied about his brother's reaction to Leander's death?"

"No. I think he started to say something quite different and substituted that instead."

"Possible. Robby, one other point. Fabe's reaction to Mariana. I happen to agree with him about that girl, but it does seem like such a swing around. First, he does anything to marry the girl and then he wouldn't have her as a gift.''

Forsythe rubbed his jaw. "Completely different from Billy O'Day's. He's overjoyed that Alexis is free to leave with him. You're wondering . . .''

"I'm wondering if Fabe saw Mariana coming out of Harriet's room, if he knows she was the one who put the drug into the chocolate. Fabe adored that little boy. Perhaps he can't bear to denounce her, but—''

"That's possible, too.''

Miss Sanderson drained her glass, stretched, and yawned. "I'm bushed, Robby. Better stagger off to bed. I suppose in the morning we go to Holly House.''

"I go, Sandy. I know Dmitri disturbs you, so you stay here and I'll drive out alone.''

"No you won't. Whither thou goeth and so on. Right now, I goeth to bed. I'd advise you to do the same.''

Forsythe didn't take her advice. He sat with the notebook in his lap, gazing down the street. His room was above the main entrance to the hotel and garish neon cast lurid tints over the snow. As he watched, two young people waded through the tinted snow. The girl wore a peppermint-striped toque and a matching muffler. Reaching out an arm, the boy grabbed her and kissed her. Both young faces were rosy with cold and alight with laughter.

Robert Forsythe had a fleeting thought of his recent weeks with Jennifer. For a moment, he saw her long, honey-scented hair and marvelous smile. Then he sighed, opened the notebook, and bent his head over it.

CHAPTER NINETEEN

Forsythe and Miss Sanderson stood before the massive gates of the Holly estate, peering between the iron bars. Lifting a gloved hand, the barrister pushed the bell again. "This place is harder to get into than Fort Knox," he muttered. "And no sign of your old cowpoke."

"Perhaps we should have phoned." Miss Sanderson turned up the collar of her coat and stamped her feet in an effort to warm them. "Let's go back to that service station and use the phone."

Forsythe took a couple of steps toward the car and then stopped. "Listen, Sandy."

Then she heard it, too: the steady throb of a motor. Moments later, a bright red snowblower appeared around a curve of the road. Seated on it was Bert Granger. His Stetson was anchored under his chin with a scarf the same shade as the machine; his wiry body was swathed in a sheepskin jacket. He peered through the mist of snow, ground the machine to a halt, and jumped down. "Hey, folks! Have that gate open pronto."

He pulled the gates wide and stepped aside as Forsythe piloted the Mercedes in. Then he and Miss Sanderson followed on foot. The secretary adjusted her woolen head scarf. "Winter came early this year, Tex."

"Ain't winter yet. This lot will be gone in a few days. You

200

want to see real winter, you come back in a couple of months."

"I'll pass; this is real enough for me. But it must make a lot of work for you."

"Keeps me busy. But I'm not supposed to hang around and open these gates anymore. Only folks allowed in are Dr. Brent and the police, and Mr. Pulos tells me when they're expected."

Forsythe had opened his window and now he stuck his head out. "Will letting us in get you in trouble?"

The shoulders under the bulky jacket shrugged. "Don't give a hoot. Me and the wife given our notice. Leave the end of this month. Our lad Eddie's got a new job in Vernon working for a nursery outfit. Eddie's a bachelor and he's bought a nice house there. Wants me and Agathe to look after it for him."

The barrister regarded the wrinkled face under the Stetson. "You're giving up a great deal."

"Know that. Agathe and me have lived in that cottage over forty years. Raised our young ones there and got a lot of good memories of this place. But it's changed something fierce. Folks dying off and then little Leander . . ." He used an end of the red scarf to wipe suddenly damp eyes. "Wife says that house is like a funeral parlor now. She can't stand working there anymore. We'll get by okay. We both get the old-age pension and we got some put by."

"What about the maids?" Miss Sanderson asked.

"Don't rightly know. Agathe says Bernice and Cassie are so jumpy, she figures they'll be pulling out soon. Those girls are good workers and won't be hard for them to find new jobs." Miss Sanderson was shivering and Granger took her elbow and urged her toward the car. "Better get in out of this wind."

"Are the Earls home?" Forsythe asked.

"Sure are. No way they could go anywhere. Had their Caddy taken away." His face split in a wide grin. "One good thing. Haven't heard them yelling or fighting. Nice quiet neighbors now. Tell you the truth, I kinda feel sorry for them folks.''

Before Miss Sanderson closed her door, she gave Bert Granger a warm smile. ''Best of luck, Tex. I hope you and Agathe like it in Vernon.''

He beamed at her. ''Happy trails, pardner.''

Forsythe put the car in gear and the Mercedes crawled down the road. ''First stop is at the house that looks like an old English inn.''

''Blimey! Maybe we'll be in luck and they won't let us in.''

Not only were the Earls prepared to admit them but Millie was posted on the step as a welcoming committee. Before they were out of the car, she was talking. ''Good to see you, Miss Sanderson.'' She shoved a fat hand at Forsythe. ''Pleased to see you again, Mr. Forsythe. You people going up to Holly House?''

Forsythe nodded and she raced on. ''Was wondering if you would speak to Harriet about us. That Dmitri won't let me anywhere near her or the house even. Know if you speak to her, she'll do something for us. Even had our car taken away. Four kids here and not even a car!''

The barrister told her he'd do what he could and Millie urged them into the hall. In the living room, Randolph Earl was sitting in the high-backed chair, clutching what looked like a glass of whiskey. On the table at his elbow, a half-empty bottle stood. The little man no longer was natty. He was unshaven, his reddish hair stood on end, and his clothes looked as though he'd slept in them. In a corner of the room, Floyd and Suzy were playing backgammon. Millie seated her guests. Miss Sanderson promptly flipped her notebook open.

Millie told her husband, ''Mr. Forsythe is going to speak to Cousin Harriet about us.''

''Fat lot of good that will do!'' Randolph savagely rubbed the red bristles on his pointed chin. ''Face it, love, your cousin won't do one damn thing for us. Waste of breath talking to her.''

Floyd swung around. "Take it easy, Dad."

"Easy enough for you to talk. *You* haven't a wife and two little kids to look after." Randolph fixed bloodshot eyes on Forsythe. "Talk about ingratitude! These kids are hightailing it out and deserting their mom and me."

Miss Sanderson expected Floyd and his sister to flare into a rage, but Suzy said gently, "We've got to, Dad. You know that. Floyd and me got friends in Sudbury who'll put us up while we look for work. As soon as we find jobs, we'll send money for you and Mom and the kids."

"This way, we won't be a burden on you," Floyd explained. "I got enough saved to get Suzy and me to Sudbury. Cheer up! I can remember when you were in worse fixes than this and you always came out okay."

"That's true," his father mumbled. "We been in some pretty tight binds."

Forsythe asked, "Mr. Earl, don't you have savings?"

"Not one bloody cent. Took all I made to keep this house going. But Millie's got some jewelry. Haven't you, love?"

His wife gave him a reassuring smile. "Cousin Harriet give me some nice pieces, those pearls and that ruby brooch. I can sell them easy."

Dreamily, Randolph looked into the amber depths of his glass. "I've got the qualifications to get a good job. Hate to work for anyone, but I'll stick it long enough to get a stake. Maybe I can start a laundromat. That's a good business to get into. Not much work and the profits will come pouring in." Lifting his eyes, he smiled warmly at his wife. "Couple of years and I'll buy you a Caddy and a nice house, too, love."

"That's the spirit!" his son said. "We got along before we came here and we'll all make out great."

Miss Sanderson was glancing from one Earl to another. Adversity seemed to have made them nicer people. Forsythe cleared his throat and Millie nodded. "I guess you want to know about Leander. We've told that sergeant all we know, but we can tell you if you like."

203

"That's why we're here, Mrs. Earl. I understand you were playing bridge on Friday evening."

"With Dmitri and Harriet and Brice. I didn't enjoy the game. Running my legs off up and down the stairs checking on Demmy and looking in on Nurse Yale and Leander. My ankles were swollen up like balloons. The things I did to make it easier on Harriet all these years and then to be thrown out like a piece of garbage."

"How many times did you leave the living room?"

"Must have been about six times. I didn't go upstairs every time. I went up . . . it was three times. Twice to check on the children and once to the bathroom. We had veal for dinner and I think it was a bit off. Got awful cramps in my stomach and thought I had diarrhea coming on. Didn't, but I sure suffered from those cramps. I was in the main bathroom just groaning with pain and that Fabe was banging on the door yelling for me to hurry up."

Forsythe asked, "Did you go into Harriet's bathroom for Bromo or Alka-Seltzer?"

"Harriet's? Of course not. If I'd wanted anything like that, I could have gotten it from the medicine chest in the main bathroom. But I got my own remedy. I went down to the kitchen and made up a glass of warm water and baking soda. That made me feel some better."

"Did you see anyone in the upper hallway?"

"When I was checking on Leander, his mother came into the nursery. I saw Dmitri going into the nursery when I looked in on Nurse Yale. And that Fabe, of course."

Forsythe turned to the sire of the clan. "Mr. Earl?"

"I was playing poker with Alexis and Floyd and that Harcourt chap. I fully expected Harcourt to make a scene. But he didn't talk much and he wasn't nasty to me or abusive."

Miss Sanderson's mouth tightened. "I can understand why you thought Fabe might have made a scene."

"You think I like what I did to him?" Randolph splashed whiskey into his glass. "I didn't have any choice. I did a lot of dirty work for Harriet Pulos and this is the thanks I got for it."

"A man always has a choice." With a certain amount of relish, Miss Sanderson added, "Now you're getting a taste of your own medicine, aren't you?"

"I am. Now I know how Harcourt must've felt." Randolph's bleary eyes wandered back to the barrister. "That evening, I left the poker table four times. Twice I went to the kitchen to get beer, twice I went upstairs. I used the bathroom both times and I stopped to get a pack of cigarettes from the room Millie and I had. The first time, I met Mariana. She had a tray with tea things on it for Nurse Yale. The second time, when I was entering my room, I saw Floyd coming upstairs. That's all I know."

Floyd nodded. "I caught a glimpse of Dad that time. I must have been in the upper hall five times. Once Mom asked me to check on Demmy and the other times I went directly to the bathroom." The boy grinned. "That room sure had a lot of traffic that night. When I came out of the bedroom after seeing to Demmy, I met Mom. She was moaning about veal and cramps in her stomach. I saw Dmitri once. He was going down toward the nursery wing. Oh yeah, Brice went into his bedroom when I was up there."

"Suzy?" the barrister prompted.

"I was only upstairs once, Mr. Forsythe. Mariana and I were playing snooker in the game room and Mom came in and told me to get Edith to bed. The kid fought like a tiger. When I was trying to get her into our room, I saw Alexis. No one else was around."

Forsythe's eyes looked from one face to another. "And all of you are positive you saw no one entering or leaving the rooms of Harriet or Dmitri Pulos?"

Four heads jerked in unison and Forsythe got to his feet. Millie Earl took them to the door. As she opened it, she whispered, "Please don't forget to tell Harriet about us. I'm sure she doesn't know what Dmitri has done." Her lips quivered and she started to cry. "None of us would touch a hair of that boy's head. Harriet should know that."

"The boy wasn't the target, Mrs. Earl. Leander's death was an accident."

"We wouldn't hurt Harriet, either. Sure, maybe we fight some and bang around the kids, but that don't make us killers." Tears brimmed and trickled down her plump cheeks. "I'm at my wit's end. That jewelry won't bring enough to travel and get settled in another place—not with two kids and one a baby."

"I'll see what I can do," Forsythe assured the woman, and hastened after his secretary.

Miss Sanderson pulled the Mercedes out of the Earl's driveway and pointed its hood toward Holly House. As they passed the Widows' House, she gave it an appreciative glance. The gingerbread trimming was glistening with snow and it looked like a Christmas card. She asked the barrister, "Are you actually going to speak to Dmitri about them?"

"They're in a difficult situation."

"It seems like poetic justice after the way they treated Fabe."

"You can blame Harriet for that."

She didn't speak again until they turned into the cul-de-sac. "No problem finding a parking space now."

In the formerly crowded area, only three cars stood. The Bentley and the Lincoln were shrouded with snow, but a yellow Toyota with a dented fender had recently been brushed off. "Doctor's plates," Miss Sanderson said. "Dr. Brent must be here."

The door of Holly House was opened by Bernice Beaton. She was taller than Cassie and had a firmer jaw, but there was a family resemblance. "Hello, Miss Sanderson," she said. "How did you get onto the estate?"

"Tex let us in." The secretary shivered. "Could we get in out of this storm?"

The maid stood aside. "Mr. Dmitri won't like this. He only lets—"

"Don't worry, Bernice." They stepped into the hall and Miss Sanderson patted the maid's angular shoulder.

Forsythe said, "We'd like to see Mrs. Pulos."

"Dr. Brent is up with her now. Agathe and me and Cassie

haven't laid eyes on Miss Harriet since . . . it must have been Friday evening."

"Is Nurse Yale looking after her?" Miss Sanderson asked.

"Nurse Yale isn't here. The doctor took her into the hospital yesterday. She has pneumonia."

"Will she be coming back?"

"I don't think so." Bernice's lips quivered. "No children left in this house, miss."

Forsythe looked up the wide staircase. "In that case, we'd better see Mr. Pulos."

"He's upstairs waiting for the doctor to finish his examination. I'll tell him you're here. Would you wait in the living room, please?"

The living room looked even more cold and forbidding than it had the last time they'd seen it. Snow flickered against the windows, echoing the white of the furnishings. There was a vase of roses on a table but they, too, were white. They waited near the archway and the secretary said, "This place looks more like a mortuary than it did the day of Rebecca's funeral." She touched Forsythe's sleeve. "Someone's coming down the stairs."

Dmitri appeared in the hall and strode toward them. He was dressed in a heavy crewneck sweater and brown slacks. His face was as calm and handsome as ever. Paying no attention to Miss Sanderson, he went directly to Forsythe. "You were right. I knew that but I couldn't budge Harriet an inch. If she'd listened to you, our son would still be alive. But I'm in charge now and I'm making sure none of those bastards will ever get near her again."

The barrister asked, "May I speak with Mrs. Pulos?"

"Tom's with her now. We'll see what he thinks."

"How is she?"

"Frankly, I don't know. She's . . . strange. I expected grief but she isn't really grieving. And she refuses to eat. I take trays to her but—" He turned his head. "Here he is now. Tom! In here."

The man who entered the room carried a black bag, but even without it Miss Sanderson would have recognized the

207

doctor. He was an older version of Tommy Brent, with flaming hair, white skin, and freckles. Dmitri made hasty introductions and Brent jerked his head at Miss Sanderson and looked with interest at her employer. "I've read a great deal about your detective work, Mr. Forsythe. I have a magazine with an interesting article about you at home and—"

"What about Harriet, Tom?" Dmitri demanded.

The doctor glanced from Forsythe to his secretary. "Do you want to talk privately?" Dmitri shook his dark head and Brent continued. "I can do no more for Harriet. Physically, she's in fair shape. Suffering from lack of nourishment, of course, but her problem is not in my field."

"Her mind?"

"Dmitri, she's retreating from reality. She's convinced that Leander is still alive. Claims she hears him playing in the hall outside her door. She has that dog in there and those toys—"

"Harriet insisted I bring Emily up to her and she wanted Leander's toy box."

"She thinks Nurse Yale is here and blames the nurse for keeping the boy from her. She thinks he'll sneak in to see her to get his toys and play with the dog." Brent dragged his fingers through bright hair. "Now it's beyond me."

"What do you suggest?"

"A psychiatrist."

"Get one! Get the best."

"I'll make arrangements at once. But, if you can't get her to eat today, she must go to the hospital."

"No!" Dmitri barked. "Harriet doesn't leave this house. Bring the equipment you need here. Get nurses—good ones. Understand?"

The doctor's keen eyes studied the younger man. "Yes, Dmitri, I do understand."

Dmitri tugged at the doctor's arm, urging him toward the hall. Brent hastily shook Forsythe's hand and allowed himself almost to be shoved from the room. They heard Dmitri's deep voice giving orders to the doctor and then the thud of the heavy front door. Again, Dmitri went directly to the barrister. "Tom says it won't hurt Harriet if you see her." He darted a look at the secretary and Miss Sanderson flinched away from him. "Only you."

Forsythe followed him into the hall and at the foot of the stairs Dmitri waited and they went up together. His magnificent eyes studied the barrister. "Do you approve of the precautions I'm taking for my wife's safety?"

"Rather drastic, but, on the whole, yes. The change of will should remove Mrs. Pulos from further risk."

They reached the top of the stairs and Dmitri paused. "The will hasn't been changed as yet. The condition Harriet is in . . . it's not possible."

The barrister looked down the long hall. It was more cheerful than the main floor of the house. The floor was carpeted in a warm chestnut and the walls were paneled in oak. "Where is the main bathroom?" he asked.

"Right here." Dmitri swung open a door and gestured.

It was large for a bathroom and Forsythe guessed it had once been a bedroom. Alexis had been right—it was posh. There were glassed-in shower stalls, a sunken tub, two toilet stalls, and an oval counter with washbasins set into it. He nodded and Dmitri closed the door and pointed. "That's the room Millie and Randolph had and that's where Suzy and Edith slept. Brice had this one and Floyd and his baby brother shared the one to its left. Harcourt was over there. At the end of this hall are two wings. The west one is the nursery wing and the other was once the servants' quarters. It's been closed off for years and is used for storage." He stopped. "This is my wife's room. Mine is down there. A bathroom connects them."

"May I see Mrs. Pulos alone?"

White even teeth worried at Dmitri's lower lip and the barrister said, "I'm certainly not going to hurt your wife."

"I don't think . . . oh, very well." Dmitri leaned against the wall and folded his arms across his broad chest. "But I'll be right here."

No doubt, Forsythe thought, with his ear pressed against the door. Harriet's room proved to be spacious and colorful.

Rose brocade hung at the windows and a lounge covered with mauve silk stood before one of the long windows. Against a heap of pillows in a four-poster was the small figure of Harriet Pulos. Her bed jacket was an elaborate confection of lace and pink satin, and ash blond hair fell in long plaits over her shoulders. She sat up and her pale lips parted in an animated smile. Slowly, the animation faded but the smile remained on her lips, as though she had forgotten it was there. Above that meaningless smile, her eyes had as much expression as the snow-shrouded windows.

"Oh," she said, "I thought it was Leander."

Forsythe stood at the foot of the bed. The dalmatian sprawled across Harriet's feet but it didn't move a muscle or even lift its sleek head. On the floor was the gaily painted toy box; it was empty. The toys were scattered over the spread—wooden soldiers, two miniature trucks, a blue and red top, a clown with a polka-dotted covering, a plush dog. Harriet clutched a battered teddy bear to her breast. She held it out. "This is Leander's favorite. He loves Teddy."

The barrister caught the empty eyes and tried to hold them. "Mrs. Pulos, do you remember me?"

"Of course. Mr. Forsythe. You visited in the summer. Leander will be happy to see you." She glanced at the door and said fretfully, "I'm going to discharge Nurse Yale. She won't let my darling come to his mother. She's always been jealous of me, you know."

"Nurse Yale is in hospital. She has pneumonia."

"That's what Dmitri and Tom told me, but I know better. Conspiring against me, all three of them." Looking slyly around, Harriet whispered, "I knew she wanted my husband but I had no idea she wants my son, too. It's shameful!"

Forsythe, his face cold and expressionless, regarded the woman. He said harshly, "It isn't going to work, Mrs. Pulos. There's no escape—not even in madness. Somewhere in your mind, you're quite aware that Leander is dead. He died in your stead."

The bear fell from Harriet's hands. In the empty eyes, a

shadow moved. "No! I hear him. Listen! He's playing in the hall. I can hear him laughing."

"Dmitri gave him chocolate and he died. Both your children are dead. Iona fell into the waterfall and Leander died in his bed in the nursery. I warned you and you wouldn't listen. *You* are responsible for Leander's death. Face it!"

For moments, their eyes were locked, and then Harriet's lips quivered and her eyes filled with tears. "How can you do this to me?" she whispered.

"Someone had to," the barrister said tiredly. He circled the bed, pulled a handful of tissues from a box, and pressed them into her hand. The coldness was gone from his face and he looked down at the woman with compassion. She wiped her eyes and he told her, "You want the name of the murderer. You want the name of the person who put that drug in the chocolate. Don't you?"

"I know who killed my son." Harriet's hands were twisting the tissue into shreds. Her eyes were alive and glinting with hate. "*Dmitri*. He was well aware of Leander's allergy and yet he deliberately gave my son chocolate."

"Mrs. Pulos, your husband was an unwitting tool. Dmitri had no idea what was in that milk. The murderer is the person who tried to kill you and killed your son by mistake."

Her eyes dropped and after a moment she nodded. "You're right. I'm still not thinking rationally. Yes, Mr. Forsythe, I want that name. I'd like to retain you to find that name."

"I've already been retained by Rebecca Holly. The person who killed your son killed her."

She grasped at his hand. Her skin was cold and damp but the stubby fingers were strong. "I'll pay you any amount."

"I want no money."

"But you will find this person?"

"Yes."

Harriet fell back against the pile of pillows. "When you do have the name, will you come to me?"

"No, Mrs. Pulos, this time you must come to me."

"I will." She started to gather the toys into a heap. "Would you call Dmitri?"

Seconds after she had said the name, the door opened, and Dmitri put his handsome head around it. "Harriet?"

"Put these toys back in the nursery and take Emily down to the run. I'd like something to eat. Light. Soup and tea and toast. After I eat, I'll get dressed." She glanced up at the barrister. "First, see Mr. Forsythe out."

His face glowing, he strode over to the bed and bent to kiss her. She turned her head and the kiss landed on her hair. "Dmitri, if Mr. Forsythe needs any help, I want you to arrange it. Mr. Forsythe, I'll be waiting."

In the hall, Dmitri said fervently, "It's a miracle! What did you do?"

Forsythe suspected the other man had heard every word, but he said, "I gave her something to hold on to." And that something, he told himself, is vengeance.

"I'm in your debt! I'm grateful—"

"I want a favor."

"Name it."

"The Earl family are in bad shape—"

"No! Let them suffer. They may have tried to kill my wife."

"This is for your wife's sake."

"What do you mean?"

"In Hollystone, Mrs. Pulos has the reputation of being kind and generous. Even if the townspeople don't care for the Earls, they won't admire the person who would throw them out in this weather with a baby and a small daughter and no funds."

Dmitri rubbed his chin. "Very well. For Harriet, I'll do it. I'll see they have sufficient funds for plane or bus fares and some to tide them over. And that's all I'll ever do for them."

That was all the barrister wanted. The ride back to Hollystone was a quiet one. Miss Sanderson didn't speak, and as she pulled the Mercedes into the hotel parking lot, Forsythe smiled at her. "Cheer up, Sandy. We'll soon be leaving this town."

She didn't return the smile. "We haven't left yet, Robby."

CHAPTER TWENTY

WHEN THEY ENTERED THE LOBBY, THEY DIDN'T SEE HIM immediately. They were busy brushing snow off their coats, unwinding mufflers, and cleaning snow from their boots. Miss Sanderson pushed damp hair back from her face and noticed the old men weren't bending over their checkerboard. Both had their eyes riveted on the entrance to the Stone Lounge. Sergeant McBride, looking even more like a poster Mountie in his fur hat and a knee-length overcoat, was standing under the neon sign. She touched Forsythe's arm and they walked over to him. Forsythe asked, "News?"

McBride shook his head. "None from my end. I was hoping you might have some for me."

It was the barrister's turn to shake his head, and Miss Sanderson breathed a sigh of relief. "For a moment," she said, "I thought something might have happened to Fabe Harcourt."

The officer smiled. "The only news on Mr. Harcourt is that he's moved into the room next to yours, Miss Sanderson. I gather he and Miss Pulos weren't hitting it off. Mr. Harcourt appealed to me and I made Bob Weston give him another room."

"Sounds like a good idea. Robby, do you mind if I share the rest of your cognac with Fabe?"

"Go right ahead. If you run out of that, there's a bottle of whiskey in my bureau drawer. Feel free."

The sergeant watched Miss Sanderson loping up the stairs. "Has she known Mr. Harcourt for long?"

"She's only seen him a few times. But Sandy has strong likes and dislikes, and she's taken a fancy to Fabe."

McBride glanced over Forsythe's shoulder. Bob Weston had joined the desk clerk and was leafing through a file box. He was paying more attention to the two men than he was his work. McBride moved farther away from the desk and the barrister followed him. "What are your plans now, Mr. Forsythe?"

"If road conditions permit, we'll be leaving Hollystone tomorrow."

The sergeant's eyes narrowed. "You said you'd never give up."

"I said nothing about giving up, but I've everything I'm going to get here. The Puloses and Earls and Brice Stevens-Parkes have said all they intend to." Forsythe smiled again, and this time there was a trace of humor in his smile. "Sergeant, I don't work with fingerprints or footprints. I work with people, what they say and, sometimes more importantly, what they don't say. What I sense they'll do, what I feel they won't do. Sandy and I have notes on conversations with all the suspects that date back to July, to the first time Sandy came to Hollystone. Somewhere in these notes is the clue we need."

McBride showed the perfect teeth in a smile that made his boyish face charming. "Luck! If you find that clue, will you share it with me?"

"You'll be the first to know. How much longer can you keep these people in town?"

"Not much longer. Until after the inquest."

The barrister extended a hand and the sergeant shook it. McBride watched Forsythe mount the stairs. A fine-looking man, he thought, with that tall, elegant body and fine-featured face. He remembered the work Forsythe had done on other cases. No doubt about it, when it came to crime, Robert

214

Forsythe appeared to have a sixth sense. This time, the barrister really needed that talent. However, if he was the murderer, he wouldn't want this man looking for him.

After buttoning his greatcoat to the throat, McBride walked toward the door. As he passed the desk, Weston called, "Anything I should know, Sergeant?"

McBride shook his head. The checker players waited until the door swung to behind his tall figure and then they bent over their table. One of them moved a man and muttered, "Bet there's another dead one out to Holly House."

His crony moved a king, jumped three men, and gave a shrill cackle. "Got news for you, Jake, you're dead, too! Chalk one more game up for me. The beer's on you!"

CHAPTER TWENTY-ONE

T HAT NIGHT, A WARM FRONT MOVED IN FROM THE PA-
cific. Snow turned to sleet and later to a steady downpour of
rain. Driving conditions didn't improve. The road through
the mountains melted into a river of slush. Regardless of the
weather, the Mercedes pulled out of Hollystone in the morning. Miss Sanderson, who was driving, was limp with fatigue
by the time they reached Vancouver. To their chagrin, they
found the city had had no snow. The secretary swore and
muttered, "What a foul climate."

Forsythe gave her a tired grin. "Much like merry old England."

For the remainder of the day, they made no effort to work,
but early on Wednesday morning they were in the library.
Forsythe was making notes at the desk and his secretary had
set up her typewriter on a side table. "Where shall I start?"
she asked.

"At the beginning. The day we met Rebecca Holly."

Her hands flew over the keyboard and as she finished a
page, she tossed it over to the barrister, who sorted the sheets
into a number of cardboard file folders. Shortly before noon,
she pulled out the final sheet, covered her machine, and
stretched. "I'd better get some lunch."

He nodded. "Then we'll go through all the interviews
together."

"Looking for what, Holmes?"

"We won't know until we find it. Will we, Watson?"

They went through the file folders exhaustively, reading, underlining words and sentences, pausing to discuss points. Finally, Miss Sanderson tossed down a folder and frowned. "I feel as though we're truly chasing that wild goose, Robby. How about you?"

"A couple of times, I've had my fingers on his tail feathers, Sandy, but there's still a number of points that won't fit."

"Leander, for one."

"Yes." Leaning back, he started to pack the carved bowl of his pipe with dark shreds of tobacco. "Better take a break."

She got to her feet. "Best suggestion you've had for a time. Brain fatigue setting in. I'm going for a walk. Want to come along?"

He flexed his knee. "The spirit's willing but this ruddy knee won't cooperate. I'll stretch out on the couch while you're gone."

When she returned from her walk, she found him sprawled on the leather couch, sound asleep, an afghan covering his legs. As she stood over him, looking down at his sleeping face, his eyes opened. "You weren't gone long, Sandy, but you're looking much perkier."

She smiled down at him. Her hair was spangled with rain, her thin cheeks were pink, and her eyes were bright. "Over two hours. I'm practically a new woman. And look what I bought."

After pushing the afghan aside, he sat up. "Spending more of your traveler's checks, eh?"

"Barely dented one. I found this in a secondhand store. I haven't seen one for years and it brought back childhood memories. Aunt Rose once had one and she let me play with it."

"A Russian doll." He pulled himself to his feet and carried her purchase to the desk. "Hand-painted, and look at the detail on it." With a long forefinger, he traced the red

217

babushka, touched the lines of the round face, and outlined the spray of bright flowers painted across the apron. He pulled the doll into two pieces and lifted out the second doll. It had an olive green babushka. "There should be nine dolls, Sandy." He took out doll after doll until a line of nine stretched across the desk.

Miss Sanderson picked up the smallest doll. "Look at the size of this, Robby. Barely as long as my thumbnail." She chuckled. "I remember the first time Aunt Rose showed me her Russian doll. When she twisted the first doll apart, I thought she'd broken it and started to wail. She told me not to be a silly girl and then she took all the dolls out. I kept crying, 'But it looked like one doll, Aunt Rose, it looked like one doll!' "

Forsythe stared from the dolls to his secretary. He took the smallest doll from her hand, fitted in the next size, and continued until a single doll stood on the green blotter. Then he sank down into the leather chair and reached for the file folders. Miss Sanderson watched him for a few moments and then she shook her head, neatly folded the afghan, and perched on the edge of the couch. Forsythe closed one folder and opened another. Time passed and all that could be heard in the library was the rustle of paper. Finally, the barrister lifted his eyes, gazed at the Russian doll, and slammed down a fist so hard that the doll vibrated. "Eureka! It looks like one. Sandy, you've hit it!"

"Don't take on, Robby. What the devil did I hit?"

"The last pieces of the jigsaw. Now I have the whole picture."

"Which is more than I have. My picture is still full of holes."

"They'll soon be filled in. Take a letter, Sandy. Sergeant McBride, Hollystone R.C.M.P." As he dictated, he paced up and down. A number of times, he paused, flipped open a folder, quoted a passage, and then continued. It took close to an hour and when he had finished, he asked, "Now do you see the whole picture?"

218

"Not only that but I can see one vital item I was completely wrong about."

He grinned. "Nobody's perfect."

"Don't rub it in." She gave him her gamine grin. "This was a horribly tangled mess. By far the most complicated case we've ever had."

His smile faded. "And it leaves a bad taste in the mouth, doesn't it? Sandy, would you type that up and get it off Express Mail. I've a phone call to make."

"To Hollystone. Robby, we aren't going back *there* again, are we?"

"No," he said grimly. "This time, Hollystone comes to us."

On Wednesday evening, the call was made to Hollystone and by late afternoon on Friday, Harriet Pulos and Dmitri Pulos were being ushered into the library by Miss Sanderson. Chairs had been placed for them facing Forsythe. After they were seated, Miss Sanderson took a chair at the end of the desk.

The secretary didn't have a notebook and she sat quietly, her hands loosely folded in her lap, studying the Puloses. This Harriet looked much different from the one she had seen a number of times at Holly House. Her clothes were quiet but the cut and materials whispered of expense. A pale mink coat was carelessly tossed over the back of her chair and the pink wool dress was cut well enough that she looked taller and slimmer. At her ears and throat, lustrous pearls glowed and her hair was drawn up into a crown of ash blond braids. She wore discreet makeup—a faint shadowing of her eyes, a lipstick that matched the color of her dress.

Dmitri made a handsome escort for his wife. His magnificent eyes roved around the library, noting the books behind the glass-fronted cases, the fireplace with a brisk blaze on its hearth, the photo of Thalia Holly propped on the mantel, the elegance of creamy Chinese rugs against polished oak. "Nice place," he said carelessly, and then he turned those eyes on

219

the woman at his side. "Harriet looks much different than she did the last time you saw her, Mr. Forsythe."

"She does indeed. You've recovered, Mrs. Pulos?"

"I'll never recover from my son's death but, yes, I do feel somewhat better. Dmitri and I would have been here yesterday, but the inquest was held in the afternoon." The pink lips tensed. "This morning, Cassie told me the Earl family are packing to leave the estate. I phoned Mr. Weston and he said Mariana has checked out of the hotel. There was no answer from Mr. O'Day's house, where Alexis has been staying. I was upset and I called Sergeant McBride. He said he'd had a letter from you and I'm not to worry. But I *am* worried. What if the murderer gets away?"

"There's no possibility of that."

Harriet relaxed against the rich froth of mink. "You relieve my mind. Now, you made a promise to me."

"I intend to keep that promise. But first you must hear me out." Forsythe glanced down at the desktop. The clutter had been removed and all that was on it was a couple of typewritten sheets under a brass paperweight and the Russian doll. Miss Sanderson noticed that his cane was propped against the desk, close to his right hand. The barrister pointed at the doll. "Have you ever seen one of these?"

Dmitri nodded. "We gave Iona one much like that for her fifth birthday. She didn't care for it."

"They aren't actually toys. But this one led me directly to the name you want." Templing his fingers, Forsythe stared down at them. "Sandy mentioned this is the most complex case we've ever worked on and I agree. And, right from the beginning, we made errors."

Harriet raised fair brows. "I suppose you mean Mother Holly."

"Rebecca Holly was one, but the most grievous of my errors wasn't directly involved with her." Picking up the doll, Forsythe pulled it apart and then started to line up the dolls. The two larger ones, he set on the right side of the blotter. The five smaller ones were lined up on the left of it. The two smallest, he set on one corner of the desk.

Dmitri and Harriet leaned forward, watching his hands. He gestured at the five smaller dolls. "The dead." His finger moved across the blotter and touched the second-largest doll, the one with the olive green babushka. "The murderer I've been searching for—cold, relentless, ruthless, a careful, methodical person with a finely tuned sense of other people's weaknesses."

Harriet was staring at the five dolls Forsythe had labeled "the dead." "Mr. Forsythe, there haven't been *five* victims."

"There have been five. Not all of them murdered but all of them victims." Forsythe studied the oval face of the woman opposite him. "My first error was in deciding that this case began on the first day of May on the plateaus beside the waterfall. Murder breeds murder, and the first crime was committed long before. Many years ago." He lifted the largest doll victim. "Kenneth Holly."

"No!" Harriet protested. "Kenneth died tragically but of natural causes."

Lifting a commanding hand, Forsythe said, "Hear me out." He lifted the paperweight and glanced down at one of the typewritten sheets. "There appear to have been two sides to Kenneth Holly. When he was sober, he was described by Brice Stevens-Parkes as 'a large, good-looking chap' with a 'boyish charm.' Brice also called Kenneth 'a perpetual adolescent.' Rebecca Holly told us that you, Mrs. Pulos, always excused your first husband's behavior on the grounds that he was 'a little boy who had never grown up.'

"But this charming boyish man changed drastically when he drank. Not only was alcohol dangerous to him physically but it was dangerous mentally. Kenneth Holly has been described as a 'beast' and a 'bounder' and a 'rogue.' I think the most accurate description was given to us by Agathe Granger. She said that when he was drinking he was a man who 'if he'd lived, I swear he'd have ended up killing someone.' The most likely person to have been killed by him was you, Mrs. Pulos."

"Are you saying I killed my first husband?"

"No. But you're the *reason* he died. Kenneth had abused you verbally many times, but the last time he abused you physically. You were described as a pitiful figure with your nose broken, your eyes blackened, hardly able to move or speak. Hollystone is a small town and news travels fast. In a short time, everyone in town would have heard what shape you were in. They also would have known that Mr. Stevens-Parkes had driven you and Thalia to safety with Rebecca Holly in Vancouver and that Kenneth was in Holly House alone.

"One person who heard that news adored you and could no longer bear the violence you were enduring. Both Stevens-Parkes and Dr. Brent love you, but both these men acted characteristically. The doctor stormed out of the house, refusing to have anything further to do with Kenneth. Stevens-Parkes made no effort to care for Kenneth, hoping, perhaps subconsciously, that the deranged man *would* die.

"But there was another man in Hollystone who loved you, a young man, at that time about nineteen. I refer, of course, to your present husband." Dmitri made a muffled sound and Miss Sanderson moved uneasily. Forsythe gazed from his secretary to the other man. "For some time, I've suspected that Kenneth Holly's death had a bearing on this case, but . . ." His eyes fastened on Miss Sanderson's face. "The logical suspect was Dmitri Pulos and something Sandy said put me right off the track. She once knew another young man, someone who Dmitri reminded her of. Raymond Harswood was also a murderer, but he killed bloodily with an ax. Sandy thought that Dmitri would be like Harswood in this respect, a hands-on killer, incapable of a more subtle type of murder. But, for once, Sandy was wrong."

Forsythe consulted his notes again. "Stevens-Parkes told us that Kenneth was 'amused' by Dmitri's crush on his wife, that he 'liked the lad and often urged drinks on him.' " The barrister held out the doll he was still holding. "Here we have a spoiled, childish man left alone on the estate for the first time. He had driven his wife and the servants away, but I would imagine he felt neglected and lonely. He wouldn't

222

have welcomed either the doctor or Stevens-Parkes, but Kenneth would have been glad to see young Dmitri.

"Probably, Mrs. Pulos, Dmitri pretended to drink with your husband and enticed him up to the bedroom that Kenneth earlier had reduced to shambles. Kenneth was used to being looked after. When he was drinking, someone always saw he got his insulin shots. Either he asked Dmitri to give him one or the boy volunteered. But what Dmitri did was give him an overdose. Then all he had to do was keep Kenneth drinking until he passed out and went into shock." Forsythe held the doll toward Dmitri. "What have you to say?"

Dmitri didn't say a word. Instead, he lunged across the desk, his hands reaching for Forsythe's throat. The barrister no longer was in his chair. He was on his feet. The cane flashed out and the ferrule drove into Dmitri's stomach. Dmitri's breath was expelled in a rasping gush and he collapsed on his chair, both arms laced over his midsection.

Propping the cane back against the edge of the desk, Forsythe sat down in the leather chair. He told the other man calmly, "Don't move again."

Under the olive skin, the handsome face was the color of ashes and the dark eyes avoided his wife. Harriet turned toward him, an expression of loathing etched across her features. "You *did* kill him," she hissed. "All these years, I've blamed Rebecca and Brice for neglect and *you* murdered him."

"Kenneth Holly's murder led to a chain of later deaths," Forsythe said. "That murder also sent you, Mrs. Pulos, into a nervous collapse. You didn't mourn a husband, you mourned a son. I doubt you've ever loved a man; your heart has only been given to children. And you regarded Kenneth Holly as your first child.

"But to return to the chain of events. After Kenneth's death, you married again. You had no affection for Dmitri Pulos but you wanted a young virile man to father your children. You were over thirty and time was precious. Both you and Dmitri obtained your desires. You bore two children; you built up a family to give them the warm childhood you'd been denied. Dmitri had the woman, the home, and the wealth of the man he'd murdered. As Rebecca told us, for many years you lived in a type of paradise. This paradise came to a shattering end on the first day of May.''

"I lost my daughter," Harriet said dully.

"And Thalia Holly witnessed a murder attempt that led first to her death and then to her grandmother's. When Sandy and I returned from Hollystone a few days ago, I came to the conclusion that Sandy was wrong in her assessment of Dmitri's character and that not only had he killed Kenneth years ago but also was responsible for the recent deaths. And that's where my reasoning ran into a number of snags. Who had Dmitri tried to push into the falls? For a time, I thought I had the answer.

"We know that Alexis Pulos often tagged along after his older brother when Dmitri visited Holly House during Kenneth's lifetime. It's possible that Alexis might have followed Dmitri to the estate the day when Kenneth Holly was supposed to have died there alone. Alexis is a bright chap and it wouldn't have taken him long to have put two and two together. It's also conceivable that Dmitri might have confessed his crime to his younger brother.

"I soon found evidence to back up this theory. On the morning of the contest, Dmitri and Alexis had a violent argument in the study. We know some of the words they were shouting. Dmitri told his brother 'I won't let you do this to my wife!' There is no difficulty in understanding what he meant. He'd received an anonymous letter telling him of Alexis's homosexual relationship with Billy O'Day and Dmitri wasn't going to allow his wife to be an object of scorn because of his brother's affair. Dmitri threatened to expose his brother, which meant that Alexis would have been driven out of Hollystone.

"But Alexis fought back. He shouted, 'I'll damn well do what I want, big brother, and you won't stop me!' Strong words to use when Alexis was supposed to be pleading for his brother's mercy. When I asked Alexis about this, he gave me a clever explanation, but he was lying to protect Dmitri.

224

What he actually was doing was blackmailing Dmitri about Kenneth's death.''

Forsythe paused to consult his notes and Miss Sanderson watched the Puloses. They sat quietly, their eyes fixed on the barrister's face. Forsythe cleared his throat and continued, "I decided that Alexis Pulos had been the intended victim, that Dmitri had tried to push him into the falls to conceal the first crime. Which could have led to Thalia's death and then Rebecca's, but—"

"But, indeed!" Dmitri interrupted. For the first time since Miss Sanderson had met him on the veranda of Holly House, she saw him smile. It should have been a charming smile. The skin around the wonderful eyes crinkled, he displayed fine teeth, and his olive cheeks were indented with the dimples his son inherited. It was far from charming. There was something frightening about a smiling Dmitri. He leaned forward, his shoulders brushing his wife's mink. "Two questions, Mr. Forsythe. If Alexis was ready to betray me the day of the wildflower contest, why hasn't he done it since my son's death? Not only did I kick him out but I also got rid of Mariana. And Alexis is fond of our sister. Also, what possible reason could I have had to put the drug into my wife's thermos?"

"Good questions, Mr. Pulos. Except for your wife, you've never had any genuine affection to give another person. But Alexis is your direct opposite. He loves you and is loyal to you and you know that. Even if you had told your wife about Billy O'Day, I doubt Alexis would have betrayed you. No matter what you'd done or will do, Alexis will remain silent. The last time I saw your brother, I think he was trying to force himself to tell me about Kenneth's death but he couldn't bear to. Instead, he said something else about you. Mr. Pulos, you knew you were safe and therefore there was no motive for attempting to murder Alexis.

"Now, your second question. I couldn't think of another person you might have tried to kill at the falls. You certainly would never harm your wife. And that is the situation I was facing when Sandy and I were working in this room on

Wednesday afternoon. Then an odd thing happened. We took a break and I had a nap while Sandy took a walk. She brought this back"—his hand flicked toward the Russian doll—"and she said something that solved the murders. Sandy said, 'It looks like one,' and at that moment, I realized we weren't looking for *one* murderer, we were looking for *two*."

Harriet's pink lips moved. "Who *was* the other murderer?"

Forsythe paid no attention to her. He gazed over her shoulder, his eyes fixed on Thalia Holly's photograph. "I immediately went through our files again and in Agathe Granger's interview found the answer. The morning of the contest was marked by only one discordant note—the quarrel in the study between the two brothers, a quarrel that sent Cassie Beaton to Agathe Granger. In turn, Agathe went to you, Mrs. Pulos, where you sat beside the pool, watching some of the younger people having their first swim of the season."

"Mr. Forsythe, Agathe did tell me but I decided not to interfere."

"That is a lie, Mrs. Pulos. You valued that day and you wouldn't allow anything to spoil it. So you entered the rose garden that is directly outside the French doors of your husband's study. When we saw you in that room after Rebecca's funeral, those doors were open. I'd hazard a guess they were open the warm and sunny day of the contest. But both men were shouting and you'd have heard them even if the doors had been closed."

Forsythe shifted his attention back to Harriet Pulos. The woman's face was under rigid control. "While you stood in the rose garden, you learned who was responsible for your child-husband's death. For years, you had hated both your mother-in-law and Brice for their parts in it. I can picture how you felt when you heard that the man who had fathered your children and had taken Kenneth's place in your life had murdered to get you. You had never loved Dmitri and now you hated him. You wanted him dead and you started to plot that death.

226

"The falls area had no guardrails. What a perfect place for a murder that would look like an accident. Coldly and remorselessly, you began your plan by ensuring that the other people present would be fully engrossed in the contest. One quality your relations have in common is greed. You played on that greed by announcing that the prize for the winner would be special."

"The lookout point," Harriet said. "If I'd been about to kill Dmitri, would I have tried where someone might have looked down and seen it?"

"You thought you had no worry on that score. The adults who looked after the children were well trained and you hardly expected one to disobey and look down. But one did. Thalia Holly, who had Iona in her charge, on a whim went to the lookout. She saw her beloved 'Mommy' sneaking up behind Dmitri with a rock poised to strike—a rock that had dirtied your hands and skirt with mud stains. You cleverly explained that by saying you'd slipped and fallen. Before you could strike your husband and send him plummeting into the falls, Thalia caught your attention by waving her arms. Her words weren't audible, but I think she was shouting something like 'Don't. Mommy, don't.'

"You dropped the rock and backed away toward the path. At that moment, Iona came running up, slipped on the moss, and—" Picking up the blue doll, Forsythe let it fall to the blotter.

Harriet moaned and covered her eyes. The barrister continued. "Your cherished daughter was dead and you blamed Thalia for the child's death. I don't think you were worried about Thalia exposing you. She was as obsessed with you as you had been with Kenneth Holly. But now, you had two lives you longed to take—Thalia's and Dmitri's. The only reason Thalia lived out those last two months was because Rebecca took her away from your estate. During this time, Dmitri and Stevens-Parkes kept both Thalia and Rebecca away from you. So . . . Thalia lived until Rebecca managed to get a letter to you. You must have been delighted. Again, you made careful plans.

227

"The Friday evening that Thalia and her grandmother arrived at Holly House for the reconciliation found the household waiting, primed by you to be nice and welcome Thalia. That way, she was unable to speak privately with you. During the night, you shut off the alarm system, crept from the house, and booby-trapped the big swing—"

"No!" Dmitri said violently. "Harriet would *never* have allowed Leander to be hurt."

Forsythe's lips relaxed in a slight smile. Above those smiling lips, his eyes were like ice. "Wrong. Mrs. Pulos put Thalia in charge of Leander and allowed the boy to have his way and use the big swing. With the covering of sawdust under the swing, she knew her son was in no danger. But it gave Harriet the opportunity to shake Thalia even more." The cold eyes shifted to Harriet. "That evening, you went to Thalia's room and—"

"When I left her room she was alive. Floyd Earl saw her. I did *not* hang my niece."

"You did something more monstrous. You drove Thalia into taking her own life. The girl was suicide-prone and she adored you. It wouldn't have been hard for a woman who knew Thalia as well as you did to find a way. If I were to hazard a guess, I'd say you admitted you had tried to kill Dmitri, that you still had every intention of murdering him. I'd say you played on the girl's guilt about Iona's accident and Leander's fall from the swing.

"You had your sewing basket with you and you took out your shears and gave them to Thalia. You told her you were through with her and she might as well cut down the curtain cord and hang herself. To confuse her disturbed mind even more, you gave her a dose of your sedative. Then you left her and outside her room you drove away Floyd Earl. Clever and cold and bestial!"

Forsythe grabbed the third doll and threw it down on the blotter. "Three victims—Kenneth, Iona, Thalia. The fourth"—he selected a doll painted a lilac color—"Rebecca Holly. When Sandy arrived at your house in July, you weren't worried. You felt you could dispose of a meddling old woman like your mother-in-law with no problem. Instead of telling Sandy about Thalia's previous suicide attempts yourself, you faked a breakdown and you left the veranda. As soon as you were gone, Brice Stevens-Parkes did just as you knew he would. He told Sandy, my vanity was hit, and I did withdraw from the case.

"But you misjudged Rebecca Holly. She was tenacious. She searched for and found the truth but it bewildered her. She had no hint of the circumstances of her son Kenneth's death. As Rebecca told her friend, 'it's unbelievable . . . there's no reason for it.' She phoned you at the hotel—"

"She did not," Dmitri said flatly. "My wife and I weren't at the hotel all day."

"You returned to your hotel at four that afternoon, Mr. Pulos. Your wife didn't feel well and she went to bed. You mixed a glass of her sedative and left. When you returned a short time later, Mrs. Pulos was apparently asleep and the glass was empty. In that interval, Rebecca had managed to reach her by phone. As far as your wife knew, you were going out for the evening with a friend."

Forsythe glanced down at a sheet of paper at his elbow. "Mrs. Pulos told us exactly what happened. She said, 'In other words, I could have emptied the sedative down the drain, dressed, walked to the park, and met Mother Holly.' That is exactly what she did. Rebecca died in that park with your wife holding the purse containing the medication and watching Rebecca Holly collapse with a coronary. Mrs. Pulos didn't lay a hand on Rebecca. She didn't have to. A few threats to a frail old woman already tense and anxious and—" Forsythe pushed the lilac doll over with the other three. "The fourth victim. Another person who died so Harriet could eventually kill you."

Dmitri pointed at the last victim, an orange one. "Leander?" Forsythe nodded and Dmitri said flatly, "It's impossible. There was no earthly reason for Harriet to put the drug into her own thermos."

"There was an excellent reason, Mr. Pulos. In July, Sandy and I went to Holly House and sat in your living room while

I tried to persuade your wife her life was in danger. What a *fool* she must have thought me. And I played right into her hands. Harriet Pulos conceived a foolproof method of achieving her desire, to kill you. All she had to do was make it look as though the murder attempt was directed at *her*. With this in mind, she had her family weekend and even invited Fabe Harcourt to stay the night to cloud the issue even further.

"On one of her many trips upstairs, your wife slipped into her own room, drugged the chocolate, and wiped the surfaces clean. As we learned from Brice Stevens-Parkes, you also are fond of hot chocolate and frequently have some from your wife's thermos. That evening, she arranged a plausible excuse for not drinking milk and she was going to see that you did. She seldom eats in the evening but that particular evening she had several sandwiches and graciously allowed you to take the thermos of milk to your room."

Forsythe paused and looked at Harriet's oval face. Miss Sanderson followed his eyes. All the woman's serenity and charm had vanished and they saw her as she actually was. A fitting mate for Dmitri, Miss Sanderson thought with a shudder. "I should imagine," the barrister said slowly, "that Harriet slept soundly that night. In the morning, she expected to hear of her husband's death, but she found Dmitri alive and her cherished son dead.

"It's understandable why Harriet went into shock, retreated from reality, and convinced herself that little Leander was still alive." Forsythe's lips twisted bitterly. "When I forced her out of that state, I made yet another error. I suppose I was slightly in shock myself and at the time didn't notice that Harriet had no interest in the person who'd put the drug into the thermos. All she could say was that *Dmitri* had killed her child. Keep in mind, Mr. Pulos, that your wife now hates you for the death of her first husband *and* also that of Leander. But Harriet is fast on her mental feet and soon realized she must pretend an interest in the thermos and that is why you're here now.

"So . . ." The barrister touched the largest doll with the

bright red babushka. "The first murderer, Dmitri Pulos."
His hand moved to the one with the olive green babushka.
"The second murderer, Harriet Pulos." He gently set the
small orange doll down beside the other four victim dolls.
"The last tragic victim—Leander Pulos."

Harriet Pulos was no longer watching the man behind the
desk. Her pale eyes were wandering around the library. "Are
you taping this?"

"No. And I'm not trying to trap you."

"What did you put in that letter to Sergeant McBride?"

"Exactly what I've told you. I also told him to allow your
relations to leave Hollystone, as they had nothing to do with
the crimes."

Harriet's pink lips relaxed and she gave the barrister a
small, vicious smile. "You have no proof, do you?"

"Nothing that would stand up in court."

One of Harriet's stubby hands touched the gleaming pearls
at her throat. "Dmitri and I can't be touched."

"Not by legal means."

"So all of this"—a stubby hand gave a wave—"is a farce.
We can't be punished."

Forsythe's eyes glinted. "Mrs. Pulos, I said nothing about
punishment. I merely said ordinary justice can't touch you."
He fitted the dolls together and set the large doll on the corner
of the desk. "As I told you, Rebecca Holly had one friend.
Her name is Augustine Spencer, and when she was speaking
with Sandy about Rebecca's death in the park, Mrs. Spencer
said she hoped I would find the person responsible. She
also said she hoped the punishment would fit the crime. I
brought you here to deliver that punishment."

Dmitri showed his deep dimples and his wife gave the
barrister a contemptuous smile. "I can hardly picture
either you or your secretary whipping out a revolver and
shooting us."

He beamed the contempt back. "Correct, Mrs. Pulos.
Neither Sandy nor I have the instincts you two have. We're
not killers. However, we are a tribunal. Sandy is your jury."

231

He turned to his secretary and asked gravely, "What is the verdict?"

"Guilty," Miss Sanderson said in her cool, clear voice.

Throwing back her head, Harriet laughed. "Ridiculous! Truly a farce! Where is the executioner?"

"Sitting beside you, Mrs. Pulos." Harriet shot her husband a look of pure venom, and Forsythe said, "Sandy?"

Miss Sanderson spoke directly to the barrister. "Another, more subtle Raymond Harswood, Robby." Her eyes moved to Harriet. "Your husband is mad, Mrs. Pulos."

Harriet shrugged. "Dmitri would never hurt me."

"He's in the grip of a dangerous obsession and the object of that obsession is you." Miss Sanderson paused and then continued evenly. "As long as you don't try to leave him, you're safe. But if you do . . ."

Forsythe nodded. "Mrs. Pulos, you're going to be caged with a madman, a man who wants you body, mind, and soul. He's already cut you off from other people. You're going to be in a prison with no escape. Other than leaving him, and taking the consequences, there's only one avenue of escape from him. You could kill him. But my letter is on file with the police. At present they can't move against you, but if Dmitri dies, they'll be on you in a flash.

"We come to your sentencing. Harriet and Dmitri Pulos! Between you, you destroyed five people. Two of them were your own children. One was a girl with a glorious talent. And you took from an old woman her last few precious years." Forsythe rose to his feet and picked up the cane. He pointed it at Dmitri and then at Harriet. "Legal punishment could never have the horror of what is awaiting you. I am your judge. My sentence is . . . *hell*!"

Lowering his cane, he said curtly, "Now, I want you out of here. I'll take you to the elevator."

Moving as though she'd suddenly aged, Harriet struggled to her feet. Her husband scooped up her coat and arranged it carefully over her shoulders. He bent and kissed her cheek. She winced away from him, but he put out a hand and pulled

232

her against him. Forsythe, still holding the cane, followed them from the room.

The patio door was wide open and cool, moist air swirled through the room, blowing Miss Sanderson's gray hair back from her face. Forsythe bent and picked up the sheets of paper that had been blown from the desk. "What in the devil are you doing, Sandy?"

"Airing the room. After that . . . blimey!"

"It's over now. Close the door. Tomorrow we head home and we can forget this."

She slid the door closed and turned. "Easier said than done. I'll have nightmares about this. What's your prognosis, Holmes?"

"Exactly what yours is. Either Harriet's going to break and make a run for it or she'll try to get rid of Dmitri. Either way, they're both finished."

"Amen to that, Robby." She opened a drawer in the desk and took out a pile of file folders. Then she picked up the Russian doll. "Do you want this thing?"

"No. I take it you don't want it, either?"

"You take it right. I'll leave it for Mark Harmon." She placed the doll on the mantel and her hand brushed the photograph of Thalia Holly. "Shall I put this in with the file folders?"

He took it from her. "Yes."

"When we get back to London, I'll file these . . ." She frowned. "I can't decide whether they belong under *C*, for Canadian crime or *R*, for Russian toy."

"Neither, Sandy." He looked down at the lovely young face in the photograph. "File them under *D*, for dancing doll."

About the Author

E. X. Giroux lives in British Columbia, Canada, just over the border from Washington State. She has written eight previous mysteries featuring the Forsythe–Sanderson detecting duo; *A Death for a Double*, *A Death for a Dreamer*, and *A Death for a Dietician* are her three most recent ones.